She wasn't what Nick expected, although he didn't know exactly what he'd expected. He sensed no fear, as if Juliette had long ago moved past such a base, primal emotion.

"I thought my son and I were safe." Her voice was barely audible. Nick leaned toward her slightly. "It's been over three months. I thought David had found somebody else . . . moved on . . . forgotten us." A small bitter laugh escaped her, riding the breeze and disappearing instantly. "I should have known he was just biding his time, waiting for us to feel safe."

"But you're using your maiden name in town. That makes you easy to find."

Juliette frowned. "I tried using a fake name for a while, but it was impossible to find jobs without a social security number."

She turned back to look at Nick, her gaze holding a steely strength. "I refuse to give my son a different name each day of the week. Besides, I'm not a criminal and I don't know how to live outside the law. . . ."

PROMISE HIM ANYTHING

Carla Cassidy

AN ONYX BOOK

ONYX
Published by New American Library, a division of
Penguin Group (USA) Inc., 375 Hudson Street,
New York, New York 10014, U.S.A.
Penguin Books Ltd, 80 Strand,
London WC2R 0RL, England
Penguin Books Australia Ltd, 250 Camberwell Road,
Camberwell, Victoria 3124, Australia
Penguin Books Canada Ltd, 10 Alcorn Avenue,
Toronto, Ontario, Canada M4V 3B2
Penguin Books (NZ), cnr Rosedale and Airborne Roads,
Albany, Auckland 1310, New Zealand

Penguin Books Ltd, Registered Offices:
80 Strand, London WC2R 0RL, England

First published by Onyx, an imprint of New American Library,
a division of Penguin Group (USA) Inc.

First Printing, July 2004
10 9 8 7 6 5 4 3 2 1

To Laura Peterson, for making me laugh and wiping my tears and always, always believing in me. Thank you, Laura, for not only being a terrific agent, but a terrific person as well.

Chapter 1

Tiny Tots Day Care was located in a quiet suburban neighborhood where the autumn leaves were neatly raked in the well-tended yards and the houses were painted in earth tones to blend harmoniously with the wooded setting.

A one-story building sporting colorful gingerbread and a merry but unobtrusive sign in the yard, the day care had been welcomed in a neighborhood where most mothers worked to provide the combined income required to live the good life.

An hour earlier the calm of the neighborhood had been broken by the wail of sirens as police responded to a 911 call from a frantic woman who worked as an aide at the establishment.

By the time Nick Corelli arrived at ten o'clock, the entire block surrounding the day care had been cordoned off and civilians in the nearby homes had been evacuated. The only people in the immediate area were uniformed cops, detectives, and the occasional reporter or photographer who managed to sneak through the police line.

Nick slid under the yellow tape and flashed his badge at the officer standing guard. In the distance he spied the police chief hunkered down behind a patrol car parked at the curb directly in front of the day care.

Chief Richard Slokem and Nick Corelli shared a relationship of mutual dislike tempered by tolerance. Nick appreciated that while in his personal opinion Slokem was an ass, he was also an accomplished politician who had managed to get more funding for the department than any of his predecessors.

Richard Slokem thought Nick to be a hardheaded, arrogant bastard who eschewed authority, but he had to admit the man was a genius when it came to catching criminals and in the psychology of defusing dangerous situations.

"Nick." Slokem greeted him with a curt nod.

"What have we got?" Nick kneeled down next to the chief, his gaze intent on the day care center.

"We're not sure. A single gunman entered the premises about an hour ago. We don't know who he is or what he wants." Slokem didn't wait for Nick's reply, but continued with the information he knew Nick wanted. "There are seventeen children in there ranging from the ages of two to five. The owner is Margaret Winfield. She's inside with one assistant. We've got one other assistant out here. She was late to work, probably the luckiest day of her life."

"Where is she?"

Slokem pointed a thumb to a young woman nearby. She was crouched down between two officers, her eyes red-rimmed as she wrote in a notebook. "I've got her listing all the names of the children inside along with their parents' names."

"Do we have a link?"

Slokem nodded and held up a telephone hooked

into a complicated piece of equipment. "We've got him on the line, but he's not talking."

"He'll talk." Nick grabbed the phone.

Slokem watched as Nick closed his eyes, drew several deep, long breaths, then reached into his shirt pocket. He withdrew a rock, touched it with his lips, and then replaced it into his pocket.

It was a ritual Slokem had seen several times. The rock was nothing special—an ordinary river rock, flat and smooth on one side and jagged on the other.

Many times, Slokem had wanted to ask the tall, dark-haired man about the rock, but something in Nick's cold gray eyes forbade invasion into the private areas of his life.

"Okay, let's get those kids out of there." Nick switched the speaker button on the phone console. Instantly they could hear the soft breathing of the man who held the day care hostage.

Nick closed his eyes and matched his breathing to that of the person on the other end of the line.

Slow.

Deep.

Controlled.

Nick frowned. No fear in the breathing, no panic. Not a good sign. Fear was an emotion Nick would twist and manipulate to use to his own advantage. Nick's guts knotted as he recognized the lack of the emotion in his opponent.

Nick breathed a natural rhythm, forcing the breaths to be audible. Despite Slokem's sigh of impatience, Nick didn't speak. He'd learned long ago the value of patience.

Seconds passed.

Seconds stretched into minutes.

Nick knew the man on the other end of the line heard him, but still not a word was spoken.

Several more minutes passed.

"Who's this?" The voice was deep and pleasant, and boomed over the speaker.

"This is Nick. Who is this?"

Another long silence fell.

Nick waited patiently. He knew sooner or later the gunman would tell his name and his demands, however bizarre they might be. Men didn't hole up with hostages unless they wanted something. Most of the time it was a desperate bid to change the past or rewrite the future that loomed before them.

"Just call me David."

"Is that your name or is that just what you want me to call you?"

Nick knew the man was weighing his options, trying to decide what was in his own best interest. Nick saw Chief Slokem approach the aide making her list. He knew the chief was checking to see if any of the fathers of the children inside were named David.

Slokem took the list from the young woman and returned to Nick's side. Nick scanned the list and cursed beneath his breath. No David was listed.

"Okay . . . so David it is," Nick said into the phone. "How you doing, David? You need anything in there? The kids all okay?"

A rumble of low laughter was his reply. "I'm fine . . . the kids are fine, and I really appreciate your concern. But, I know the reality here, and I know I'll probably be dead when this is all over."

"If you don't do anything stupid, you won't be dead," Nick countered.

"Ah, but I just might do something stupid. It wouldn't be the first time."

Nick and Slokem exchanged glances. What exactly did they have here? A poor, tortured fool who'd momentarily gone over the edge, or a seasoned criminal with nothing left to lose?

"David, why don't you let the kids go? You've still got two adults in there."

Again a deep, resonant laugh. "Sorry Nick, no can do. And if you don't stop those officers who think they're sneaking up on me, I'll throw a little body out the window." The words were punctuated by an explosion as he fired his gun out the window.

Everywhere people hit the ground. In the distance the sound of women screaming, wailing, rent the air, and Nick knew the mothers of the children had begun to arrive.

He clenched the phone more tightly. Dammit, there had been no warning, no increased stress in the man's voice to indicate his intent. Unpredictable. Unemotional. And unafraid to shoot the gun. Not good signs.

Slokem called the SWAT team members back, cursing soundly beneath his breath. "David, you don't want to hurt the kids," Nick said. "Think about it, David."

"What do I care? Only one of them is my brat." Again the chilling laugh came across the line. "But I think it's nice that you say my name so often, that you're trying so hard to bond with me."

The man wasn't stupid. He knew the rudiments of hostage psychology. Nick drew a deep breath. "Okay,

David, let's cut through all the bullshit and get down to business. What happened today, David? Your boss fire you? The tax man choking you? Your wife tell you to get the hell out?"

"*Juliette!*"

The cry pierced the morning air, sending chills up and down spines with its mournful intensity.

He looked down at the list of parents once again and spied the name Juliette Monroe.

Juliette. An unusual name.

He stabbed the name with his finger and looked at Chief Slokem. "Find this woman and get her here now . . . before this son of a bitch explodes."

Chapter 2

Davick Blankenship stood at the window, the semi-automatic rifle like a lover in his arms. A stiff, unyielding, cold lover, like his wife, Juliette.

She hadn't been stiff and cold when they'd first married. Oh no, she'd been hot as fire. They'd spent the first six months of their marriage in bed, and she'd promised him it would always be like that.

Lying bitch. He stroked the stock of the gun. Cool metal. Like Juliette's eyes had been in the days before she'd left him.

He glanced over to the corner, where the children were huddled together, a clot of sobbing, slobbering, squealing bodies. The two adults were attempting to shush them, their gazes furtively darting from the children to him.

One child sat slightly apart from the others, his blue eyes dry and somber.

Billy. He had eyes like his mother's. Mocking. Judging. No tears. Never tears. For just a moment David imagined putting the barrel of the gun to his son's head and pulling the trigger.

Adrenaline pumped through him. He felt the kick of the gun, smelled the acrid scent of gunpowder min-

gling with blood and death. The images were so vivid;
it took him a minute to realize he hadn't already
pulled the trigger.

Billy's gaze remained on him, as if he were privy to
David's thoughts. David smiled at his son. Soon, he
thought. But not yet. He wouldn't kill Billy until Juliette
was present.

He wanted Juliette to see the death of her son, the
end of her world. Perhaps then, finally, he would see
her cry.

He stared out the window and watched the cops
scurrying between the cover of parked patrol cars.
Their uniforms splashed bright blue amid the red and
gold of autumn leaves. Like squirrels gathering nuts
for the winter to come, and he was the nut they were
after.

He wasn't crazy. Crazy was baying at the moon or
wishing on stars. Crazy was believing you were Santa
Claus or thinking your dog spoke to you in your head.
Crazy was believing in fate.

No, David wasn't crazy; he was merely determined
to get what he wanted. And he wanted it the way it
had been—before things had gotten so screwed up, before Juliette had given birth to the brat and she'd gone
just a little crazy.

He fired another shot out the window, just to keep
them on their toes.

Juliette Monroe was working for the fifth day in a
row as a substitute third grade teacher at the Maple
Tree Elementary School. It had been a good five days.
The students had been well-mannered and the other
teachers had been friendly.

They were in the middle of the morning reading group when the principal, Mr. Cook, tapped on her door. In that rapid tattoo, Juliette heard trouble.

"Ms. Monroe, could you come to my office, please?" He gestured to the teacher's aide standing next to him. "Brenda will take over your class."

Juliette grabbed her purse and quickly followed Mr. Cook, who walked with long, purposeful strides down the polished hallway floor. In the five days she'd been working for the attractive silver-haired principal, she'd noticed that he always smelled of expensive, spicy cologne. Now the scent mingled with a sense of foreboding inside her.

When she reached the office and saw the two uniformed police officers waiting for her, she knew she hadn't been wrong. Trouble was here, and that could mean only one thing: David had found her again.

"Juliette Monroe?" The thin, young officer had pockmarked cheeks and eyes that were dark pebbles, cold and angry.

"Yes."

"You got a husband named David?" This from the older cop, whose eyes showed a shadow of sympathy.

"Ex-husband," she replied.

"You need to come with us." Again the young officer. He attempted to take her by the arm, but she stepped back from him.

"Ma'am. Please."

Juliette nodded to the older cop and together the three of them left the school building. They placed her in the back of the police car and the minute they pulled away from the school, the lights and siren came on.

She asked no questions and they offered no explanation. She hoped they were taking her to identify David's body, for his death seemed to be the only thing that would finally, irrevocably grant her peace.

For almost a year she and Billy had been on the run, going from city to city, state to state, seeking asylum from a madman. And in the past three months, she'd thought they'd escaped him. She'd begun to hope.

As the police car shot through intersections and hurtled through traffic, Juliette realized they were traveling toward the Tiny Tots Day Care. Panic welled up inside her and she found it difficult to draw a breath.

Billy.

Her son's name echoed in every chamber of her heart, and a nearly overwhelming sense of dread overtook her. Keep Billy safe, she prayed. She could handle anything David chose to do to her, but if he hurt Billy, she would never recover.

She closed her eyes, summoning the strength she knew she'd need to deal with whatever lay ahead.

Just as she had feared, the patrol car eased down the block where the Tiny Tots Day Care was located. But before they got anywhere near the building, they pulled to the curb and the two officers escorted her from the car.

The peaceful quiet of the residential block had disappeared, replaced by the crackle of police radios, the hum of equipment from several press vans, the whir of cameras as photos were shot, and the constant wail of a group of people who clung to one another.

Juliette walked between the two officers, her heart pounding a rhythm of disbelief and horror. As they drew closer to the day care, the officers pulled her down into a crouch and the three of them darted from patrol car to patrol car until they reached the vehicle directly in front of the day care.

At that point, the two officers left her in the charge of a slightly overweight, balding man in a three piece suit, and a dark-haired man in a navy windbreaker who didn't acknowledge her presence in any way, but rather stared intently at the day care building.

"Mrs. Monroe." The balding man nodded a terse greeting. "I'm Police Chief Richard Slokem. We seem to have a situation here." Despite the coolness of the autumn day, perspiration dotted Richard Slokem's forehead. "We have two adults and seventeen children inside there, along with a man we believe is your husband . . . David Monroe. He has a gun, and he's threatening to kill the children."

"Blankenship," Juliette corrected him. "His name is David Blankenship. Monroe is my maiden name."

For the first time, the dark-haired man turned to look at her. He was ruggedly handsome, but his eyes radiated with a dark intensity. "We need to know everything we can about your husband."

"Ex-husband," she replied.

"Since when?"

"A little over a year ago."

"Does he take medication?"

"Not that I'm aware of."

"Does he take illegal drugs?" The questions shot out of him with the force of bullets from a gun and all the while he stared at her, as if the answer to David rested someplace hidden inside her.

"He didn't when we were married."

Those dark gray eyes studied her soberly. "Is he crazy?"

"Oh, yes," she replied.

He raked a hand through his unruly hair. "So, what's this about?"

"Power. Control." The answers came from Juliette without hesitation.

"What do you think he wants?"

Juliette closed her eyes for a long moment. "Me."

She opened her eyes and stared at the day care where inside was the boogeyman of her youth, the monster of her every nightmare, her ex-husband.

Chapter 3

She wasn't what Nick expected, although he didn't know exactly what he'd expected. She was a winter kind of woman, her hair a cool blond and her eyes a glacier blue. Slender, she leaned forward slightly, as if afraid without her conscious effort the autumn breeze might blow her away.

He sensed no fear, as if she'd long ago moved past such a base, primal emotion. It had been over an hour since he'd told David that his ex-wife was present. There had been no further communication between David Blankenship and anyone else on the outside. He had not asked to speak with Juliette and had stopped talking altogether to Nick.

The parents of the children had grown silent as well, as if their fears were too deep for tears, too immense for mere human cries.

"Maybe we should try the SWAT team again," Slokem suggested, his frustration evident in the stiffness of his shoulders, the deep frown that tore into his forehead. His term as Chief of Police was up in three months and Nick knew he was hoping to serve another term. The death of little children did not play well either in the press or on the political scene.

"No. I'm not convinced this bastard won't shoot a kid."

"I thought your job was to make sure he doesn't shoot a kid," Slokem replied thinly.

Nick turned and stared at him. "I'm a cop, a negotiator, not a magician." Nick raked a hand through his hair and directed his attention back to the building.

He was concerned. David Blankenship had been holed up for a little over two hours and other than yelling his ex-wife's name, he'd made no demands, given no indication of what had brought him to this place in time.

He'd feel better if David was demanding a million dollars in unmarked twenties, the release of a dozen skinheads from the local jail, and a Black Hawk helicopter to assure his escape from this mess.

Silence made negotiation impossible. Without demands, there was nothing to negotiate.

Juliette Monroe had been helpful in filling in some information about David Blankenship. Thirty-three years old, David was the only son of a Philadelphia entrepreneur and his socialite wife.

According to Juliette, on the day of her marriage to David eight years ago, his parents had given him access to an obscene trust fund, then had cut all ties with him and his new bride.

Nick looked over to where Juliette stood. Although surrounded by officers, she looked alone, isolated and somehow removed from her surroundings. Somebody had given her a cup of coffee, but she held it as if she had no idea what it was or what to do with it.

Nick motioned her to him. She showed no emotion

as she approached. No fear darkened her eyes, no weary resignation slumped her shoulders.

In his years of experience, Nick had occasionally seen female victims of spousal abuse. They all had the same eyes, filled with denial and shame and a suppressed edge of panic. He saw none of that in Juliette Monroe's pale eyes.

"Try talking to him again."

She took the phone from him, her fingers as icy as her eyes. She might look utterly nerveless, but her frigid fingers told another story.

"David . . . talk to me," she said into the receiver.

Nick flipped a switch that would allow him to hear the conversation as well.

"David . . . for God's sake. Hasn't this gone on long enough?"

The result was the same as it had been the last three times she'd attempted to initiate a dialogue. Silence, then an audible click as David broke the connection.

She handed the phone back to Nick and for the first time he saw a hint of fear whisper in her eyes. "You have to get my son out of there."

"I'm doing the best I can," Nick replied.

"No, you don't understand." She grabbed him by the arm, her fingertips biting into the flesh beneath Nick's windbreaker. "Billy is the one most at risk here. David hates him." She looked down at her fingers gripping him and flushed, as if aware for the first time that she was touching him.

She sank down onto the ground behind the patrol car, as if her legs would no longer hold her upright. Nick sat next to her, his gaze lingering on her.

The last thing he wanted to do was share any of the

emotions that were obviously at work inside her. Emotions were dangerous, particularly in situations like this. Nick had to remain unemotionally involved, ready to form a relationship of sorts with the man with the gun inside the day care.

"I thought we were safe." Her voice was barely audible despite the unnatural silence that had fallen over the area. Nick leaned toward her slightly, catching for the first time the faint smell of spicy perfume that emanated from her.

"It's been over three months. I thought he'd finally forgotten us." A small bitter laugh escaped her, riding the breeze and disappearing instantly. "I should have known he was just biding his time, waiting for us to feel safe."

"You've been in Riverton three months?" he asked. She nodded.

"Why Riverton?"

For the first time her lips curved into a small smile. "You mean, why on your turf?" The smile was quicksilver, sparkling in her eyes. But it was there only a moment, then gone, swallowed by the cool facade. "My parents lived here for two years before they died. I visited them here and thought it seemed like a nice, peaceful town, a good place to raise a child. I thought he'd never find us here."

"But you're using your maiden name. That makes you easy to find."

She frowned and stared at the day care building. "I tried using a fake name for a while, but it was impossible to find jobs without using a social security number."

She turned back to look at Nick, her gaze holding a

steely strength he was unaccustomed to seeing in survivors. "I refuse to give my son a childhood of having to remember a different name on different days of the week. Besides, I'm not a criminal and I don't know how to live outside the law." She stood and brushed off the seat of her pants. "Now, tell me what we have to do to get my son out of there."

Nick stood as well. "I wish I had a definitive answer for you, but I don't. All I know at the moment is David has all the cards, nineteen cards to be precise, and at the moment he's making no demands. He's not even talking to us. So right now we have no alternative but to wait."

"Wait for what?"

"Wait for him to play his cards," Nick replied. Or force him to play, which was always a dangerous gamble. He picked up the phone and punched in the number that would connect him to the phone in the day care. It rang three times before it was answered.

"David, this is Nick Corelli again. Listen, it's after noon. I'm sure those kids are getting hungry. Maybe you're getting hungry, too. Can we get you all anything?"

For a long moment there was silence.

"Yeah. We are getting hungry," David finally said.

A rush of adrenaline swept through Nick. Contact had been made once again. "You want us to send something in for you? What sounds good? We'll get you what you want, David."

"Pizza, Nick. Pizza sounds good."

"Great. What kind do you like?"

There was another moment of silence. "Have Juliette order the pizza. She'll see that they get the order right." With these words, David once again broke the connection.

Nick turned to Juliette. "They want pizza. David said to have you order it, that you'll make sure they get it right."

For the second time, a flicker of emotion darkened the depths of her blue eyes. She pulled her turtleneck sweater down just enough so he could see a two-inch pale white scar that marred the smooth skin of her throat. "This is what happened the last time I ordered pizza for David and I didn't get the order right." She patted the turtleneck back into place. "Trust me, I'll make sure it's right."

Chapter 4

The first news bulletin of the hostage situation at the Tiny Tots Day Care Center aired at 11:23 A.M.

SuEllen Maynard sat forward on the sofa in the double-wide trailer where she lived with her mother and her mother's latest lover, Max.

She turned up the volume of the nineteen-inch television as a picture of David Blankenship flashed across the screen. Her heartbeat quickened. He was as handsome as a movie star and his liquid brown eyes seemed to be peering straight into her very soul.

The photograph was on the television screen for only a few moments, then gone and the interrupted soap opera picked up once again.

But SuEllen couldn't get back into the soap, not with those beautiful brown eyes haunting her. She leaned over and from beneath the coffee table grabbed a notebook and a pen.

She would write to David Blankenship. His eyes had demanded she contact him. She'd recognized the torment in his eyes, and at eighteen years old, SuEllen was already a survivor of life's torment.

A mother who lived in the bottom of a whiskey bottle had stolen her childhood, and at fourteen SuEllen had been raped by one of the men her mother had brought home, stealing whatever innocence she might have had left.

Her life began at sixteen, when, for the first time, her mother had taken her to the Leavenworth Penitentiary to visit the father who'd been arrested for first-degree murder a month before SuEllen's birth.

That day, SuEllen was exposed to a group of men like she'd never known before. Men filled with danger, with overwhelming passion. Here were men who had railed against the unfairness of their lives, whose passions had driven them to the ultimate extremes. They had not allowed society's rules or God's law to stop them in their fury.

SuEllen knew that fury; it had lived inside her for as long as she could remember. She'd seen the same thing in David Blankenship's eyes and knew somehow he was her destiny, her soul mate.

She had no idea what forces had compelled him to take the day care hostage, but she sympathized with him. She knew sometimes you had to go to extremes to get people to listen to what you needed to say. SuEllen had never had the guts to go to the extreme, but she sure as hell admired those who did.

She'd take the letter to the Riverton jail, where he'd be held until his arraignment. She had no doubt that he would answer her letter. She had running correspondence with a dozen prisoners, including the father she'd never hugged, never even touched, but who professed to love her dearly.

As she began the letter, her heart sang. She knew David Blankenship was the man she'd been waiting for. He was going to change her life forever.

*   *   *

The pizza had arrived and Nick had negotiated the release of five children in return for the pizza. That had been hours ago.

The police were itching to end the situation, the parents of the children still inside were once again growing noisy, demanding action, afraid of action, needing nothing more than their babies back safe in their arms.

However, nobody was eager to escalate the situation with the children still held hostage inside. Nick had never been so frustrated in his life.

He couldn't get a handle on David Blankenship. They'd had several conversations, but in each of them Nick hadn't been sure who was controlling whom. And then there had been the long periods of silence, when the phone in the day care rang and rang, but David refused to answer, refused to talk.

Those periods of silence were always ended by a single gunshot out the window that sent screams into the air, and cops scurrying like frantic hamsters running on exercise wheels.

Throughout the afternoon, Juliette Monroe had sat behind a patrol car, her lovely features void of emotion. Nick had never seen anyone so self-contained.

As twilight fell, the evening air grew cooler and the hysteria surrounding the scene seemed to intensify. Reporters jockeyed for position, cops set up bright lights to illuminate the building when darkness fell, and the parents' wails grew louder, as if they believed the coming of night stole all hope.

Nick could only remember one other time when he'd felt so frustrated with a hostage situation. Like now, at that time his stomach had clenched with the anticipation of catastrophe. Like now, that time he'd had a foreboding sense of tragedy. While he'd been negotiating that particular situation, he'd had no idea how sharply, how personally the resulting tragedy would affect him.

He reached up and absently touched the small lump of river rock in his pocket, swallowing hard against the grief that always threatened to consume him when he thought of that day two years ago.

"I can get him out of there."

Nick jerked around to see Juliette standing next to him. Those cold blue eyes of hers gazed at him intently. "How?" he asked.

"Give him what he wants. Promise him I'll go back to him, be a wife to him again."

"I can't let you do that," Nick said brusquely.

"Why not? Nothing you're doing seems to be working." For the first time a flash of anger darkened her eyes. "Is there some sort of unwritten rule? Don't lie to a psychopath?"

"Of course not," Nick replied curtly. "We lie all the time in hostage situations, but we're careful about what we lie about."

"Then let me lie about me and I'll get him out of there." She looked away from Nick and gestured to the men setting up additional spotlights, preparing for a nightlong siege. She looked back at Nick, those eyes of hers chilling, intensifying the bad feeling in the pit of Nick's stomach.

"He'll kill Billy. If you don't do something, he'll kill my son."

Nick believed her. Even though David Blankenship

had shown no indication of his intent to specifically kill his son, something in the depth of Juliette's eyes indicated otherwise.

But Nick also knew you never gave a hostage everything he wanted. That's why it was called hostage *negotiation*. Nick stared back at the day care center and raked a hand through his hair in frustration. "So, what do you have in mind?" he asked.

She picked up the phone and hit the single digit that speed-dialed the phone inside the day care. Nick's first impulse was to instantly disconnect her. He squelched his impulse and instead hit the button that would allow him to listen in on the conversation.

The phone rang ten times before it was answered. "David, it's me."

Her voice was softer, smoother than Nick had heard it before, and yet her eyes remained arctic cold. She fascinated him, but it was a fascination he couldn't indulge. He knew better than to invest any emotions whatsoever in anyone involved in this situation. Emotions made errors and at times got people killed.

"David . . . are you there?" she asked. There was no reply. "You don't have to talk to me, but I'd like to talk to you."

Her voice was positively silky and created a pit of warmth in Nick's stomach, a warmth that warred with the chill of his increasing sense of impending doom.

"About what?" David asked.

"Us." Still not a flicker of emotion in her eyes.

"There is no us," David replied, a trace of bitterness in his deep voice.

"David, I've been thinking about you a lot lately." As she spoke, one hand reached up and touched her neck where she'd shown Nick the scar. "It used to be so good between us. Remember?"

David disconnected. However, before Juliette could hand the receiver back to Nick, it rang.

"So, what have you been thinking lately?" David asked.

"I've been thinking a lot about that first year of our marriage. It's the only time I can remember being truly happy."

Again Nick noticed that her eyes said one thing, her voice quite another.

"You left me." His voice was guttural, and choked with emotion. Nick's adrenaline level increased.

"I was confused, David. I needed some time to figure out what was important to me. And in the time we've been apart, I've realized that you're important to me."

"You're lying. They are telling you to say these things. You're just working with them to get me out of here." Again he disconnected.

"I'd better talk to him," Nick said. "This wasn't a good idea, he's getting agitated."

"Wait," Juliette said, refusing to relinquish the phone. "He'll call me back." As if to prove her point the phone rang again.

"Why did you have to have the kid? Everything was perfect before then."

"I know . . . I know," she replied smoothly. "I thought I wanted to be a mother. It's what other women want. But I was wrong. I didn't realize how it would ruin things between us."

Again Nick was struck by how compelling, how earnest her voice sounded while her eyes betrayed no emotion whatsoever.

"Do you believe in second chances, David?" her voice was a near whisper. "Is it possible we could have a second chance together?"

A collective gasp went up from the crowd as Kathy Rogers, one of the adult workers, appeared at the small front window, a gun to her temple.

"Son of a bitch," Nick gasped softly. He should have known better than to have allowed her to talk to David. Suddenly the situation had escalated to a dangerous level.

It was obvious he was using Kathy as a shield against any sniper who might try to take a shot. "The only way we have a second chance is if the kid is dead." David's voice was no longer cool and calm, but agitated and harsh as he spoke into the phone. He was speaking loud enough that his voice carried out the open window.

Nick knew if this went bad, he'd be haunted for a long time, not only by the terror on Kathy's face, but by a vision of the children still inside who were also being terrorized.

Nick motioned for her to give him the phone. He needed to defuse the situation. He needed to get that gun barrel away from Kathy's head.

But Juliette refused to relinquish the phone. As she gazed at her ex-husband in the window, not a flicker of emotion darkened her eyes and Nick found himself wondering what kind of woman she was.

"David, if you kill that woman, we'll never get our second chance. If you kill Billy, you'll spend the rest of your life in prison." She paused a moment, as if to allow her words to set in. "Why don't we just take him to child welfare and dump him there? You and I can head back to Philly and pick up the pieces of our own life."

There was a long silence and Nick's stomach rolled with nervous tension. Juliette looked as cool as if she were talking about the weather.

"You're lying. You won't get rid of the kid."

Nick noted how David never referred to his son by name. A bad sign. Billy was apparently utterly depersonalized in his father's mind.

"David, I'm tired of the kid. I'm tired of having to pick up after him, and listen to his whining. Did you know he still wets the bed? I have to change his sheets every morning. Trust me, I'm ready to give him up. David, let him go, let them all go and come out. I promise you we'll go back to the way things were. We'll be so happy again."

Kathy disappeared from the window and David hung up. Nick released a ragged breath and grabbed the phone from Juliette. "Jesus, lady. You're one hell of a gambler."

"Now we'll see if I win or lose." She sat on the curb, no outward appearance of emotional trauma.

Nick stared at her for a long moment, intrigued by her strength, her cunning in offering up herself as a sacrificial lamb. She was like nobody he'd ever dealt with before.

The phone rang once again and Nick again focused on his single task: apprehend the suspect before anyone was hurt.

"If I decide to walk out of here, what would happen?" David asked.

Relief coursed through Nick. By David's even mentioning the possibility of giving up, the battle was half won.

Chapter 5

David stood at the window and stared out. According to Nick Corelli, if he came out now with his hands up, he and Juliette could walk away and Nick would see to it that the kid was taken to child welfare.

"You haven't hurt anyone," Nick had said. "You've provided us all a little excitement, but no harm, no foul."

David didn't know if he could trust Nick Corelli or not. He doubted very seriously that they would just allow him to walk away from all this.

They'd probably demand he have a psychiatric evaluation. At the very least, he'd be held for a couple of days then released.

Still, it would be nice to think he could walk out, lay down his gun, grab Juliette, and ride off into the sunset.

Juliette. His heart cried out her name as he remembered the scent of her, the smooth silk of her skin, the way he had once been her moon and stars, her very world.

Was she lying? He didn't know. He couldn't tell. She'd promised him things would go back to the way they had been. Without the kid, David would once again be the most important person in her life. And that's all he had ever wanted.

Could he trust her?

David tightened his hands around the gun. She'd been right about one thing. If he killed anyone, they'd never have a future together.

Oh, but he'd wanted to kill Billy. He'd wanted to explode the boy's brains right there at the window, where Juliette would be able to see her son die. Then she'd understand who was in control.

But so far he hadn't hurt anyone. No harm, no foul, as Nick had said. Even if they lied and arrested him, he'd be able to make whatever bail was set. And Juliette would be waiting for him, ready to begin their future together.

Surely what she'd said was true—that she'd had time to think about what was important to her, that he was all that was important to her.

He rubbed his forehead, a headache of indecision pounding fiercely. Could he trust her? Was she sincere in the promises she'd made? She'd never find another man like him, surely she knew that. Nobody would ever love her as he had—as he still did.

He frowned, becoming aware of one of the children's sobbing. He turned and glared at her. A little dark-haired girl in a yellow dress, her crying jarred in his brain, intensifying his headache.

"Shut her up," he snarled at the teacher who sat on the floor next to the girl. "Shut her up before I do it for you."

The teacher grabbed the child and placed her on her lap, then pressed the little girl's face against her chest, somewhat muffling the sobs.

David turned back to the window. Darkness would be falling soon. Beneath the cloak of night, they would come for him. There was no way he'd even see them coming.

He picked up the phone. Nick answered instantly. "If I walk out of here, no cuffs, no arrest. I take Juliette and disappear."

"David, you know I can't make any firm promises until the hostages are out of there and we see that everyone is safe and sound."

"I haven't hurt any of them," David replied. "I don't want to bother anyone, Nick. I just want to take my wife and go home."

"Then come out, David. Throw out the gun and step out the door with your hands in the air. We'll talk about what happens next when everyone is out of there."

"No cuffs," David demanded. "I don't want to be handcuffed."

"You come out like a gentleman, we'll treat you like a gentleman," Nick replied.

Indecision tore through David. "Let me talk to my wife."

"David," she said.

The sound of his name on her lips sent desire swooping through him. She was his world, his heart, his soul, his very life. Without her, he knew he would die. He felt it in the pounding of his heart, in the ache within his soul.

"Promise me," he said. "Promise me when I walk out of here, wherever I go, whatever I do, you'll be with me."

"Right by your side," she replied.

"And we'll dump the kid and things will go back to the way they were when we first got married. Promise me."

"I promise," she replied. "I promise because that's what I want, too."

"I'm coming out."

David hung up and smiled at his son. "Hey pissy boy, you're going to go live with foster parents. Your mother doesn't want you anymore and I never did want you."

David laughed, euphoria swelling inside him as Juliette's promise echoed through his head. He'd always known deep in his heart that she would return to him. How could she not? They were soul mates, destined to be together through eternity. Without each other, they were nothing.

Outside the day care, preparations were made for all contingencies. The SWAT team members moved closer to the building, officers drew their weapons and aimed at the doorway.

Everyone knew that this, the point of surrender, could be the most deadly moment of all in a hostage situation. David Blankenship had two choices: He could play by the rules or not. Everyone was on edge and ready.

"David. Open the door and throw out your gun," Nick instructed over the phone.

"Hold your fire," Richard Slokem's voice thundered through the air.

The door to the day care center opened and the gun hit the ground just beyond the stoop. Dusk painted the entire scene with a surreal light. The only sounds were the slight rustling of officers moving through the grass and a dog barking in the distance.

"Okay, David. Put the phone down and step outside with your hands high in the air."

The minute David Blankenship stepped out of the day care, officers moved in. Two officers grabbed him and within seconds had his hands cuffed behind his back. Six more officers flew into the day care and quickly ushered the children and their teachers to awaiting EMTs.

Nick approached where David stood between the officers. "How are you doing, David?"

"Not good, Nick," David said, obviously recognizing Nick by his voice. "I thought we agreed no cuffs." David's voice held a touch of irritation, but his gaze swept past Nick to where Juliette stood in the distance.

"Juliette." He called to her, his body vibrating with what Nick considered a disturbing energy.

Even from this distance, Nick could feel the cold stare emanating from Juliette's eyes as she looked at her ex-husband.

For a moment, as Juliette's and David's gazes remained locked, Nick felt like an intruder in their private world. He saw and felt the moment David realized her betrayal.

"You fucking bitch," David whispered softly.

At that moment Billy left the emergency crew and went to stand by his mother. Again Nick was struck by how unnaturally controlled Juliette was. She didn't grab her son to her breast or cover his face with kisses. The only sign of anything between mother and child was when Billy reached up to hold his mother's hand.

"Juliette!" David screamed, his face twisted into a

mask of rage at the sight of Juliette and Billy, united in their stance against him. "You fucking bitch, you promised. You fucking promised me."

"I lied." Her voice rang clear and strong.

All the rage melted away and the coldness in David's eyes chilled Nick to the bone. "I'll get you, Juliette. Eventually I'll get out. They can't hold me forever. I'll find you again and you'll pay for your lies, Juliette."

"Get him out of here," Nick said to the two officers who held him.

It wasn't until David Blankenship was safely ensconced in the back of a patrol car that Nick walked back to where Juliette and her son stood.

"I guess I should thank you for all your help," Nick said.

"I don't want thanks. I did my part. I got him out of there, now you do your job. You make sure he stays in jail. You make sure he rots in a prison somewhere."

She didn't give Nick an opportunity to reply. She whirled on her heels and together she and her son headed down the sidewalk.

Nick stared after her and absently rubbed the river rock in his pocket. He hoped to hell David would spend plenty of time in prison for this, but all he knew for certain when it came to the judicial system was that there were no guarantees.

The best Nick would have been able to offer her was the fact that since it was so late on a Friday night, David would be held over the weekend for arraignment on Monday concerning charges.

With this disturbing thought in mind, Nick decided it was definitely a good night to get rip-roaring drunk.

Chapter 6

It wasn't until they were back in the tiny furnished dump of an apartment they called home that Juliette fell to her knees and grabbed her son in a fierce embrace.

She needed to feel the beat of his heart against her own, smell the sweaty scent of his little-boy head, assure herself that he was really and truly okay.

For a few moments she couldn't speak, so overwhelmed was she with the emotions of a mother who had seen her child in mortal danger.

If he'd been born a month earlier he'd have been in kindergarten instead of day care. He would have been safer in a school where authorities were on guard against guns.

She ran her hands down his back, across his thin shoulders. She wished she could rip off his shoes and count every toe like she'd done when he'd been a newborn. She needed to know that everything was where it belonged, that David had done nothing to physically hurt him.

A sob caught in her throat and Billy's arms tightened around her neck. Another sob escaped as the trauma of the day replayed itself in her mind, as she realized how close she'd come to losing the only thing she loved in life.

"Mommy, it's okay," Billy finally said. "I'm okay." He patted her back, and the gesture of her child attempting to console her stopped her tears. He never liked to see her cry.

"Well, of course you are," she said and finally released her death grip on him. She cupped his face between her hands and looked at his beautiful little face.

It had been love for Billy that had kept her alive through the worst of David's abuse. And it had been love for her son that had finally given her the strength, the courage to leave David.

"You are the strongest, most brave boy I've ever known," she said, fighting against the tears of relief that once again threatened to fall.

He nodded, then his gaze turned slightly accusatory. "I don't pee the bed anymore."

She stopped the half-hysterical laughter that started to burst from her. After all he'd been through, after all he'd experienced that afternoon, the thing that had him most upset was that she'd said he still wet the bed.

"He called me a pissy boy," Billy said.

"You and I both know you aren't a pissy boy," Juliette said. "But you understand why I had to say that, why I had to say all of those things."

He nodded, his pale blond hair gleaming in the artificial light from overhead. "Want to color with me?"

Once again intense love welled up inside her. "I'd love to color with you."

Minutes later mother and son sat at the kitchen table coloring together. This had been one of the few activities mother and son had enjoyed when living with David. When David fell asleep, Juliette often sneaked into her son's room, where they would quietly color together.

She was pleased that Billy was coloring a happy picture, one with the brightest crayons from the box.

There were nights she couldn't sleep because she worried about the emotional damage he'd already suffered in the five years of his life.

She'd tried to make things as normal as possible for him, but the life they'd led while with David and even the life after David had been anything but normal.

Billy awed her. He had an inner strength, a well of courage, and a resigned acceptance far beyond his five years. They were traits he'd seemed to have been born with, as if the angels had known he would need to be a special child in order to survive.

He'd been a baby who hadn't cried, a toddler who hadn't fussed or whined. He'd learned at an incredibly early age to play alone, amuse himself, stay hidden in his room, and wait for the times when Juliette could sneak away from David and in to him.

Mother and son had shared a conspiracy. No hugs, no kisses, no signs of affection at all if David could see, but the moment they were alone, she held him and rocked him and kissed him, forging a bond of love that was unbreakable.

Was this finally the end of their running? Their fear? She'd like to think that David had finally, irrevocably crossed a line that would see him behind bars for a very long time. But she'd long ago lost faith in the judicial system.

"Mom?" Billy looked up from the bright yellow sun he'd been coloring.

"What, honey?"

"Are we gonna leave here?" He eyed her somberly, his gaze holding neither anticipation nor dread, merely curiosity.

"I don't know, honey," she answered truthfully. She picked up a purple crayon from the pile in the center of the table. "If the police keep David in jail, then maybe we'll stay."

She never referred to David as "your father" or "your dad." She had long ago, in her mind and in her heart, severed any familial relationship between David and Billy. She thought it was healthier for her son that way.

By ten o'clock Billy was in bed in the only bedroom and Juliette made out her bed on the sofa even though she knew sleep would be a long time coming.

Before settling in, she went to stand in the doorway of Billy's bedroom, just needing to look at him one last time before going to bed.

He slept on his back, legs and arms sprawled so that he took up the entire space of the twin bed. A tiny snore emitted from his open mouth and a fierce love welled up inside her. Whatever it took. She'd promised herself from the moment he'd been born that she'd do whatever it took to keep Billy safe.

She fought the impulse to go into the room, crouch down beside the bed and run her fingers over his face, feel the warmth of his sweet cheeks, the feather softness of eyelashes, the rhythmic breathing that came during sleep.

She left his doorway and went back to the sofa.

Turning off the light, she snuggled into the blankets and stared at the dark ceiling overhead.

How she wished her parents were still alive. How she ached for the comfort of their love and support. Losing them both in the space of a six-month period had been one of the most devastating blows in her life and had left her vulnerable to David's manipulative charm.

She had only herself to depend on. She hoped and prayed the police department would do their job and keep David in jail for a very long time.

With the darkness of night to conceal her, she released the sobs that had been welling up inside her. Tears ran down her cheeks as she relived how very close she'd come that afternoon to losing her son.

Nick spun the black rock on the top of the bar, then slapped his hand on it to stop the spinning and ordered another beer.

The Riverton Roadhouse was noisy and Nick welcomed the loud voices, the raucous music, and the clink of glasses and beer bottles that filled the air.

The Roadhouse was owned by an ex-cop and had become a favorite hangout for off-duty officers as well as half the town of Riverton. Nick often wound up there when he needed to unwind.

He spun the rock a second time and took a sip from his beer and tried not to think about the woman and boy who had been at the heart of the day's excitement.

The image of the two of them walking away, not speaking to each other, not touching except for their hands, remained burned in his head. There had been such dignity in the set of her shoulders, a dignity that had echoed in the smaller shoulders of her son.

"There he is, the man of the hour."

Nick turned on his barstool to see three fellow officers approaching. All three had been at the Tiny Tot Day Care Center.

They sat at a nearby table and gestured for him to join them. He pocketed his rock, grabbed his beer, and moved to the table. "Ted," he yelled to the bartender. "A couple of pitchers for my friends."

"So, you must be feeling pretty good." Bob Triplett slapped him on the back. "Slokem is happy, the press is happy, and all those parents want to give you a trophy."

"Any praise should go to Juliette Monroe," Nick observed. "She did more than anyone to get Blankenship out of there."

"She was some looker, wasn't she?" Jack McCain, the youngest of the four, whistled beneath his breath. "Some babe, but definitely ice in her veins."

Sammy Bellows, the eldest of the four and one of Nick's closest friends, shook his head. "If I was her, I wouldn't exactly be sleeping well tonight. Did you see Blankenship's face when he realized she'd fucked him over?"

"Definitely a nutcase," Jack said. He smiled wryly. "He'd probably benefit from the new anger management classes."

They all hooted and laughed derisively. A local psychologist had arranged with a friendly judge to offer anger management to first-time offenders exhibiting violent behavior. For the most part the Riverton cops thought it was a bunch of crap. Violent offenders belonged behind bars, not in a classroom.

Nick sipped his beer and listened to the others recap the day's events, talk about other criminals, other cases and their own wives and girlfriends.

Although he nodded and laughed in the appropriate places, his head was filled with thoughts of Juliette Monroe. She'd been more than a babe. Her pale blond hair had been pulled back in a clip at the nape of her neck, giving a false severity to her delicate features.

There had been just a moment, a split second in time when he'd watched her talking to David and he'd wanted to unfasten the clip and let her hair spill around her shoulders. It had been a crazy thought, completely inappropriate on all levels.

He shoved thoughts of the cool blonde from his mind and refocused on the conversation at the table. By eleven Nick was ready to call it a night. He threw a handful of bills on the table and stood.

"Wait . . ." Jack stopped him and Nick sank back in his chair. "We've got a little bet going on."

"A bet?"

"About that rock in your pocket." Jack paused a moment to take a deep swallow of his beer. "Now, I think it's from the first time you got laid, that your first sexual encounter took place on the rocky shore of some lake and you picked up that rock to remind you of the bliss of the moment."

Sammy punched Jack in the arm. "You're young enough, boy, that you have sex on the brain. I figure that rock is from the lake shore of a fishing cabin Nick intends to buy when he retires."

Bob shrugged his burly shoulders. "I just think you're nuts."

Nick laughed and stood. "Good night, guys."

"So aren't you going to tell us?" Jack protested.

Nick touched the rock in his pocket. "Nope." He turned and left the bar.

Chapter 7

David sat on the upper bunk in his jail cell, staring at the concrete wall in front of him. Thankfully, he had a cell to himself and didn't have to expend any energy defending his personal space from some moron.

Despite a miserable night on the stinking mattress, his thoughts and his emotions were focused more clearly, more sharply than ever before.

Where once he'd loved Juliette more than anything in the entire world, he now hated her. His hatred knew no boundaries, was as timeless, as fathomless as evil itself.

He'd been a fool to trust her, to believe her promises, her lies. His faith in her had been a test, and she had failed.

He stretched out and stared up at the ceiling. She was so sly. He'd never had an inkling that she would leave him, that eventually she would choose her son over him. He hadn't known what she'd planned until she was gone and he'd been served with divorce papers.

"Hey, Blankenship." Deputy Traylor knocked his baton against the steel bars. David had been in the cell less than twenty-four hours, but already he knew

Traylor was an asshole. "Hey, wacko, I'm talking to you."

David sat up. "Yeah, well unless you're here to tell me I'm being released, I don't have anything to say to you."

Traylor smirked. "By tonight you'll have a couple of roomies. Saturday night always fills up the cells with drunks and dopeheads. Maybe one of them will be the father of one of those poor little kids you kept at gun-point yesterday." He laughed and scratched his pro-truding stomach.

David said nothing, knowing that in refusing to be baited he irritated the deputy more than if he spoke.

Traylor stared at him for a long moment, frowning his disappointment at David's lack of response. Finally he reached into his back pocket and withdrew an en-velope. "Appears you've got a fan. Hand-delivered no less."

He tossed the envelope through the bars and it slid across the floor and disappeared beneath the lower bunk. Traylor shook his head as he turned to leave. "Fucking fan mail for a fruitcake."

Long after Traylor had left, David remained on the top bunk, his thoughts racing. Was the letter from Juliette? Was she sorry for lying? Somehow he didn't think so. He'd seen those cold blue eyes of hers just be-fore she'd turned to walk away.

He'd see those eyes of hers again, only the next time they wouldn't be cold and distant. He smiled, imagin-ing those blue eyes weeping in despair and in terror.

Energy raged through him and he jumped down from his bunk and grabbed the letter that had slid be-neath the lower bunk. The envelope was unsealed and it was obvious he wasn't the first person to read the letter.

> *My dearest David,*
>
> *We haven't met yet, but I knew the moment I saw you on the news today that you would be important in my life . . . that we would be important to each other.*
>
> *When I looked into your eyes, I saw that you had been disappointed and deceived by the people closest to you. I, too, have known disappointment and heartache, and I understand the rage that builds within.*
>
> *At the moment I work as a cashier at a Dairy Shack, but I know my real purpose, my true destiny is to love you, to be the Cleopatra to your Mark Anthony, the Juliet to your Romeo.*

The letter went on for several more poetic paragraphs and was signed, "Crystal, the gleaming gem of your future."

David tossed the letter on his bunk. It was obvious the author was young and deluded. His destiny, indeed.

The only destiny David had was to punish Juliette for her betrayal . . . and he intended to punish her to death.

"Blankenship." Traylor appeared once again. "Your lawyer is here to see you."

Once again energy soared through David. He stood patiently as Traylor entered his cell and handcuffed him. His arraignment was first thing Monday morning. All he needed was a good lawyer, and thankfully he had one of the best.

Traylor led him to a small conference room where Jeffrey Beacham awaited him. The middle-aged lawyer frowned but spoke not a word until Traylor had uncuffed David and had left the room.

"Thank you for coming."

Jeffrey ignored David's outstretched hand and instead gestured him into a chair at the table. "Sit down, David. We have a lot to discuss."

Jeffrey opened his briefcase and pulled out a file folder, then eyed David dispassionately. "I spoke to the D.A. this morning and they intend to charge you on Monday with everything from reckless endangerment to kidnapping."

He looked at David, a trace of distaste in his gaze. "Jesus, David, a day care. What were you thinking?"

David looked down at his hands. "I don't know. I wasn't thinking. All I knew was the need to talk to my ex-wife. I guess I just snapped. I never intended to hurt anyone."

Jeffrey stared at him for a long moment, then sighed and raked a hand through his thin, sandy hair. "Look David, over the last couple of years, I've managed to keep your record clean, but I don't know if we'll be so lucky on this one."

"I know, I know." David held out his hands, palms up in a gesture of supplication. "I don't know what happened. I just went a little crazy. I'm ashamed of myself."

Jeffrey looked at him for a long moment, and in the deepest recesses of his brown eyes, David saw the lawyer's repugnance for him.

David didn't give a shit what Jeffrey Beacham

thought of him. David didn't pay the lawyer to judge him.

"I'll do what I can on this one, but after this, I think it's best we part ways." Jeffrey didn't quite meet David's gaze. "After we get this squared away, I'll send you the remainder of your retainer."

"You get me out of here and you can keep the rest of the retainer as a bonus," David replied.

Greedy little prick, David thought as Jeffrey nodded. As Jeffrey outlined what he intended to do in order to secure David's release, David contemplated what the dapper lawyer would look like with his throat slit open, and smiled.

Chapter 8

Nick left the Riverton Police Station around four on Monday afternoon and pulled into his apartment complex a few minutes later. It had been a quiet day and he'd managed to spend most of it catching up on the mountain of paperwork that comprised a large part of his job.

He was now looking forward to a cold beer, a sizzling steak, and an evening of reading the latest Jonathan Kellerman novel.

He parked his car, but instead of going directly to his apartment, he veered left and knocked on the apartment next door to his.

There was no reply, although he knew she was there. She was always there. He knocked again. "Diane?" he called.

"Nicky?" The feminine voice was barely audible through the heavy wood of the door.

"Yeah, it's me."

The door creaked open and, as always, Diane Borderman stepped away from the open door as if she were afraid Nick would pull her outside.

Nick closed the door behind him and waited a moment for his eyes to adjust from the glare of the late afternoon sunshine to the dark interior of the apartment.

Although it was still early and there was plenty of daylight left, in Diane's apartment it was always night and the rooms were lit by artificial means.

"Good day? Bad day?" he asked as he gave Diane a quick hug. Her thin body trembled slightly against his before she stepped back from him.

She shrugged, walked over to the sofa, and curled up on one end. "Okay day," she replied, but Nick didn't miss the dark shadows beneath her eyes or the lines of strain that belied her words. "You want something to drink? I've got juice and soda in the fridge."

"Sure, a soda sounds good." He walked into the kitchen. In this room as well as every other room of the apartment, the shades were pulled down tight, not allowing in a single shaft of sunshine or a single peek of the outside world.

He grabbed a Coke from the refrigerator, then returned to the living room and sat next to the young woman he was bound to through tragedy and guilt.

For a moment neither of them spoke. The hum of the state-of-the-art computer in one corner was the only sound. The computer was Diane's link to the outside world. Only by entering cyberspace would she venture beyond the safe confines of her apartment walls.

"You keeping busy?" he asked.

She nodded. "I've got contracts to build four Web pages, one more intricate than the next." Diane had built a thriving business for herself in building Web pages.

"Have you spoken with Dr. Holloway lately?" Dr.

Holloway was the psychiatrist who had been treating Diane for the past year and a half.

"I talked to him yesterday."

"I thought the goal this week was to open the curtains at one window."

Her cheeks flushed and she averted her gaze from his. "It was. But I told Dr. Holloway I'd try next week."

Nick sipped his soda and tried to think of something else to say. They never spoke of his work, and he had little in his life other than his job.

They also never spoke about Miranda.

"Have you heard from Tony lately?" she asked.

"Yeah, I got a letter from him yesterday." A wave of guilt swept through Nick as he thought of his younger brother. Two years ago Tony and Diane had been dating and planning a wedding and a life together.

"How is he doing?"

"Okay. He still hates California, but likes his job okay. He finally got tired of renting and has made an offer on a house. He isn't sure if they'll accept the offer or not. He's planning on coming back to visit at Christmas."

"That will be nice for the two of you," she said, and in her voice Nick heard the slight wistfulness that was always there when she spoke of Tony.

"Yeah, but I'm still planning on you and me going ice skating together out at Tanglewood Lake before the winter is over."

She smiled, and in that gesture he saw a glimmer of the vibrant, lovely woman she had once been. "I'm counting on it," she said, although they both knew it was probably an unrealistic goal.

Nick finished his soda and stood. "I guess I'll get

home. I've got a date with a medium-rare steak." She got up and walked with him toward the door, stopping when she was about two feet in front of it. "You need anything?" he asked, his hand on the doorknob.

"No, I'm fine. That's the joy of the Internet. Whatever I need, I can order and have it delivered to my door."

Nick nodded, although he knew some things she couldn't get online. She'd never find a Web site to sell her sanity. And no matter how high-tech she got, she'd never be able to turn the clock back to that single moment on a Saturday afternoon two years ago when her life had been destroyed.

They embraced briefly, then Nick stepped out of her apartment. He drew a deep breath of the outside air and touched the rock in his breast pocket.

There were moments during the course of his days when he sometimes forgot that the rock was there close to his heart. After a visit with Diane, the weight in his pocket became that of a huge, crushing boulder.

His apartment held all the welcome of a cheap motel room. After the stuffiness of Diane's place, Nick went around opening windows, allowing in the unusually warm early October air.

He'd moved here eighteen months earlier, when Tony had left town and Diane's agoraphobia and panic attacks had grown extreme. Diane had no family and with Tony gone she was utterly alone. Nick had stepped in, driven by the knowledge that it had been his failure that had taken all she cared about away from her.

He unwrapped a T-bone and sprinkled it with seasonings, then grabbed a can of beer and popped it open, and pulled out a TV tray.

He'd never even bought a kitchen table set to fill the

space in the eat-in kitchen. Any extra money he got he spent on the fishing cabin he'd bought for a song because it was in such disrepair. He hadn't told anyone about the cabin yet, was waiting until he had it all finished before he invited any of his buddies to join him for a weekend there.

He took a deep pull of his beer and grinned inwardly as he thought of the conversation with his fellow officers at the Riverton Roadhouse on Friday night concerning the rock he carried.

Nobody had come close to guessing what the rock meant. There was only one person on earth who knew where the rock had come from and why he kept it.

He took another drink of his beer, then stood and stepped out on his deck to ready the grill for the steak. He'd just lit the charcoal when his cell phone rang. "Yeah?"

"Nick, it's me."

Nick recognized Sammy Bellows's voice. "Sammy, what's up?"

"I'm here at the courthouse and I thought you might be interested to know your fruitcake from Friday just walked."

"Son of a bitch!" Nick slammed his hand down on the deck railing. "What happened?"

"He had one sharp lawyer, and he talked Judge Bishop into setting bail. Blankenship put up a million dollar bond without blinking an eye."

"Sammy, do me a favor. Find Juliette Monroe's address for me." He had to be sure somebody had warned her that her crazy, abusive ex-husband was free.

Chapter 9

After Nick left, Diane paced her living room. Restless energy and a vague sense of anxiety swept through her.

As always, Nicky's visit had been both welcome and yet torturous. Often, when she looked into Nicky's dark gray eyes, she saw the specter of Miranda and the pain that Diane constantly fought against would come crashing down around her.

She walked over to the living room window, her footsteps faltering as she got close enough to touch the wand that opened and closed the miniblinds.

She'd promised her doctor that this week she would try to open one set of blinds in the apartment. It was time, past time, to force herself to face the demons that kept her a prisoner in her own home.

Her heart began to pound. The beat of rushing blood banged at her temples as she thought of what lay outside the window.

The world.

She reached out and grasped the wand. Her fingers trembled uncontrollably, making the plastic slats chatter like teeth. Her knuckles quickly turned white from her death grip on the narrow piece of plastic.

Just twist the wand, she instructed herself. Take just one little peek outside, then you can call Dr. Holloway with your success.

Just twist the wand. A sob wrenched from her as her fingers refused to respond to her mental command. One peek. One sliver of sunlight.

The air grew thinner, harder to breathe. She sucked in what was left of the air, her chest aching with the effort.

The world.

A place of danger.

Death at any moment.

Devastation in the space of a heartbeat.

The air was gone and she coughed, fighting a wave of light-headedness. She knew, of course, that the air wasn't really gone, but her jaws were clenched so tightly, her lips pressed together so firmly, she couldn't draw enough to sustain.

Closing her eyes, she tried to imagine herself ice skating on Tanglewood Lake. By Christmas the trees that lined the huge pond would be heavy with snow and dripping sparkling icicles.

The icy wind would bite at her face. She could taste the woodsmoke from the fires that burned in barrels to warm the skaters, feel the glide of her legs beneath her as she skimmed over the glasslike surface.

A hand reached for hers, warm and strong, and it wasn't Nicky's hand, but Tony's.

She realized at that moment why Nicky continued to spend time with her. His pain was as great as hers. The only difference was he continued to function in the world while she had retreated from it.

She opened her eyes and discovered that she had

dropped the wand, although her hand was still tightly clenched as if she still held it.

A drop of perspiration trickled down the side of her face and she drew a deep breath, knowing the panic attack that had momentarily gripped her had passed.

Curling up on the sofa, she gave in to the exhaustion that crushed her.

Chapter 10

Within minutes Sammy had contacted Nick with the Monroe address, and Nick headed to the small apartment complex on the north side of town.

He learned from Sammy that David Blankenship had waived his right to a jury trial and was set to face the charges pending before a judge in two and a half months' time.

Smart move, Nick thought as he turned into the complex. A jury of his peers might find the act of holding children hostage unforgivable. Now, Blankenship and his lawyer had only one person to convince that he wasn't a menace to society.

The Wood Tower Apartments were a dreary testimony to low-income housing. The wooden shingles of the buildings were weathered to the gray of hopelessness. Window screens were torn or missing altogether and children with dirty faces and runny noses seemed as plentiful as the cockroaches he knew inhabited such places.

He pulled up in front of number 2212 and parked. A group of older teenagers standing nearby eyed him warily, then sauntered away. Although Nick wasn't in uniform, and he wasn't driving a patrol car, he knew they had identified him as a cop.

It never ceased to amaze him how unerring the gangbangers were at sniffing out a badge.

He knocked briskly on the Monroe door and saw the heavy curtain at the window flutter, then fall once again into place.

Juliette answered the door, surprise lighting her eyes as she recognized him. He'd been right about her hair. It was loose, and she looked softer, more feminine than she had that horrendous day at the day care. Of course, here, she was in her comfort zone, a zone he was about to break with his news.

"Mr. Corelli. Please, come in."

As he stepped by her to enter the small apartment he smelled the scent of her, a subtle, spicy perfume that seemed as mysterious, as intriguing as the woman herself.

The furnishings were shabby. A brown sofa, threadbare in places, a scuffed and scarred coffee table, and a small television on an equally small stand comprised the sum total of the living room. Everything was spotlessly clean.

It was obvious he'd interrupted her dinner preparations and the smell of browned hamburger and spices filled the air. Billy peeked in from the bedroom, his blue eyes wide and somber.

"Hi, Billy," Nick said, wishing he'd come with any news other than what he had to tell her.

"Hi." The young boy offered a shy smile, then disappeared back into the bedroom again.

"Please, I need to stir." She waved a finger for him to follow her.

He walked behind her into a kitchen the size of a postage stamp. She went to the stovetop and stirred something inside a pan and he remained standing in the doorway.

The one thing he'd noticed as he'd walked through the living room was that there was not a single personal item of either hers or Billy's around. The kitchen was the same way. Nothing of the occupants other than the pot of whatever she was cooking on the stove.

She finished stirring and turned to look at him. "Do the police always make a follow-up call on victims or has something happened?"

He didn't want to tell her. He didn't want to see her eyes lose the glint of life that lit them at the moment. He didn't want to watch her crawl into herself, into the place she had been during the day care debacle. "Something's happened."

She held his gaze for a long moment, then sank down at the scarred wooden table. "What?" Her shoulders had stiffened, as if she was ready to receive a physical blow.

Nick had an irrational impulse to pull her to her feet, wrap his arms around her, and hold her tight. At that moment he recognized that something about this woman made a touch of heat sizzle inside him.

He focused on his reason for being here. "He's out."

"Out?"

"On bail."

"On bail?" She echoed his words without inflection, her gaze never leaving his.

"He walked out of jail about an hour ago."

Her body tensed and her gaze darted around the room as if seeking an escape route. "Then, we have to go." One of her slender hands unconsciously reached up to her neck and touched the scar Nick knew lay beneath the sky blue turtleneck sweater she wore.

"Go where? His trial is set to start in just a little over two months' time. The prosecution will want your testimony."

Her gaze focused on him once again. "He'll never go to trial. In two months' time I'll be dead. Billy will be dead. Trust me on this."

"We'll make sure that doesn't happen." Nick took the chair across from her.

"Oh please," she replied scornfully. "You couldn't even keep him in jail for longer than a weekend."

"My job was to get him out of that day care with no harm done to the hostages. With your help, I managed to do that. But I won't take any responsibility for our screwed-up judicial system."

"Did you hear the promises I made him? Do you have any idea the price of betrayal?" Her voice was unsteady and low, barely more than a whisper. She grabbed his hand, her fingers cold as they gripped his and yet the simple physical touch made the sizzle inside him rise a bit in temperature.

"You have no idea how smart he can be, how vengeful." She released his hand and stood. "We have to leave here. I have to get Billy away from here."

"And so you move, start over, build a life and wait for him to find you again?" He rose from the table as well.

She eyed him coldly. "The alternative is certainly less appealing."

"We could get a restraining order in effect." Nick knew the suggestion was stupid and the look she gave him sent heat to his cheeks. He held up a hand to still the protest she was about to make. "I know, I know, a piece of paper isn't going to keep you safe."

She remained silent as Nick's thoughts raced. "If we get a restraining order and he shows up here, his bail will be immediately revoked. We could put you and Billy someplace safe for a couple of days and I could get some officers to be here."

A glimpse of hope altered her expression.

"Where would we go?" she asked. The question let him know she was considering his scenario.

"Do you have any friends David wouldn't know about? Any distant relatives?"

She shook her head. "No friends. No relatives."

Nick wasn't surprised by her answer. He'd never met an abused woman who hadn't been systematically isolated from friends and alienated from family. "Then we'll put you in a motel."

She frowned. "I don't have money for a motel room. I have to save what little I've got in case this doesn't work and Billy and I have to take off once again."

"I'll take care of the room," Nick said. He knew he was stepping over boundaries. His duty, his responsibility to this woman and her son had ended the moment David Blankenship had walked out of that day care center.

"How fast can we get a restraining order?" she asked. And in that question Nick knew she had made her decision.

He looked at his watch and frowned. "Court is closed for the day, but I can call in some favors. We may be able to get one tonight." He looked back at her.

"How long will it take for you to pack your bags and get ready to move?"

"Billy?" she called. The boy instantly appeared in the doorway. "Do you remember Mr. Corelli?" The boy's gaze flickered to Nick, then back to his mother. "Get the suitcases. We're leaving."

The child disappeared from view and reappeared a moment later, lugging two large suitcases. Juliette stepped forward and took one of them from him. Nick grabbed the other. "That's it?" he asked.

"We never unpack," she replied.

Those three simple words reflected a life of chaos and instability.

They stepped out of the apartment and Nick waited while she carefully locked the door. "Should we follow you in my car?" she asked. She gestured to the old Ford parked in front.

"No. We'll leave it here. We want Blankenship to believe you're inside."

Within minutes they were settled in Nick's car, Juliette in the passenger seat and Billy in the back. As Nick put his key into the ignition, Billy leaned forward and tapped him on the shoulder. Nick turned to meet the boy's somber gaze.

"I don't pee the bed."

For a moment, Nick wasn't sure what the boy was talking about, then he remembered. Juliette had told David that Billy was a bed wetter, that she had to change his sheets each morning.

"I never believed that you did, partner," Nick replied.

Billy nodded, as if satisfied, then sat back and buckled his seat belt. Nick started the car and they took off.

Chapter 11

Freedom.

It sang through David's soul as he left the jail behind and headed for the apartment he'd rented a week before he'd stormed the day care.

He breathed deeply of the autumn-scented air, a welcome relief from the fetid, stale stench of incarceration. The early evening sunshine was warm on his back as he got into his car, which Jeffrey had arranged to be waiting for him.

It took him only fifteen minutes of driving time to reach the place he now called home. He parked his car in the underground parking lot. He considered the parking one of the blessings of luxury living, but had been disappointed to learn that the underground lot offered no security.

He took the elevator up to his apartment on the tenth floor and opened the door to the apartment where he would be staying until he'd completed his goals.

His feet sank deep into the plush beige carpeting and the rooms held the scent of fresh paint and new furnishings. All the comforts of home, but this wasn't home.

Home was the mansion in Philadelphia where he and Juliette had lived since their wedding day. There each and every item had been chosen with care to create the perfect world David wished to live in. It wouldn't be perfect again until the stupid bitch and her spawn were dead.

He threw his keys on the kitchen table and added what little change jingled in his pocket. He took a moment to sort the pennies, nickels, dimes, and quarters into separate little piles. He'd never liked the way they looked all jumbled up together. Satisfied with the neat results, he opened the refrigerator and grabbed a bottle of vodka, Bloody Mary mix, hot sauce and a half a lime.

With controlled, efficient movements, he made himself the drink, then carried it into the living room and to the bank of floor-to-ceiling windows that overlooked the town of Riverton.

She was out there. In that hole of an apartment she called home with the brat that had ruined everything. Did she know he was out of jail? Had somebody told her he had been released? Was she frightened?

He took a sip of his drink, savoring the taste on his tongue. It was cool and biting, the way he imagined fear would taste.

It had taken him months of tracking her social security number to discover she was substitute teaching at several schools in Riverton, Kansas. Research had indicated that Riverton was a small town.

David had left Philly for Riverton and it had taken him only two weeks to find his bride. For three days after that he'd shadowed her, discovering the day care where she took Billy on the days that she worked.

That's when he'd come up with his plan to invade the day care.

He left the windows and sank onto the sofa. Propping his feet up on the marble-topped coffee table, he leaned back and smiled.

He knew the police would probably be watching him, waiting for him to screw up so they could throw him back into jail to await his court date.

Patience. It had always been one of David's strong suits. The cops couldn't watch him forever.

He sat up as the phone rang. Nobody had this number except his lawyer. Something must have happened. He answered on the second ring.

"David, it's Jeffrey." The lawyer's smooth voice filled the line.

"Yes, Jeffrey?"

"I just spoke with somebody from the police department. At some point this evening or first thing in the morning, you will be served with a restraining order. Juliette and Detective Nick Corelli are with a judge now getting it signed into effect. You know what a restraining order means?"

"I'm not to contact her in any way. I have no intention of bothering Juliette again." The lie tripped smoothly from his mouth.

"Good, good. And don't forget the ten o'clock appointment tomorrow morning with Dr. Pippersom."

"I won't forget."

"Make sure you don't. It's important, David."

"I understand. I'll be there."

"And we'll set up a meeting in the next couple of weeks? I'm flying back home first thing in the morning, but I'll call you and we'll figure out our strategy for keeping you from serving any time."

"I appreciate it," David replied.

The phone conversation ended and David once again leaned back, his thoughts racing.

So, Juliette had gotten a restraining order. It didn't matter. She'd had them before. He knew they weren't worth the paper they were written on. She'd never waited around to see if the cops would do anything to him. Always before when he'd found her, she'd packed up and run. Interesting.

Perhaps Nick Corelli, the smooth-talking cop, had talked her into staying to testify. He wondered if Nick was fucking her? The thought sent a burn through him, obscuring his vision with a red haze while his head rang with the bells of rage.

Maybe that's why she'd betrayed him. Because of the cop. David drew deep, cleansing breaths, forcing the fury to recede until the hot rage was replaced by controlled calm.

David had the money, the cunning, and the patience to fulfill his destiny. All he needed was to work out the details.

Chapter 12

Riverton, Kansas, was just off the interstate, and the road into town was littered with motels. Although mostly frequented by tired truckers who wanted no more than a clean bed, there was a motel for every taste and budget.

Nobody spoke a word as Nick drove from Juliette's apartment to the Twilight Time Motel where Nick had once spent a night of passion with a woman whose name he now couldn't remember.

He chose this particular motel for a couple of reasons. The first was that although relatively small and cheap, it had a nearby coffee-shop cafe that delivered to the rooms. Second, it had been built in the seventies, about twenty years before the Holiday Inn that now obscured its view of the street. Longtime Riverton residents knew it was back there, but most travelers never noticed it, tucked as it now was behind the three-story hotel. It was perfect for cheating spouses and one night-stands—and, Nick hoped, for hiding from David Blankenship.

Nick knew the desk clerks at the Twilight Time Motel didn't keep good records, didn't demand identification, and didn't care less who was in the room as long as the room was paid for in advance.

It took him only minutes to go into the office, pay for two nights' stay and be handed a room key. He returned to his car, where Juliette and her son sat in the same silence they'd been sitting in when he'd left the car.

"Room 114," he said and handed her the key.

He backed away from the office and pulled to the end of the building and around the corner where room 114 was located. "You and Billy go on in. I'll get the bags," he said as he turned off the car engine.

She nodded and together she and Billy left the car and a moment later disappeared into the room. Nick pulled the suitcases out of his trunk, wondering vaguely what in the hell he was doing. He set the suitcases down and leaned against the car for a moment.

What in the hell was he doing? He'd never gotten personally involved in a case before. Was he involved now because he really believed David was stupid enough to come after his ex-wife and son?

Or was he involved because the scent of her dizzied him just a little bit and he wondered what those eyes of hers would look like if the threat in her life was permanently removed?

On a physical level he was intensely aware of her— of the press of her breasts against her sweater, the length of legs he could easily imagine wrapped around his hips.

Was it compassion or testosterone that drove him? He rubbed his pocket where the rock nestled against his heart. Or was it simply a need to atone for past sins?

It didn't really matter. He was in for the game.

The department would never reimburse him the expense of the motel room or the food costs she and Billy might incur. He hoped to hell he could convince Slokem to put a few men on the apartment she'd just vacated, hoped to hell they could get David Blankenship off the streets until his trial date.

Even then, there was no assurance Blankenship would spend any real time in jail. All he needed was a liberal judge and compelling arguments from a good lawyer.

A burst of anger swept through Nick. It was always the same. The cops arrested the bad guys and far too often the judicial system let them go. A revolving door that put thugs and thieves back on the streets.

But Nick knew that David Blankenship was something more than a thug or a thief. He was more than a spouse abuser and garden variety creep.

There had been only two times in the course of his career that Nick believed he had confronted true evil. The first time had been nine years ago and at that time evil's name had been John Michael Fontaine.

John Michael Fontaine had brutally raped six young women before he finally killed one of them and left behind enough forensic evidence for the cops to nail him.

Nick had been one of the cops who had gone to arrest him in the small, neat two-bedroom home where the thirty-year-old man lived. Fontaine had greeted them at the door, waived his right to a lawyer, then had proceeded to confess everything, including the murder of his mother a year before.

As he'd spoken of the details of his crimes, his eyes had held no remorse, no shame. His voice was matter-of-fact and without emotion. He'd killed his mother because she had been an irritating nag. He'd explained that he'd asked out each of the women but they'd all refused to go out with him. He'd been enraged by their rejection and had raped them. The last woman he'd killed because she'd not only rejected him, but she'd laughed at him as well.

The older cop, Mike Mathias, who had been Nick's partner at the time, had called Fontaine a perverted, creep scumbag. Fontaine had smiled pleasantly and told the man that eventually when he got out of prison, he would rape his daughters and kill his wife.

It was at that moment that Nick had recognized the pure evil that existed inside the man, a man with no conscience, no empathy for anyone. A chill had swept through Nick, as if the finger of death had lightly stroked the back of his neck.

Fontaine didn't wear his evilness on his facial features, which were pleasant and almost handsome. It didn't ooze from his voice when he spoke. Rather he harbored it deep inside himself and nurtured it with the terror, chaos, and death he inflicted.

The mental picture of Fontaine faded, leaving in its wake a vision of David Blankenship. Nick had watched Juliette and her son walk away, and as David had been cuffed and shoved into the back of a patrol car, the look on his face had made the same kind of damp chill streak through Nick.

Nick couldn't explain his feeling of dread, couldn't testify about the ice-cold shivers David invoked in him. But he knew in his gut the man was dangerous. He knew without doubt the man was capable of murdering both his wife and child.

Compassion or testosterone? Maybe a little of both, he thought as he picked up the suitcases once again and entered the room.

Billy was already in front of the television on one of the double beds, and Juliette stood near the other bed, staring around her as if trying to figure out what she was doing here.

Nick set the suitcases near the doorway to the bathroom and frowned as he viewed the room. Apparently in the years since he'd stayed here, the place had gone downhill.

The beige carpeting looked dirty and was worn slick in some areas. The bedspreads on the two double beds didn't match and the room smelled of stale cigarettes and the scents of strangers.

"I apologize. I didn't realize this would be quite so dismal."

"There's cable TV," Billy said, not taking his gaze from the television set.

Juliette smiled. It was the first time he'd seen her smile. Instantly, the frost thawed in her eyes, and her features softened and warmed and Nick felt the warmth in the pit of his stomach.

"We'll be fine here. We have cable," she said, the smile lingering for a moment longer.

Nick nodded and looked away from her. He dug into his back pocket for his wallet. "I wrote down my cell phone number for you. You can reach me day or night at this number." He handed her a slip of paper with the number written down.

"Don't leave this room for anything. Whatever you need to eat, order it from the cafe and they'll deliver it.

Pay for it in cash." He pulled out five twenties and held them out to her.

Her smile instantly disappeared as she looked at the money he held out. For a long moment neither of them moved. She didn't reach out to take the bills, and he didn't drop the hand that offered them.

He knew she had no money to spare, but he also sensed in her a pride that made reaching out for the money nearly impossible.

He took her hand in his, unsurprised to find her fingers icy cold. He placed the bills in the palm of her hand and gently folded her fingers over it, then released her.

"Why are you doing this for us?" she asked softly.

"It's my job," he answered easily.

"No, it isn't," she replied, her gaze compelling him to look at her. "It's beyond your job."

Nick shrugged. "Let's just say I have a weakness for boys who don't pee the bed."

Again a whisper of a smile lit her eyes and curved her lips. Nick wondered what kind of a woman she might have been had she never encountered David Blankenship. He also wondered what other scars her body bore besides the one she'd shown him on her neck.

How many scars did she carry inside her, where nobody could see? Certainly, Nick knew about those soul scars. He'd seen firsthand with Diane how devastating they could be.

And what of the scars that had already been seared into Billy? Nick shoved this thought aside and suddenly felt the need to escape from this woman and boy.

"Don't leave the room and don't answer the phone

if it rings," he instructed briskly as he backed toward the door. "I'll come by sometime tomorrow to check in with you and let you know how things are progressing."

She nodded and followed him to the door.

"Chain this and leave it chained at all times. It won't stop anyone indefinitely, but it might slow somebody down."

He opened the door and started to step out, but she stopped him by calling his name softly. He turned back to look at her.

"I'll kill him if I have to. If I get the opportunity, I will kill him." It wasn't a threat, it was the promise of a woman tired of running, tired of hiding—the vow of a woman determined to end her torment.

Nick acknowledged her vow with a nod of his head. "Let's hope it doesn't come to that." He stepped out into the lengthening night shadows and closed the door behind him. He heard the distinctive click of the locks being turned.

Fifteen minutes later Nick walked into the Riverton Police Department. At one time the ancient brick building had housed the jail in the basement. But two years ago a new jail had been built on the property adjacent to the police department.

Everyone in the department was hoping that the taxpayers eventually would spring for a new police department building as well. As it was, the building was stifling in the summer and frigid in the winter and always smelled unpleasantly musty. The pipes banged and clanged and the plumbing had a tendency to back up for no obvious reason.

Nick's desk was next to one of the windows and he opened the window to allow in the crisp, clean-smelling night air.

"Hey, Nick, what are you doing here?" one of the younger officers greeted him.

"Just stopped by to talk to Sammy," Nick said.

"He's in the back, getting a cup of coffee. Should be out in just a minute."

Nick nodded and sat at his desk. He shared the desk with Sammy Bellows. Nick worked a day shift and Sammy the night. When Nick had worked the night shift, he and Sammy had been partners for a while. Sammy was not only an ex-partner, but also a good friend.

The first thing Nick did was take the framed photograph that rested on the top of the desk and shove it in the top drawer. It was a picture of Marilyn Monroe . . . the infamous shot from *The Seven Year Itch*, where she was standing over a subway grate trying unsuccessfully to hold down the bottom of her white dress.

He yanked open the desk drawer on his bottom right and withdrew a framed photograph of his great-grandmother, a humorless woman who closely resembled a pit bull.

It was a game he and Sammy played.

He pulled the rock from his pocket and worked it between his fingers as he thought of the best ways to approach Slokem with his request.

He wanted men at Juliette Monroe's apartment or a tail on David Blankenship. He knew eventually Blankenship would blow the restraining order and Nick wanted a cop there to put the dangerous man back behind bars.

A meaty hand fell on his shoulder and he turned around to see Sammy standing next to him, two cups of coffee in hand. "What's the matter? Can't get enough of this dump?"

Nick grinned and took the coffee cup Sammy held out to him. "Actually, I'm here because I need to talk to you."

Sammy pulled up a chair from another desk. "I'm listening."

"You just rented a room at the Twilight Time Motel."

"I did? How long am I staying there?"

"I'm not sure. Two days minimum, maybe longer."

"I hope to hell there's a gorgeous blonde waiting for me there."

Nick nodded. "A gorgeous blonde and her son."

The teasing grin fell from Sammy's face. "Ah, Nicky, what in the hell are you doing?" There was a touch of censure in the old man's voice.

Nick slid the rock back into his pocket and leaned back in the chair. "I don't know. I think I'm doing what I have to do."

Quickly, he filled Sammy in about the restraining order, Juliette's move into the motel room and what Nick hoped to achieve.

Sammy frowned. "You know the chief will never okay the manpower to stake out her apartment or put a tail on Blankenship. As far as he is concerned that case is closed."

"I'm hoping I can change his mind."

Sammy snorted. "Yeah, and I'm hoping Marilyn is waiting for me in the afterlife, but I gotta feeling we're both gonna be disappointed." The two were silent for a moment. "When are you going to talk to him?"

"I thought I'd swing by his house when I leave here." Nick looked at his wristwatch. "I figure by now he's had dinner and he's probably downed a couple of stiff martinis. Maybe that sweet little wife of his has rubbed his back and he's basking in front of the television dreaming about his promising future."

Sammy snorted once again. "The only back Meredith Slokem is prone to rub is her own. He probably grabbed something to eat on the way home, downed a couple of beers, and fought with Queen Meredith over her charge card bills. He's now breathing smoke through his nose and waiting for some hapless cop to stop by so he can bite his ass."

Nick grinned at Sammy's scenario. "My ass has been bitten by Slokem before." His grin faded and he leaned forward once again. "I got a bad feeling about this, Sammy. I got a feeling if we don't do something to help those two, something bad is going to happen."

Sammy studied him for a long moment. He'd known Nick for years, and knew Nick rarely dramatized for drama's sake. He also had, over the years, come to respect Nick's gut instincts.

"You really think Blankenship is stupid enough to jeopardize his bail by coming after Juliette?"

Nick thought back to that moment in front of the day care facility when David had realized his ex-wife had lied to him, made promises she had no intentions of keeping. "Yeah, I do. It isn't that he's stupid, but I think he has a rage inside him that he can't control. He'll come after her and I figure it will be in the next couple of days. I don't think he'll be able to help himself."

"So what are you going to do if Slokem turns you down?"

Nick frowned. "I don't know. All I know is that I'm not backing away from this." He thought of Juliette and her son. "Whatever it takes, whatever I have to do, I intend to make certain that nobody gets hurt by David Blankenship."

Thirty minutes later, Nick sat in Richard Slokem's driveway. The Slokems lived in the one exclusive housing development Riverton offered. Surrounding an expensive apartment complex, the homes in the Whispering Oaks subdivision were large and elegant, with treed lots that gave the new homes an aura of old permanence.

The Slokems' house was a massive two-story with thick columns across the front giving it the look of a southern plantation. Nick knew Slokem had married money, otherwise he'd never be able to afford this house in this location on his salary.

Nick had been here only once before, at a Christmas party Meredith and Richard had thrown three years before. It had been a stiff, formal affair that the cops had all joked about for months. The general consensus was that Meredith probably had the house fumigated after entertaining the commoners.

The lady of the manor answered the door. Meredith Slokem was an attractive woman—the attractiveness of high maintenance. Not a single strand of silver threaded her dark hair, and her skin had the unnatural smoothness of a woman who frequently visited a plastic surgeon.

"Yes?" She eyed Nick blankly.

He fought a surge of irritation. He had talked to the woman at various functions over the past ten years yet she never remembered him. "I'd like to speak with the chief."

"And you are . . .?"

"Corelli. Nick Corelli."

"Of course. Well, Officer Corelli, it's rather late."

"It's rather important." Nick held her gaze.

"I'll tell him you're here."

She disappeared from the door without inviting him in.

Nick remained on the porch and reminded himself he was known for his negotiating skills. He just had to figure out what was the best way to negotiate with an asshole.

Chapter 13

Her scent lingered in the apartment where she and her son had lived. It was the first thing Nick noticed when he'd reentered the place, a faint spicy flower scent that rode on the otherwise stale air.

He'd spent the night in a chair at the front window of Juliette's apartment, watching, waiting for any sign of Blankenship.

For the first time in his career, Nick almost felt sorry for Richard Slokem. The chief had looked more stressed than Nick had ever seen him when Nick had gone to plead the case of protection for Juliette and her son.

"Hell, Nick, I've got people screaming at me from all sides on this issue. The entire community is outraged that Blankenship is out of jail. Between the mayor's office and mine, we've logged hundreds of protest calls just since the news of his release broke."

"Then give me enough men to make sure that Juliette and her son are safe," Nick had said.

"If I do that, then every parent who had a kid in that day care will demand the same kind of protection." Slokem had heaved a tired sigh. "I got outraged citizens screaming at me from one side, and on the other side I've got the town's attorneys warning me that if we harass Blankenship in any way he'll sue and this town can't afford those kinds of legal repercussions."

"So we just leave him alone and hope that he doesn't kill anyone?" Nick had asked bitterly.

Slokem had gazed at him slyly. "You got a ton of vacation time built up, don't you? I can't keep track of what my officers do in their off-duty time."

So Nick was now on vacation time. When he ran out of vacation days he'd use up his sick leave. When his sick days were gone Slokem had promised him they'd figure out something else.

All Nick knew was that he couldn't walk away and leave Juliette and Billy vulnerable to David Blankenship.

At seven he poured the last cup of coffee from the thermos he'd prepared before he'd arrived at her apartment. The coffee was cold and his eyes felt gritty with lack of sleep.

All the blinds in the apartment were closed except the one at the window where Nick sat. They were cracked open only enough so Nick could see Juliette's car parked at the curb and the street beyond it.

There hadn't been much traffic throughout the night or so far that morning. He'd hazard a guess that half the tenants in this particular apartment complex didn't have the money to own or operate a vehicle on a regular basis.

He drank the last of the cold coffee then stood and stretched with arms overhead. His left shoulder popped as his body unkinked from the position it had been in for too many hours.

He'd just dropped his hands to his side when a rapid knock fell on the front door. Adrenaline spiked through him as he drew his gun and approached the door. Who would be calling at this time of the morning?

He unfastened the chain lock with one hand and flipped the safety off the gun with the other. He yanked open the door.

"Hey, Nicky," Sammy greeted him.

"Jesus Sammy, what the hell are you doing here?" Nick holstered his gun and at the same time yanked the big cop through the door.

"I'm the cavalry." Sammy grinned at Nick.

"What's that supposed to mean?"

"It means I told Slokem I was feeling a little puny and needed to take some time off and and help out a buddy."

Nick stared at Sammy in surprise. "I . . . I don't know what to say."

"Say you'll never take down my Marilyn picture again to put up that photo of your butt-ugly relative."

"Consider it said," Nick replied.

"You look like hell, Nicky boy. Go home, eat something, and get some sleep. I'll stay here and watch for scumbags. Go on. Get out of here. You can come back after you've slept a couple of hours."

A minute later Nick was out on the sidewalk heading for his car that he'd parked on the next block. Before this was all over he was going to owe Sammy big-time. It wasn't every cop who would give up precious sick days to help a friend, but Sammy was that kind of man and Nick was grateful.

He just hoped the whole ordeal didn't take too long. He hoped that if David Blankenship intended to screw up he'd do it soon.

Blankenship's trial date was December eleventh, but Nick wanted him back behind bars in the next week. Blankenship's incarceration would make a fine Christmas gift for Juliette and Billy. Now, all Nick had to do was wait until Blankenship screwed up.

David had no intention of screwing up. Parked in his car down the street from Juliette's apartment, he saw the big burly man go inside and the familiar dark-haired cop leave and he'd known with a gut-wrenching certainty that Juliette and the boy weren't there.

Fury pulsed inside him. They were trying to catch him. They wanted to put him away and keep him from what was rightfully his.

The bastards. Didn't they understand that Juliette would always be his?

What God had joined together let no man rip asunder. Juliette would be his until he put a gun in her mouth and pulled the trigger. She would die for her betrayal.

As David drove back to his own apartment, his thoughts whirled in his head. The cops wouldn't be going to all the trouble to stake out her apartment if she wasn't cooperating with them. That meant she and the kid were still in town.

Hide and seek. David was good at the game. No matter where Juliette tried to hide, he always found her. And he'd find her this time, too. It was just a matter of time.

At nine that morning David met with Dr. Pippersom, the psychiatrist his lawyer had arranged for him to see. David was properly contrite for his actions; the tall, gaunt doctor was appropriately nonjudgmental, occasionally nodding his head to encourage David to continue exploring his feelings where life and his ex-wife were concerned.

It was a waste of David's time, but necessary to keep him out of jail. Red tape crap. Jeffrey thought it would be good to show the judge that David was willing to undergo therapy and seek professional help.

By the time David left the doctor's office he had a plan. At noon he walked into a Denny's restaurant carrying a briefcase. Inside the briefcase was a manila envelope containing ten thousand dollars. Enough money to buy help, enough money to buy a soul.

He requested a seat at a window booth and slid into the side that faced the door, putting the briefcase on the bench seat next to him.

He ordered a grilled chicken salad and ate it while watching the door. He'd just finished the last bite when the man entered the restaurant. David checked his wristwatch. Precisely one o'clock. Good. The man was punctual. David didn't tolerate tardiness.

It hadn't been too much trouble for David to find a young man willing to do a little work for a lot of money. All he'd had to do was hang out at a local pool hall and ask a few questions. The bartender, an ex-con, had given him a phone number to call.

The two men acknowledged each other with a nod of their heads, then Byron Camp approached the booth. "Mr. Smith?" he asked, and David nodded his head.

David ignored the hand held out to him. "Sit down, Mr. Camp," he said.

The man was younger than David had expected. He

looked to be in his late twenties, but his cold, dark eyes spoke of a lot of hard living in those years.

Byron was whip thin with acne scars across his cheeks and what appeared to be a homemade tattoo on his forearm. "Don't jerk me around, Mr. Smith," he said as he slid into the seat across from David. "Anyone who lives in a fifty mile radius of this shithole knows your face."

They didn't speak again until the waitress had poured Byron a cup of coffee and refilled David's cup. Only when they were relatively assured of no further interruptions did Byron continue. "I don't give a damn who you are or what you've done. All I care about is that you mentioned to me over the phone that you need some help and are willing to pay well."

"As I explained on the phone, I have a job for you, Mr. Camp."

"Yes, you said something about finding somebody."

"A woman. My ex-wife. I have reason to believe she's still here in town, but she's gone from her apartment. I want you to find her."

It took only thirty minutes for David to conduct his business with Byron Camp, even less time to know that Camp was perfect for the job. The man had asked no questions as to why David wanted to find Juliette, had no interest in anything but the huge payday a positive result would yield.

It was obvious Camp was a man familiar with the wrong side of the law, and David was comfortable that fate had handed him the perfect tool to find Juliette.

As Bryon left the restaurant, David focused on what came next in his plans. He sipped a last cup of coffee, in no real hurry, savoring the knowledge that he was one step closer to killing Juliette.

Dessert. He'd always had a sweet tooth. But Denny's had nothing on their menu that interested him. What he wanted was an ice cream cone and he knew just where to go to get it. A place called the Dairy Shack, where they not only had fifty flavors of ice cream on the menu but also a girl named Crystal who had written him a love letter.

It was just another day at the Dairy Shack. Business was slow and SuEllen moved slower. She drew an ice cream cone for a squalling four-year-old and dreamed of being anywhere but there.

She had a head full of dreams, and a heart full of misery.

She wanted to escape the trailer park where she lived and the Dairy Shack where she worked, but she had no place else to go. At seven bucks an hour it would take her years to save up enough money for a new life and that was only if her mother kept her mitts off SuEllen's money.

Everytime SuEllen had a nice sum of money saved, her mother would find her hiding place. Next thing she knew she was starting all over again from scratch.

SuEllen didn't have to read cards or tea leaves to see her future. She'd probably work at the Dairy Shack until retirement. She'd marry some low-life dope dealer and buy a trailer near the one where she'd grown up. She'd have babies with running noses and her man would slap her around whenever he was drunk or high.

She couldn't help but wonder how different her life

might have been if her daddy hadn't gone to prison before she was born. Maybe then her mama wouldn't have become a drinking whore and they would have never heard of the Sunshine Trailer Estates.

Her mom, her dad, and she would have had bacon and eggs in the mornings in a sun-filled kitchen and on Sundays they would have pot roast with buttered potatoes and carrots that melted in your mouth. They'd share conversations about love and family and they'd laugh together all the time.

It would have been so wonderful to be a real family, to have picnics and holiday dinners and go to the movies. Her father would have taught her to ride a bike and work on a car engine, he would have hoisted her up in his arms and tickled her silly.

"SuEllen, you can take your break now." Harley McClean, the manager, popped his head out from his office. "Janice will cover for you while you're gone."

SuEllen finished wiping down the countertop then grabbed her cigarettes and lighter and headed out the back door. As she lit a cigarette she let her mind wander free into fantasies of make-believe and what might have been.

She saw the car first, a sleek, shiny black sports car that looked as out of place at the Dairy Shack as a duck in the desert.

The car pulled into a parking space near where SuEllen stood and she watched as the driver got out. Him! David Blankenship.

She would have recognized him anywhere. Her heart pounded with an excitement she'd never felt before—it was the excitement of possibility. She tossed her cigarette to the ground.

He was even more handsome in person than he'd been on the television. His hair was more blond than brown and the dark pants and tailored shirt he wore looked expensive.

As he approached she felt dizzy with anticipation. What was he doing here? Had he gotten her letter? Or was it just a weird coincidence that he was here?

A smile curved his lips as he approached her and she thought she might die. "Hi, I'm looking for a Crystal," he said.

"It's me . . . I mean, I'm her," she stuttered and felt a blush sweep over her cheeks.

"That's not what your name tag says." He smiled, and in that smile she felt as if he knew every secret in her soul, every dream in her heart. "Now why would you want to call yourself Crystal when you have a pretty name like SuEllen?"

She'd never thought her name pretty until it fell from his lips, then it sounded like a sweet melody. "I just . . . uh . . ."

"You do know who I am, don't you?" he asked. She nodded. "I can't tell you how much I liked your letter. It was the brightest spot I've had in my life for a long time." Again he smiled and warmth fluttered through her stomach.

"I just had to write it."

"I'm glad you did."

For a moment they stood silent and she desperately wished she could think of something witty, something enchanting to say. But she was neither witty nor enchanting. "I like your car," she finally said. "It's a beauty."

"Want to take a ride in it?"

"I . . . I can't. I only got five minutes left of my break."

He smiled and held out his hand toward her. "Take a chance, SuEllen. Come with me. It might just be the start of something wonderful."

Almost without her volition her hand reached for his. After all, anyplace had to be better than the place she was in.

Chapter 14

Juliette couldn't remember the last time she'd slept so well. It was amazing what an anonymous motel room could do for one's sense of safety.

She awakened just after nine when Billy turned on cartoons and the sound of Rugrats filled the room. She remained in bed with her eyes closed for long minutes, her head full of thoughts of Nick Corelli.

Why was the handsome cop helping them? She'd had contact with lots of cops over the year she and Billy had been on the run, but none of them had done a fourth of what Nick had already done for them.

What made him different? What had made him reach out to them? What made him care?

She had no answers, only gratefulness that he was making an attempt to help them and a touch of wariness that came naturally after all that she'd been through.

Still, because of Nick she'd had her first good night's sleep in a year and because of Nick her son was enjoying a moment of cartoons without the fear that at any moment the boogeyman might appear at their door.

She stirred against the sheets, reveling in the fact

that for the moment she felt no need to be on guard, no underlying compulsion to pack up and run. She couldn't remember feeling so . . . so normal. Certainly she hadn't felt like this since the very first days of her marriage to David.

She rolled over and looked at her son, feeling the warmth of love flood her. He lay on his tummy facing the opposite end of the bed, his attention captured by the colorful animation on the television.

"I could eat a horse," she said.

Billy turned his head and grinned at her. "I could eat a cow," he replied.

"Maybe we should just compromise and order in some bacon and eggs." She got out of bed and padded to the desk. "I think I saw a menu from the cafe here last night. Aha!" She opened the menu and read her son the breakfast offerings.

Soon they were eating pancakes and watching cartoons. Then Juliette went into the bathroom to shower after cautioning Billy not to open the door for anyone.

She stripped off the extra large T-shirt that served as a nightshirt, then paused as she caught her nearly naked reflection in the cracked mirror on the back of the bathroom door.

Her body bore the testimony of a man's rage—and when David's rage had erupted, his choice of weapon had always been a knife. He liked to make scars, to remind her of her mistakes, to teach her not to make the same mistake twice.

One of David's marks half encircled one of her breasts—carved into her when he thought her dress had exposed too much of her feminine curves. Two inches of ropy raised skin on her lower belly had been the punishment for overcooking a roast. But the worst of them all was a scar in the shape of the letter D, a brand placed on the upper inner thigh of her left leg for being too friendly to a UPS deliveryman.

They were marks of David's abuse, his madness, but they were also symbols of her shame. She'd spent a lot of time analyzing how she'd become his victim, how an intelligent woman like herself had fallen through a dark portal and into hell.

She turned away from the mirror and focused on getting showered and dressed as quickly as possible. Twenty minutes later she sat on the edge of her bed, wondering how they were going to spend the long hours of confinement.

She thought about calling Nick to find out if anything had happened with David, but she knew if anything had happened he would have come to tell her. She knew she just wanted to make the call to hear his voice, to know that she and Billy weren't all alone.

She also knew it wouldn't take long for Billy to get bored watching cartoons. There was only so much sedentary activity a five-year-old boy could handle.

Sure enough, by noon Billy was tired of watching television. The only toys he had to call his own were his crayons and paper and a set of Matchbox cars, easily packed and taking little space in the suitcase whenever they went on the run.

He got out the cars and Juliette helped him make roads by using all the towels the bathroom had to offer. They played together for almost two hours and every minute of that time Juliette's heart ached for the little boy whose life had been nothing close to what she'd dreamed for him.

When she'd left David she'd vowed that she'd not only provide Billy with all of her love, but also build a life for him filled with happiness and all the things that little boys loved. She'd failed dismally so far.

It was difficult to build a life when you constantly had to run and hide from somebody wanting to take your life. It was almost impossible to build anything substantial when you were constantly looking over your shoulder and wondering when it all would crumble to ruin.

Maybe this time, she thought. Maybe this time things would be different.

Nick was right. It was time to stop running and take a stance. Billy would never have anything if they continued to run. Hopefully David would screw up and go to jail for a very long time and Juliette could finally give her son the life she so desperately wanted for him.

It was just after two when a knock fell on the door. Juliette froze, her heart banging frantically. "Billy . . . go into the bathroom and lock the door," she instructed.

He asked no questions, but did as she bid. Only when he was safely secure behind the locked door of the bathroom did Juliette approach the door.

"Juliette, it's me, Nick."

She breathed deeply, and shoved the familiar panic back inside as she opened the door. "Ah, I see the stress of a night in a dump hasn't done any physical harm to you," he said as he entered the room and dumped the shopping bags he'd carried in on Billy's bed. "Where's Billy?"

Odd, how the dimensions of the room seemed to

shrink with his presence. "In the bathroom," she replied. She knocked on the bathroom door. "Billy, you can come out now."

Nick wore a pair of tight jeans that looked as if they'd seen many a wash and clung to his long legs. The black T-shirt he wore emphasized broad shoulders and sinewy muscles. David would have gutted her had he known how her heartbeat raced just a little bit faster at Nick's nearness.

"Hey, sport," Nick greeted her son with a smile as he came out of the bathroom. "I brought you something." He dug into one of the shopping bags and pulled out a handheld video game. "Thought it might help you pass the time."

Billy didn't reach for the game, but instead looked at his mother, who looked at Nick. "Nick, you're already doing so much for us. We can't accept—"

He held up a hand to still her protest. "Please, don't. I know how long the hours can be cooped up in a single room. It's not a big deal." He tossed the game to Billy.

Once again Billy looked at his mother and she saw the want in his eyes. She nodded her head and Billy whooped with excitement. She looked back at Nick. "I'll pay you back," she said. "Someday when all of this is over, I'll pay you back for everything."

"Okay, but we'll worry about it later." He dipped into the bag and withdrew two more games. "Hey Billy, try these. The guy at the store told me they were lots of fun."

Billy took the games from him, his blue eyes shining brightly. "Thanks." Before the single word was out of his mouth he was on the bed and engrossed in the new toy.

Nick shoved his hands in his jeans pockets and returned his attention back to Juliette. "The other bag has some magazines in it for you . . . women kind of magazines."

His thoughtfulness nearly undid her. It was enough that he was trying to keep her and her son safe. But the fact that he'd thought of creature comforts as well as their safety touched her more than anything or anyone had in a very long time.

She was afraid to completely believe in his goodness, afraid to trust the utter steadiness of his gray eyes. More than anything she was afraid to trust that somehow this time would be different, that she and Billy would finally be able to not be afraid anymore.

"Thank you," she said, aware that the simple words were inadequate.

He nodded, then checked his watch. "I've got to get out of here. I've got a buddy sitting at your apartment and it's time for me to relieve him. You doing okay?"

"Yes, we're fine." She walked the few steps with him back to the door. "So, nothing has happened so far. He hasn't shown up yet." She kept her voice low.

"Nothing yet. It's early. He hasn't been out of jail that long. He may be lying low for a bit."

"But what if he waits? What if he waits a week, or two weeks or even a month before making a move? How long are the police going to be willing to stake out my apartment?"

Nick averted his gaze from hers and something in his expression alarmed her. "The police aren't at my apartment, are they? They aren't involved in this at all."

His ruggedly handsome features pulled into a frown. "There are police there. I'm there and my buddy Sammy is there."

"But it's not official."

He sighed, his gaze still not meeting hers. "No, it's not exactly official. It's complicated, Juliette. Slokem gave me and my buddy time off to watch your place, but there isn't an official police presence at the moment."

Any hope that she might have foolishly entertained vanished beneath his words.

She should pack. She and Billy shouldn't hang around to await the moment when David would outsmart them and find them. She should get out of town before David tried to extract his revenge.

"Juliette." Nick reached out and grabbed her by the wrist, as if he had read her thoughts and needed to make an attempt to stop her escape. "If you ever hope to end all this, you have to trust somebody and it might just as well be me."

He held her wrist firmly, but not hard enough to hurt her. His fingers warmed her skin and she had a sudden impulse to throw herself against him and feel his strong arms surround her.

She had been alone for so long, long before she'd made the decision to leave her abusive husband. But she didn't know this man and she couldn't afford to be weak. She drew a steadying breath and pulled her wrist from his grasp.

"At the moment it seems I have no other choice but

to trust you," she said. "At the moment my life and my son's life depends on this plan of yours working out."

He smiled, although there was no humor in his gray eyes. "My job may depend on it as well. I'd say we both have reasons to want this plan to be successful." He opened the door. "I'll be back tomorrow to check in." With these words he left.

Juliette locked the door after him, then leaned against the door in thought. What was driving Nick Corelli to put his life on hold for a woman and a boy he'd never met before that Friday afternoon at the Tiny Tots Day Care?

Was she a fool to trust a man she hardly knew? Certainly she'd been a fool plenty of times in the past. After all, she'd once trusted David Blankenship.

She grabbed the bag off Billy's bed and carried it to her own. She sat down and pulled out the items contained within. A *Cosmopolitan*, a *Woman's World*, a *Redbook*, and a crossword puzzle book and beneath the magazines, two chocolate candy bars and several packages of batteries for Billy's new games.

"Mom? Is everything all right?" Billy's childish eyes gazed at her with a touch of concern.

She wanted to cry. She wanted to laugh hysterically. They were stuck in a disgusting motel room with all their worldly belongings, dependent on a man she barely knew to keep them safe from a man who wanted to kill them both.

She picked up one of the chocolate bars. How could she not trust a man who'd brought her chocolate? "Everything is fine, honey," she said and prayed that she wasn't telling herself and her son a lie.

Chapter 15

"Are you going to tell me what's going on?" Diane gazed at Nick, who sat on the sofa in her semi-dark living room. Nick had stopped by for an early morning visit with his friend before returning to Juliette's apartment for another day of surveillance.

"What do you mean?" he asked.

"For the past three days I've heard you coming and going at all hours and you didn't even mention to me that you were going to take some vacation time."

Nick looked at her in surprise. "How did you know I was on vacation?"

"I hacked into the Riverton Police Web site. It's all in there if you know how to access it—employment records, medical information—you never told me you had a BB lodged in your skull."

"Jeez, Diane. I could have you arrested for hacking into those files," Nick exclaimed.

She flashed him a quick grin. "But you won't. So, tell me about the BB in your head."

"There isn't much to tell. When I was eight Dad bought me a BB gun for Christmas. Tony was only five at the time and he was mad because he hadn't gotten one. Anyway, that afternoon I went out in the backyard to try out the gun. Tony went with me but before I could shoot it, he started fighting me for it. We tussled around until the gun went off and the BB hit me in the side of the head."

Nick smiled at the memory despite the fact that at the time it had happened it had been damned traumatic. "Mom thought I was dying, Tony thought he'd killed me, and Dad was cussing up a storm. They rushed me to the emergency room, where it was discovered the BB had lodged harmlessly in my thick skull. One of the few times it has paid me to be hard-headed."

She sighed and curled her legs beneath her on the chair where she sat. "I miss him," she said softly.

Nick leaned forward. "Then call him. Diane, that's all he's been waiting for. A phone call from you and he'd be back here in a minute."

"Back here to what?" Diane asked, an edge of bitterness in her tone. "What kind of a life can I offer him? One where he has to enter my world of mental illness? No thank you. I miss him, but I care about him far too much to call him."

Nick fought the impulse to argue with her. Nick missed his brother, too, and there was nothing he'd like to see more than the two people he loved happily together as they'd once been.

He knew his brother, and he knew there would always only be one woman for Tony and that was Diane. But Nick couldn't put two stubborn people together any more than he could take back the day of tragedy that had exploded their whole world.

"So, are you going to tell me what's going on with

you?" Diane asked, obviously unwilling to talk about Tony any further.

Nick considered her question, wondering why he hadn't told her about Juliette and Billy before now. He settled back against the sofa cushions. "I'm trying to help out a woman and her son."

"Help them by doing what?"

"You saw the news reports about the hostage situation at the day care?"

"Of course," Diane replied. "Half the country saw it."

"I'm trying to keep David Blankenship away from his ex-wife and little boy. He wants them dead."

He quickly filled Diane in on what had been happening since Blankenship had been arrested, explaining to her that he and Sammy had been splitting time at Juliette's apartment in an attempt to get David on a violation of the restraining order.

Frustration filled him as he explained to her the situation. In truth, Nick was surprised that their mission hadn't already been accomplished. But there had been no sign of David Blankenship anywhere near Juliette's apartment.

Nick couldn't believe he had misjudged Blankenship. He'd been so sure that the man would violate the order—that David would find it impossible to ignore his unhealthy obsession and stay away from his ex-wife and son.

But Blankenship appeared to be behaving, and it looked like Nick and Sammy were probably wasting their time. Nick didn't mind so much for himself, but he hated like hell that Sammy had given up his vacation time.

"Something special about this woman and her

son?" Diane asked. She gazed at Nick steadily, as if knowing something he didn't.

Nick hesitated a beat before answering. "Not necessarily. Only that I feel in my heart that their lives are in danger and the department couldn't do much to help them, so I decided to do what I could."

Diane's brown eyes continued to study him thoughtfully. "You've had people in danger before but you've never taken this kind of a personal interest."

"I've never been so sure of the danger before," he replied. "I talked that man out of the day care center. I saw the hatred in his eyes as he was led away. It was a kind of hatred that doesn't just go away on its own."

Her gaze continued to linger on his with speculation. "Is she pretty?"

Nick raised an eyebrow in surprise, wondering what had prompted her question. "That has nothing to do with the situation."

Diane smiled, a soft smile that he hadn't seen on her features for a very long time. "So, she is pretty. It's all right, Nicky."

"What do you mean? What's all right?" The conversation was starting to make him distinctly uncomfortable.

"It's all right that you're finally moving on. It's time. It's way past time," she said.

He laughed uncomfortably and stood. "Diane, I'm just doing my job. I'm just doing what I feel is necessary in this particular situation. And speaking of jobs, I need to get going." He wanted to stop by the motel and check in before he returned to Juliette's apartment for a day of surveillance.

"Okay, Nicky. Whatever you say," Diane said, obviously not believing him. She stood as well and walked over to where he stood.

She wrapped her arms around his neck and kissed him on the cheek. "You've been a good friend, Nicky, a lifesaver. But it's time for you to stop babysitting me. Time for you to find a life for yourself."

"I haven't been babysitting you," he protested.

"No, but maybe you've been doing penance." She kissed him on the cheek once again. "Just promise me you'll be careful."

"Always," he replied.

It wasn't until he was in his car and driving toward the apartment that he thought of what she'd said to him about moving on.

Was that what this thing with Juliette was all about? He wanted to think that his only involvement in this case was as a cop trying to protect a vulnerable woman and her child. But he'd been fooling himself if he didn't acknowledge the fact that he was intensely physically drawn to her.

Over the past three days he'd kept his contact with her and Billy at a minimum, checking in briefly with them each day to see if there was anything they needed. Each day he saw the wear of the wait on her face, but she made no complaints and asked for nothing.

After the tragedy of two years ago when Diane had lost her only daughter to a bank robbery gone bad, Nick had put his life on hold, trying to cope with his sense of loss while at the same time trying to ease Diane's crippling grief. Penance, was that what he'd been doing?

Moving on? Moving past the grief and looking outward instead of inward? He touched the rock in his shirt pocket as he thought of the little girl he'd not been able to save.

Was he finally moving on or was he attempting to gain some forgiveness by saving one child in the place of the one he had lost?

It had been like stealing candy from a baby. Seducing SuEllen Maynard had been easier than anything David had ever done in his life.

She'd been hungry for male attention, overwhelmed by David's lush style of living and eager to believe that he was a man worried about the safety of his son and that's what had prompted his temporary walk outside the limits of the law.

He was now seated at his kitchen table, working on his laptop and checking into the business that kept him financially healthy while SuEllen slept in the bedroom.

Blankenship Enterprises and a two million dollar trust fund had been his legacy from his parents when he'd married Juliette.

His parents were still alive, but had essentially paid David off to keep him out of their lives. That was fine with him. He had no use for his workaholic father or insipid mother. He'd always been stronger and smarter than either of them.

He'd taken the money and the computer software business and run with both. The money he had invested wisely and the business had grown to four times its size since he'd taken the helm. David was worth more money than he'd ever spend in one lifetime. But none of that meant anything to him. Not while Juliette was alive and well and separated from him.

He looked up as SuEllen came out of the bedroom. She was dressed in her Dairy Shack uniform and walked with the clumsy gait of both reluctance and the residual effects of the drug David had given her before she'd fallen asleep.

He frowned as he saw her uniform. For the past three days she'd worn one of his shirts and a pair of his jogging pants. "Hey, hey, what's going on? What's with the uniform?" He jumped up from his chair and approached her.

She stared down at the floor, her long bangs half hiding her eyes. "I've got to go. I need to get back to work, otherwise I'll lose my job altogether."

David placed his hands on her shoulders. "And that would be a bad thing?"

She looked at him then and her dark brown eyes held the conflict of a young woman who wanted it all, but was afraid to believe that having it all was possible for herself. "That job is all I've got."

David moved his hands to caress her shoulders. She had thick shoulders, unlike Juliette's slender, fragile ones. He forced a caring, tender smile to his lips. "SuEllen, that's not true. Now you have me."

Hope battled with disbelief on her features and her disbelief won out. "What do you want with me? I'm a nothing, a nobody and I'm not even pretty," she scoffed, shame deepening her voice. "You're handsome and rich and could have any woman on earth."

No, not any woman. He couldn't have Juliette but he'd make sure nobody else could have her either. To do that he needed SuEllen. She was an integral part of his plan and he wasn't about to let her run out on him.

"But no other woman understands me like you do. I like having you here with me. I need you here with me." His voice was seductively smooth and she leaned toward him, as if his voice had the power to physically move her. "Besides," he continued. "You are pretty." She eyed him skeptically.

He smiled again and swiped her long bangs away from her forehead. "Okay, you could use a good haircut and some new clothes, but that's all. Why don't we do that this morning? Get you into a salon for an updated hairstyle, then go shopping."

"Really? You really want me to stay here with you?"

"I've never wanted anything more in my life," he replied.

A shimmer of tears shone from her eyes and she threw her arms around his neck and hugged him tightly. "I want to be here with you," she whispered, her voice fervent with longing.

"And I need you here with me," David said. Oh yes, he needed her all right. If his plan worked the way he intended, SuEllen Maynard would be what kept him out of prison when he killed the betraying bitch Juliette and the snot-nosed kid who had destroyed everything.

Chapter 16

The handheld video game Nick had brought Billy was Godsent, keeping him entertained during their days of being cooped up in a motel room.

Maybe children experienced the passage of time differently than adults, Juliette mused as she thumbed through one of the magazines for the fourth time since Nick had brought them to her.

Apparently Billy didn't feel the frustration of their lives at a standstill, of the hours and days lost to the whims of a madman.

She'd already lost so much time, so many dreams to David Blankenship. Six years of pure hell and too many dreams to count.

She touched the raised skin of the scar on her neck. This scar, along with all the others that decorated her body and soul, were evidence not only of David's torture, but of her own stupidity, weakness, and fear.

She dropped her hand and gazed at her son.

He was stretched out on his tummy on the double bed next to hers, the video game player in his hands. His fingers bounced and popped against the buttons and, depending on the outcome of his play, he either emitted a disgusted sigh or whispered an excited "Yes!"

Her heart swelled with grief. She grieved the fact that running, hiding and making do was a normal life as far as her son was concerned. In his entire five years of life, he'd had nothing near approaching normal in his childhood.

She ached over the fact that everything he owned fit neatly in a small suitcase, that his beautiful eyes held a wariness that no child should possess.

She mourned for all the things Billy was missing in his life: things like best friends and baseball games and campouts and just being free to play in a park.

For the past twenty-four hours she'd been examining her options. It was now the evening of their ninth day in the motel room—nine days of accepting the charity of a virtual stranger.

How much longer could Nick continue paying for this room and how much more of his generosity could she accept without losing the last ounce of what little self-respect she still owned?

The problem was that her alternatives were grim. She and Billy could leave once again and go on the run, looking over their shoulders with the certainty that eventually David would find them again.

This was the first time he'd done something to force him into a courtroom. She hated to run, knowing that her testimony might possibly help put him away for a couple of years.

She closed her eyes, reveling in the thought of a year or two of no fear. How wonderful it would be. The thrill of her thoughts was momentary, replaced by a sense of despair and hopelessness that was far too familiar.

A heavy fist hammered on the motel room door. She jumped and Billy's gaze, wide and uncertain, locked with hers.

"Go," she said and pointed to the bathroom. She got up from the bed. "And lock the door," she told her son as she moved across the room to the door.

A rapid series of loud knocks resounded once again, each bang accelerating the frantic beat of her heart. She hurried to the window by the side of the door and, with trembling fingers, moved the curtain aside an inch.

Damn.

The vantage point was all wrong. She couldn't see who stood at the door. She let the curtain fall back into place, her heart beating a rapid tattoo. Was it David? Dear God, had he found them?

"Carol . . . honey, it's me, Bernie," a deep, unfamiliar voice yelled. Another knock followed the words. "Come on, bunny baby, let me in so we can talk. I swear, she didn't mean anything to me. It was all just a big, stupid mistake."

Juliette released a trembling sigh of relief. It wasn't David. He hadn't found them after all. She moved to the door. "You've got the wrong room," she yelled through the thick wood of the door.

"Ah, come on, snuggle bunny, don't be like that. Open the door. Open up and let old Bernie in."

"This isn't Carol's room," Juliette shouted. "There is no Carol here."

"You can't fool me, baby bunny. Come on, open the door."

The man sounded as if he'd acquainted himself with more than a bit of liquor at some point during the afternoon. She didn't think he was just going to go away with only her voice through the door proclaiming she wasn't his beloved "bunny."

She hesitated a moment, then unlocked the door and opened it the inch or so that the fastened chain would allow. The man at her door was tall, with broad shoulders and greasy dark hair that hung around his acne-pitted face. He wore a pair of jeans and an oil-stained T-shirt and his eyes darted from left to right as if unable to maintain a steady gaze. He was either drunk or high, she thought.

"Hey, you aren't Carol," he exclaimed as if he'd just received an epiphany from God.

"That's what I've been telling you. You have the wrong room. There is no Carol here."

"Sorry to bother you. Guess I made a mistake," he said and backed up.

"No problem," she replied. She closed the door and locked it once again, then wondered if she should call Nick and report the incident. She decided against it. After all, there was really nothing to report.

"Billy, you can come out now," she called through the closed bathroom door.

The door opened and Billy appeared, looking too small in the doorway. "Is everything all right?"

"It's fine. It was just somebody looking for somebody else and he had the wrong room. Hey, slugger, want to play a game of Go Fish?" she asked.

Billy smiled and nodded and for just a moment, with the beauty of his smile warming her heart, she felt a flicker of hope deep inside her—the hope of a future without fear, a future without David Blankenship.

Bingo!

Byron Camp walked away from the motel room trying to keep his feet on the ground. He felt as if he could fly. He'd done it. He'd found her and the bankroll David Blankenship had given him would instantly double.

He hadn't seen the child, but assumed he'd been somewhere inside the room. Just to be sure, when he got back in his car Byron pulled out the wallet-size picture Blankenship had given him and gazed at it.

Even though he'd only been able to see her through a crack in the door, his view of her had been enough to assure him that she was the same blond, pretty woman as the one in the photo.

Blankenship hadn't had a photo of his son, which Byron thought rather odd, but it wasn't his place to question anything. He'd been hired to do a job and now it was done. Hot damn!

It had been laughable when Blankenship had introduced himself as Mr. Smith, like Byron wasn't smart enough to watch the news. Byron had watched with interest the hostage situation at the day care when it had been broadcast over the television. It wasn't every day Byron got to see another criminal at work. Of course, had it been Byron in that day care he would have never surrendered. He would have taken out as many cops as possible on his own way out.

Byron didn't care what fake name David Blankenship called himself as long as he paid with real money.

It had taken him and three young punks that he'd

hired for next to nothing a little over a week of pounding pavements and knocking on motel room doors to finally find her.

Byron was a happy man. Now, all he needed to do was contact Blankenship, arrange for the final payoff, then give the man her location. He didn't waste a minute wondering what Blankenship intended to do to his ex-wife. It was none of his business. All Byron cared about was the twenty thousand dollars the information had earned him.

Since getting out of prison eight months ago, Byron had had trouble adjusting to life on the outside. He wasn't cut out for legitimate work and the money he'd managed to get from knocking off gas stations and convenience stores wasn't enough to satisfy his needs or wants.

This score would get him out of this shit town before the first snow flew. He'd go west, where the sun shone all the time and the cops didn't know his name.

He picked up his cell phone and punched in the numbers that would connect him to Blankenship and the ticket to his new life.

David got the call at 5:25. He and SuEllen had only been home for about an hour after a day of shopping and beauty work. He'd bought SuEllen not only new clothing and underwear, but also good cosmetics and jewelry and a half a dozen new pairs of shoes.

She had wept happy tears with each new purchase as well as when she'd looked at herself in the mirror after getting the works in a beauty salon.

It had been an interminably long afternoon as far as he was concerned. SuEllen had babbled about her bad childhood, her miserable adolescence, and the drunken, doping mother who had been more child than parent. She'd also spent much of the day telling David about her father, Big John Maynard, a man she obviously adored who was spending the rest of his life in prison for murder.

The more she talked, the more David hated Juliette for forcing him to invite into his life this low-life, trailer trash woman child.

"I think we need a toast," he said after he'd disconnected from Byron Camp. "To celebrate a wonderful day spent together."

She jumped up from the sofa, her hand patting her hair as if to assure herself that her movement hadn't messed up the new style. The hairstyle, short and curly, was a vast improvement over the long, lank hair that had done nothing to emphasize her almost attractive features. "I'll get something for us."

David motioned her back to the sofa. "Sit and relax. I'll get it."

He went into the kitchen and pulled a bottle of champagne from the refrigerator. He then grabbed two tall fluted glasses from the cabinet and set them on the countertop.

As he opened the champagne and added the strong tranquilizer to SuEllen's glass, his blood rushed with the knowledge that Juliette was within reach.

He'd make the bitch pay. She'd pay for leaving him, then she'd pay for lying to him. He'd make her sorry she'd destroyed everything.

He returned to the living room, the two glasses in hand. SuEllen had never tasted champagne before hooking up with him, so she had no idea that the slightly bitter aftertaste from the dissolved tranquilizer wasn't normal, which definitely had worked to David's advantage.

Within thirty minutes SuEllen would be sleeping soundly enough for him to sneak out, kill the bastard kid and Juliette, then sneak back in before she awakened. When he returned, he'd awaken SuEllen, who would provide him an alibi. He'd kill his wife and that kid and never spend a day in prison.

"A toast," he said as he handed SuEllen her glass. "To a wonderful day shared together. May there be many more in our future."

"I'll drink to that," she said, her eyes shining brightly. She downed the drink in three big swallows as David did the same.

Now, all he had to do was wait a few minutes for the drug to begin its work. "How about a movie?" He picked up the remote for the television. "I feel like just kicking back and relaxing."

"Me, too," she agreed. She scooted over on the sofa so she could lean her head against his shoulder. He put an arm around her and turned on one of the movie channels that was showing an old Burt Reynolds movie.

Within twenty minutes SuEllen was out, snoring faintly in the throes of deep sleep. He got up, easing her down to a prone position on the sofa, then went into the bedroom and from a drawer withdrew a length of thin plastic-coated wire.

He wrapped the wire and placed it in his pocket, then from the wall safe he withdrew a manila envelope filled with cash. After checking that SuEllen was still soundly sleeping, he slipped out the front door of the apartment.

Minutes later he was in his car and driving toward the destination where he would meet with Byron. Adrenaline pumped through him as he congratulated himself on choosing Byron, a man who'd obviously been motivated to get the job done.

He'd set their meet behind a Kmart store that had shut its doors three months before due to a failing economy. He knew the area would be deserted and without security. Perfect for David and Byron's final appointment together.

David arrived first. Even the golden kiss of twilight couldn't soften the area behind the abandoned store. Empty wooden crates stood stacked high, like sentries on either side of the back door of the building.

Parked in one of the empty spaces, a Dumpster overflowed with crushed boxes and broken hangers and shelving units. Trash not only filled the Dumpsters, but littered the area as well.

He tapped his fingers impatiently on the steering wheel as he waited for Byron to arrive. The rush of anticipation soared through him, along with the flames of anger. He let both take possession of him, consume him.

He knew there were some people in the world who feared anger, who spent their entire life fighting against a simmering internal rage, but David believed he'd been born with it and he'd embraced it from an early age.

The secret was to not allow the rage to rule you, but rather make sure you ruled the rage, and David was an expert at it.

His fingers stopped their tapping as a rusty blue Chevy rounded the side of the building. He relaxed as he recognized Byron as the driver. Byron pulled his car next to David's and David got out of his car and slid into Byron's passenger seat.

"Been waiting long?" Byron asked.

David shook his head. "Just got here myself. Did you tell anyone about this?" He tried to ignore the fact that the interior of the car smelled of old fast food, cat piss, and sweat.

"I never tell anyone about my business." Byron figured there was no reason for Blankenship to know about the three street punks he'd hired.

"You kept no notes, nothing like that that could tie you to me?" David asked.

Byron grinned, the gesture doing nothing to improve his looks. He tapped the side of his head. "I keep all my notes in here."

"And you have the information for me?"

Byron smiled again. "She's in room 114 at the Twilight Time Motel. I didn't see the kid, but I'm assuming he was someplace inside the room, too."

Of course the kid was in the room. Juliette wouldn't allow him to be anyplace else but with her. Again David felt the flush of rage, of power filling him up.

It was as seductive as love-making, as pure an emotion as he'd ever experienced. He embraced it as hot blood ran thick through his veins, giving him the beginnings of a hard-on.

He withdrew from one of his pockets the envelope filled with cash. "Here's your final payoff. I appreciate the expediency with which you accomplished this job."

"It was a pleasure doing business with you." Byron threw the envelope with the cash onto the dashboard.

David smiled at the man, then snapped his fingers. "I forgot something. I brought you a little gift, kind of a 'thatta way, boy' reward. Hang loose, I left it in my car." He slid out of Byron's passenger door and returned to his own car.

He had nothing to retrieve from inside his car, but leaned through the driver's window as if to grab something. When he approached Byron's car again, instead of returning to the passenger side, he walked to Byron's side, forcing the greasy-haired punk to roll down the window.

In the blink of an eye, David had the thin wire not only in his hands, but wrapped tight around Byron Camp's thick neck.

Byron made no noise. He couldn't. David had the ends of the wire in a death grip and by leaning backward and pushing against the car with his thighs the wire instantly pinched off all air to Camp.

Camp couldn't make any noise, but his hands clawed up first in an attempt to grab David, then at his own neck in an attempt to loosen the garrote.

He thrashed, legs flying apart, as if trying to move his body off the seat and out the window, anything to loosen the killing choke of the wire. He was effectively pinned between the steering wheel and the seat, making David's job all the more easy.

The harder David pulled, the redder Byron's face grew. His eyes bulged and within seconds he'd passed out. David tightened the wire and held it for another couple of minutes, making certain that there would be no gasp for breath and no recovery when he removed the wire.

When he finally released his hold, Byron's head lolled back against the seat, his eyes unnaturally wide and reddened and appearing to stare straight ahead at the big Dumpster. His mouth gaped open, his tongue splayed out like a thick piece of liver.

At least there was no blood, David thought as he placed the wire back in his pocket and wiped down the car door with a handkerchief. That's why he preferred the coated wire. It rarely cut the skin as long as he used a skillful touch.

He retrieved the envelope of money he'd given to Byron, then wiped down the passenger side door handle and every place else he might have touched, then he got into his car and drove off.

As he drove he checked his watch. The meeting had only taken about fifteen minutes from beginning to end, leaving him plenty of time to get to the Twilight Time Motel and take care of Juliette and Billy.

As he drove he whistled to the tune of "Ain't Misbehavin'." It had always been one of his favorite songs.

Chapter 17

"Mom? Someday could we get a dog?" Billy asked as they were seated at the little table in the motel room finishing up the last of their dinner.

Billy's favorite channel on the television for the nine days that they'd been in the motel room had become the Animal Planet. Juliette supposed she should be grateful he hadn't asked if someday they could have a snake or some other reptilian creature.

"Maybe eventually, when we get into a house," she replied. "If you could have a dog, what kind would you get?"

He chewed a french fry thoughtfully. "I dunno . . . maybe a big black one."

Juliette hid a smile by taking a bite of her hamburger. "What would you call him?"

"King," Billy said instantly, as if he'd already given it a lot of thought. "And he'd be big and have sharp teeth and he'd scare away bad people, but he'd love me and you." He tilted his head sideways. "Or I might call him Nick."

Juliette sat back in surprise. Each time Nick had come to see them here, she'd noticed Billy watching him intently, smiling shyly whenever Nick looked at him.

Apparently there was a touch of hero worship going on. Juliette didn't blame her son—she thought she might be entertaining a bit of hero worship herself where Nick Corelli was concerned.

"Either name is a good one for a dog," she said.

"He'd be real smart and I could teach him all kinds of tricks, and he could sleep in my bed with me."

"Whoa . . . I don't know about that," Juliette said with a laugh.

They both froze as a fist banged on their door. Juliette motioned toward the bathroom with her head and Billy hurried from the table and into the smaller room.

As she made her way across the room to the door she heard the reassuring click of the bathroom door lock. Billy had gone from a pleasant talk about a dog to being locked into the tiny room for his own safety.

Maybe it's the same man who'd been here earlier, she told herself. Maybe he went out and had a few more drinks and was back again looking for his "bunny."

The knock came again, nothing tentative or hesitant about the banging thuds. Juliette peeked out the window, but as before she couldn't see who stood at the door.

She moved from the window to the door and placed her hands on the solid wood. The knocking stopped for a moment and she didn't know if she should call out or not.

When the next thud came she gasped. Instead of a

knock, it was as if somebody had thrown themselves against the door with all their body weight.

Whoever was on the other side of the door, they weren't knocking to be allowed in, they were trying to break down the door to get in.

This wasn't some drunk once again at the wrong room looking for his bunny. This was something worse.

David! She knew in her heart that on the other side of the door was David.

Although she wanted to throw herself against the door and try to physically stop the door from opening, she knew she needed to get to the phone.

She threw herself across the room, sprawling over Billy's bed and grabbed up the phone receiver and punched in 911. Thankfully an operator answered immediately.

"Room 114, Twilight Time Motel. Somebody's trying to break into my room. Hurry!" She didn't bother to attempt to hang up the phone, but rather dropped the receiver and raced back to the door, where the crashing thuds continued to sound.

There was no doubt in her mind. She knew. It wasn't just any intruder. It was David. His evil emanated in the air. An icy spike of terror walked up her spine. He'd found them and she knew if he managed to get inside she would die, along with her son.

She had no time for her terror, rather felt the death of anything remotely emotional inside her as a pure clarity of thought descended.

Not knowing how long it might take for the police to arrive, she knew she had to do whatever it took to save herself, to save Billy.

She ran to Billy's bed and with Herculean effort grabbed the top mattress and stood it on its side, then tried to maneuver it against the door, thinking it would be one more barrier if he managed to break the lock on the door.

The fact that he didn't say a word, made no effort to communicate with her whatsoever, only let her know the depth of his desire to destroy her.

He was through talking. There would be no more attempts for reconciliation, no efforts to somehow try to win her back into his life. He didn't want them back in his life.

He wanted them dead.

She heard the sirens in the distance quickly coming closer and the pounding, the thudding, everything stopped. She leaned against the upturned mattress and time seemed to stand still.

There was only one thought in her head. He'd found them again. He'd found them again. That thought echoed in a numbing refrain, chilling her to her very core.

The siren became piercingly loud, then abruptly stopped.

"Ma'am?" A knock on her door. "Ma'am? It's the police. Is everything all right in there?"

The voice was definitely not David's, but still Juliette hesitated. What if he was out there, just waiting for the door to open?

What if this had been his intention all along? To create a scene, have her call for police, then when the police got here to open the door, he'd rush in and kill them all?

She knew most people would believe her thoughts

to be the height of paranoia, but those people didn't know David Blankenship. David wouldn't blink an eye over killing a cop if he also got her and Billy in the process. In his mind the ends would justify the means.

"Ma'am . . . open the door," the officer's voice called again with a slight edge of impatience.

"Is there anyone out there?" she asked. "Anyone at all?"

"Just me and my partner."

"Look around . . . make sure there's nobody who can come in with you when I open the door for you."

"Nobody is going to get in but me and my partner. Now, open the door."

Juliette shoved the mattress aside and cracked open the door. "Please . . . be careful. He's very dangerous. Make sure he can't get in."

"Nobody is getting in but us, ma'am." A middle-aged man, the officer's eyes held the weariness of years on the job, but there was also kindness there. His partner, a younger man, had his hand on the butt of his gun, an eager expression on his face as if he couldn't wait to see some real action.

Juliette prayed he wouldn't see any action on this day. She unlocked the door, took off the chain, and allowed the two officers to step inside. The moment they were in, she slammed the door and locked it once again.

"Billy." She called her son from the bathroom and it was only when he was by her side and she sat on her bed that the numbness fell away and she began to shake uncontrollably.

"I'm Officer Kent James," the elder of the two said as he pulled a notepad from his pocket. "Want to tell me what's going on?"

"Before I tell you, I need to do something." With trembling fingers she reached and hung up the phone receiver. She waited only a moment, then dialed the number Nick had given her.

Fuck.

David slammed his fist on his steering wheel as he drove away from the motel. Who would have thought the cops would respond so quickly? They must have had a fucking patrol car in the next block.

Three more minutes and he would have been inside. The door would have finally given way and he would have been in. Three more minutes and he would have been exacting his own personal revenge against the wife who had betrayed him and the child who had destroyed his life.

Fuck! He slammed his fist down once again. And who would have thought the doors of that dump would have been so solid, the locks so effective?

Breathe, David, he commanded himself. Breathe slowly and think. All right, so he'd been unsuccessful this time. And perhaps he'd brought about the demise of Byron Camp a bit precipitously.

Within the hour she'd be gone, hustled to a new location for her safety by the cop bastard who'd talked him out of the day care center. Yes, he might have been a bit premature in saying a permanent good-bye to good old Byron.

He reached his apartment and pulled into the underground garage and within moments crept back into his apartment.

SuEllen was still sprawled on the sofa, unconscious

in sleep, blissfully unaware of the fact that David had been absent.

He went into the bedroom, put the money and the wire in the wall safe, then removed his jacket, rolled up his shirt sleeves and returned to the living room. He turned on his laptop, then stood next to the sofa and shook SuEllen by the shoulder.

"Hey, sleepyhead," he said. "Wake up, I'm getting lonely and hungry."

She stirred and sat up, her eyes bleary with grogginess. "Wha . . . what time is it?" she asked.

"Almost eight. You went out like a light and I've been sitting here waiting for you to wake up. I thought maybe we'd go into the kitchen and fix some omelets for dinner."

"That sounds good," she said. Always agreeable, the little sow. "I'm sorry I fell so sound asleep. I've got to stay away from champagne."

He held out his hand to her and she took it, letting him pull her up and off the sofa. "Nothing wrong with drinking champagne. You'll eventually get used to it."

As they walked into the kitchen he placed an arm around her shoulder and smiled down at her. "I love watching you sleep," he said. "You look like my own little angel."

Her lips trembled as a joyous smile swept over her features. "Oh, David. You make me so happy."

David squeezed her against him. "And you make me happy, too." Oh yes, she made him happy. She was the perfect alibi, devoted to him and dumber than a rock.

*   *   *

"He found us."

Nick pressed the cell phone tighter against his ear. "Are you all right?"

"We're okay. Two police officers are here now."

"I'll be right there." Nick was out of the door of her apartment and in his car within seconds.

Dammit. How in the hell had David found them? The man wasn't a psychic. He wasn't God. He sure as hell wouldn't have been able to pick up a phone and call information and learn their whereabouts. But, somehow he'd managed to locate Juliette and Billy.

The only person who had known where they were was Sammy and Nick trusted that man with his life. There was no way Sammy had told anyone where the two were hiding. So, how had David found them?

Nick had been careful whenever he went to the motel. He'd checked for tails and driven a round-about way that would have exposed anyone following him. He was ninety-nine percent certain he hadn't been followed. So how?

It was a question with no answer and in any case the most important thing now was getting them to another place of safety.

A single patrol car was pulled up outside of her room. Nick stepped into the room and was greeted by Juliette, who instantly threw herself into his arms.

Surprised by her uncharacteristic display of emotion, realizing she must be on the edge of falling apart, he wrapped his arms around her and held her tight against him.

Billy sat on a chair at the table talking to one of the two officers in the room. The other officer, Kent James, stood nearby. He looked away as if to give some semblance of privacy to Nick and Juliette.

Nick was having difficulty concentrating on the scene around him. It was difficult to focus on anything but the sweet warmth of Juliette intimately against him.

The top of her head fit neatly beneath his chin, making them a perfect fit for dancing or making love. Her breasts snuggled into his chest and her hips were almost aligned with his, making the embrace almost painfully pleasurable.

As he felt himself responding to her, he reluctantly unwrapped his arms from around her and stepped back to gain an inch or two of distance between them. He placed his hands on her shoulders. "Are you sure you're okay?"

She hesitated a moment, then nodded and seemed to pull herself together as she straightened her shoulders and drew a deep breath.

Nick dropped his hands from her shoulders and looked at Kent. "Kent," he said in greeting.

The older man nodded, then gestured to the younger officer. "This is my partner, Greg Templeton. Greg, this is Detective Nick Corelli."

Nick walked across the room and ruffled Billy's hair. "How you doing, Billy?"

"Okay now," the little boy replied.

"So, somebody want to tell me what happened here?"

"We were two blocks away and got a call to investigate a possible break-in," Kent explained. "When we arrived we saw nothing suspicious and nobody hanging around the place."

"He was here," Juliette said fervently.

"She says her ex-husband tried to get into the door,

but she didn't see him," Officer Templeton said. "There's no sign of forced entry around the door." There was a touch of skepticism in the young officer's voice.

"And I'm telling you it was David Blankenship and he tried to force his way in here and in doing so he violated a restraining order." Juliette's voice was cool as she gazed at Officer Templeton.

"But you didn't actually see him," Templeton returned.

A faint flush crept into Juliette's cheeks. She hesitated, then shook her head. "No, I didn't actually see him." She turned and looked at Nick. "I couldn't see the door from the window. But it was him. You know and I know it was David."

Nick also knew that unless there was an eyewitness putting David at the scene, there would be no arrest for violation of a restraining order. He also knew the odds of anyone in the motel complex admitting to seeing anything were slim to none.

"Pack your things," he said to Juliette. "We've got to get you out of here."

A flutter of relief lit her eyes and he realized at that moment that she hadn't been at all sure he'd believe her. He believed her. There was no way she could make up the dark terror that lingered in her eyes, no way Billy could pretend the haunted look that possessed his features.

"Nick, could I speak with you for a moment?" Kent gestured toward the door, obviously wanting privacy.

"Sure." Nick looked at Juliette. "I'll be right back. Be ready to leave."

Together Nick and Kent stepped out of the motel room. Night had arrived earlier than usual and Nick knew there were storms in the forecast. The cool night air did little to ease the heat of anger that coursed through Nick. How in the hell had David found them?

"Just to tidy things up a bit I asked for an officer to go to David Blankenship's place and check things out," Kent said. "He called me to report back just before you arrived."

"And?"

"And he found David and some young thing cozy in the kitchen making omelets. The girl insisted to the officer that David had been with her all day and all evening."

Nick frowned. "Who's the girl?"

Kent opened his notepad. "A SuEllen Maynard, age eighteen. She yelled and threw a fit about his ex just trying to make trouble for him, that he'd done nothing wrong. The officer left with a reminder to Blankenship that he wasn't to have anything to do with his ex-wife."

Nick had no idea what to think about this new turn of events. "Thanks for the info."

"There's really nothing more we can do here," Kent said. "Before we leave we'll knock on a few doors, see if anyone can corroborate Ms. Monroe's story."

"In this dive you'll be lucky if anyone answers a door," Nick replied.

"Yeah well, I'll write up a report but you know probably nothing will come of it."

Nick nodded and within minutes the two officers had left and he loaded Juliette's and Billy's suitcases into the trunk of his car. All he had to do was figure out where in the hell he was going to put Juliette and Billy.

Chapter 18

There was no way Nick could chance taking the two to his apartment. Blankenship knew his name, probably already knew where he lived.

Diane's. He reached up and touched the river rock through the fabric of his shirt pocket. If they stayed at Diane's, then they would be just next door so Nick could keep an eye on things, and surely David didn't know about Nick's friendship with the woman.

As he drove away from the motel, Juliette told him about the man who'd come to her door earlier seeking somebody named Carol.

"Did you recognize him?" Nick asked. He kept an eye on his rearview mirror. He wanted to make damn sure they weren't being followed. He still couldn't believe the bastard had found her in the motel.

A slash of distant lightning rent the skies in the southwest. A storm was moving closer by the minute. Nick felt as if the storm was inside him, a storm of frustration and anger that Blankenship seemed to be one step ahead of them.

"No. I'd never seen him before in my life."

Nick digested this new information. Although he'd guessed David as a loner, strictly depending on his own devices, he supposed it was possible the man had hired somebody to help him search for Juliette. He checked his rearview mirror once again.

"Do you know somebody named SuEllen Maynard?" he asked.

"No . . . should I?"

"She's an eighteen-year-old who gave your ex an alibi for the time you said he was at the motel."

"Then she lied. He was there, Nick. I didn't have to see him. I didn't have to hear him speak. I know it was him trying to get through that door."

"You don't have to convince me, Juliette," he said softly.

"Nick, would you mind pulling over?"

He shot her a quick glance, wondering if she was going to be sick or something. He pulled his car to the curb and shut off the engine, then checked the rearview mirror yet again.

"Mom, are you okay?" Billy asked from the backseat.

"Fine, honey. I just need a minute to think." She leaned her head back and closed her eyes. She raised her hand and rubbed her forehead, as if attempting to erase an irritating headache.

Nick sat patiently. The only sound in the car was the noise of the video game Billy had turned on.

After several moments she opened her eyes and gazed at him. Her eyes glowed electric blue in the deepening dark of the night. "Maybe it would just be best if you let us out right here and we disappear."

"That's not an option."

"I think it is," she replied.

Aware of Billy listening from the backseat, Nick

opened his car door. "Why don't we get a bit of air? Billy, you sit tight, we're just going to step outside for a minute."

He could tell she didn't want to have a private conversation with him. It showed in the slowness of her movements as she opened the passenger door and pulled herself up and out.

He stepped up on the sidewalk and waited for her to join him. She wore the same turtleneck sweater she'd worn the first night he'd met her, the night they'd manipulated David out of the day care center.

In the illumination from a nearby street lamp, he couldn't help but notice how the material clung to her full breasts and emphasized her slender waist. He couldn't help but remember how those breasts had felt thrust against his chest as he'd embraced her in the motel room.

But there was nothing inviting in the cool distance of her eyes, nothing remotely seductive in the rigid cast of her shoulders and back.

"I just think it would be best for everyone if Billy and I left," she said before Nick could speak.

"Why? So you could get a month, maybe two of peace before he finds you again? How many times are you willing to start over? How many times are you willing to uproot Billy? Best for who if you pick up and run again now?"

"I don't know what else to do." There was an edge of anger in her voice, and underlying that, an edge of desperation. "How long are you willing to put your life on hold for us? How long can you afford to rent motel rooms to keep us undercover? I know you're a cop and I know what cops make. Unless you're independently wealthy, this will be a hardship on you financially."

"Why don't you let me worry about that."

She crossed her arms, as if closing within herself. "This has already gone on too long. We've accepted your generosity for too long. Why are you doing this?" she asked. "Why are you so intent on helping us? Are you expecting to get something out of it?"

The question offended him. "Yeah, I'm looking to get something out of it. The thing all men are hoping for when they help a damsel in distress. I'm hoping you'll be so indebted to me you'll have hot sex with me in positions I've only fantasized about." He held her gaze until she looked away, a slight flush coloring her cheeks.

"I've made you angry."

"Yeah, a little," he agreed.

She released a sigh. "I'm sorry. It's just that in the last year since I left David, nobody has stepped up to help us in any way." A flash of lightning, closer than the last flash he'd noticed, illuminated her tense features. "Do you have some sort of hero complex or what?"

He jammed his hands in his pockets and stared down the quiet residential street. "When I was twelve I watched a bully beat the shit out of my younger brother. When I tried to intervene, that bully beat the shit out of me. I decided at that moment that for the rest of my life I'd work to see that the bullies in this world didn't win. Your ex-husband is the worst kind of bully, a man who targets women and children. I don't want to see him win. If you run again, he wins." It was the longest, most impassioned speech Nick could remember making in a long time and he still wasn't finished.

He pulled his hands out of his pockets and instead took her by the shoulders. "Do I have a hero complex? Maybe. All I know is that it's important to me to keep you and Billy safe. I don't expect anything in return except the knowledge that one more bully is behind bars and you and Billy will be able to live a happy, normal life. Besides, we're ten days closer to David's trial date."

For a long moment they held each other's gaze. Nick dropped his hands from her shoulders and was surprised when she reached for them. As he'd come to expect, her fingers were cool.

"Okay then, I guess we should get going," she said and he knew any question of her running was answered for the moment. She dropped his hands and turned toward the car.

Moments later they were headed toward his apartment building. Nick had no idea how Diane would react to the arrival of two unexpected guests, but he knew she wouldn't turn them away.

Just for a night or two, he told himself. He'd tell Diane it was a temporary situation until he could figure something else out.

Maybe it was mentioning having sex with her, or maybe it was because of the brief embrace they had shared, but the minute they were settled back in the car he was acutely conscious of her on a physical level.

It was as if her physical presence assaulted him on all levels. He could smell the scent of her, the faint sweetness of exotic flowers with a hint of mysterious spice. He wondered what it would take to warm up her hands. Would kissing her make her blood warm? Would slow, deep, intimate kisses make the tips of her fingers warm and welcoming?

Her strength amazed him. It wasn't just a physical desire that grew by the moment for her, but he admired that strength and her determination to keep her son safe at all cost. At the moment he was caught up in the pleasure of the scent of her, the need to warm her from the inside out.

He hated the direction of his thoughts, knew that if she could read his mind she'd run for the hills. She'd believe him to be just another man wanting to use her.

What she didn't know was even though Nick had thoughts about kissing her, making love to her, he didn't intend to follow through on those thoughts. He would not be another man in her life taking from her.

He could be most helpful to her by remaining emotionally detached. He'd learned the hard way how being emotionally involved were dangerous.

"Where are you taking us?" she asked, breaking the silence that had filled the car. He realized he hadn't heard the beeps and whistles of Billy's video game for a few minutes.

He looked in the rearview mirror and saw that the young boy had curled up in a fetal ball and was asleep. The boy had no idea where they were headed, had no idea what tomorrow would bring, but still he slept peacefully, certain that his mother would keep him safe. A new burst of admiration for Juliette filled him. She had to be some kind of mother.

"I'm taking you to a friend's place. She lives in the apartment next to mine. You'll be safe there with her for a day or two, at least until I can figure out our next move."

"Does she know we're coming?"

"No, but it will be fine. Diane and I are very close. I'd do anything for her and she'd do anything for me."

"We seem to be going in circles," she observed a moment later.

"We are. If David hired somebody to find you, then it's possible we were followed from the motel. I won't stop at Diane's until I know for certain we aren't being tailed." He flashed her what he hoped was a reassuring smile. "Just relax. Everything is under control."

Just relax. Yeah right, Juliette thought. Just relax and let your life be handled by others, drift along like a wind-tossed leaf in a storm drain.

Nick had been right about one thing. They were ten days closer to David's trial and she and Billy were still okay. In eight weeks David would face a judge and hopefully be put into prison for a long time to come.

If he didn't face a judge on that day, if he blew off his court date, then a bench warrant would be issued for him and eventually he'd face stiffer penalties. Now was not the time to run.

As they drove through the dark of night, she cast quick glances at Nick, whose features were illuminated by the light of the dashboard and the occasional flashes of lightning that rent the sky.

Everything about him radiated strength, from the chiseled features of his face, to the broadness of his shoulders and the deep tones of his voice. And yet, the strength she felt radiating from him didn't threaten her like David's strength had.

During the past nine days she'd watched Nick interact with Billy. He'd been gentle and kind and had displayed a genuine affection. That, as much as anything, drew her to Nick.

She turned and glanced at Billy in the backseat. He looked like a little blond-haired cherub. How she wished her parents had been able to live long enough to see him, hold him.

If they'd been alive when she'd met David would she have married him so quickly? Had she not been reeling with grief over their deaths would she have bound her life to his? She liked to believe she wouldn't have made the same mistakes had her parents survived that car accident and been alive to support and guide her.

She pulled her thoughts from the what-ifs of her life and instead focused on the present. It was difficult for her to totally depend on Nick, to trust him or anyone else for that matter. She'd been so accustomed to being so alone in the terror, the pain, and the regrets of her life.

She cast Nick another surreptitious glance. She found it interesting that despite the fact that most of her emotions had been stolen from her through years of sheer survival, desire had apparently endured. Something about Nick stirred a physical awareness that she hadn't felt for years.

It was an emotion she didn't trust, one she believed was prompted by the fact that Nick was the first and only man who had tried to help them.

"Tell me about your friend, Diane," she asked, needing something else to occupy her thoughts besides the scent of his subtle masculine cologne and the thoughts of those moments in the motel room when he'd held her tight against him.

Another flash of lightning illuminated Nick's features and she saw the smile that curved his lips. "Diane Borderman. She's a peach. She and my brother dated for a long time, then two years ago they broke up."

He hesitated a long moment and a frown replaced the smile. "I should warn you, Diane is agoraphobic and it's a pretty severe case. She not only doesn't leave her apartment, she keeps all the blinds pulled tight in every room."

Dismay swept through her. "Oh Nick, then surely we'll be too much for her."

He shot her a sideways glance. "Do you think I'd put you someplace where things would be difficult or awkward? Diane is a bright, loving woman. She's a computer whiz and has a heart of gold. Trust me, it will be fine. Besides, the fact that she keeps her curtains and blinds all tightly closed works to our advantage."

"How?" she asked.

"All the neighbors, garbage men, delivery services, and the mailman know about Diane, and her having her blinds and curtains closed is nothing unusual. Pulled curtains and blinds not only make it impossible for her to look out, it makes it impossible for anyone to see in."

Juliette frowned and looked back at her son once again. What were they doing to him? Now he would know what it felt like to be a mushroom, to be in a dark place, devoid of sun and light.

"Juliette, it's temporary, I promise," he said. "Just until we can figure something out."

She nodded. "You mentioned a brother."

"Yeah, Tony. He's three years younger than I am. He moved out to California about eighteen months ago and has done quite well writing and developing computer software."

"The two of you are close?" She already knew the answer. She could hear the obvious affection in his voice.

"Very. Tony is a great guy, full of an exuberance for life that's contagious. I miss him a lot."

For a few more minutes they drove in silence. Juliette leaned her head back against the seat, her gaze lingering on Nick. "Have you ever had a single moment in time that you wished with all your heart you could take back?"

He didn't answer right away and she felt a sudden tension radiate from him. "Sure, everyone has those moments," he finally answered. "What's yours?"

"Mine is easy. It was the moment when I said 'I do' and became David's wife. What about you? What's yours?"

He shrugged. "It doesn't matter. You can't go back and change those moments. You only have to figure out how to live with the consequences. I'm just hoping we can help you and Billy have a good future."

She nodded and stared out the passenger window. The fact that he hadn't answered her question reminded her that he wasn't an intimate of hers, he was merely a cop doing a job. The truth was that even though she had him on her side, she was basically as alone as she'd ever been. She'd do well to remember that.

It was ten minutes later that he pulled into the parking lot of an attractive apartment complex. The storm had moved close enough that thunder could be heard rumbling overhead and the cool night air held the scent of approaching rain.

He pulled into the driveway of one of the units and gestured to the one next door. "That's my place." He shut off the engine. "Why don't you just sit tight and let me talk to Diane. I'll be right back."

She watched him walk from the car to the front porch. She couldn't help but notice the tight fit of his jeans across his backside, the slight roll of hips that gave him a sexy saunter.

David had been her first and only lover and she was surprised by the curiosity that now sizzled through her. What would it be like to make love with Nick? What kind of a lover would he be?

He knocked on the door and the door opened. He remained on the porch, obviously talking to somebody who stood inside, then he returned to the car.

He opened Juliette's door. "Come on. I'll get Billy and come back for the bags in a minute." As she got out of the car he leaned into the backseat and pulled the sleeping child into his arms. Billy's eyes opened wide, then as he recognized Nick he relaxed and curled his arms around Nick's neck.

Juliette's heart constricted at the sight of her son trusting Nick enough to wrap his arms around him and return to the vulnerable state of slumber.

For just a moment Juliette wished she were small enough to curl up into Nick's arms and feel the security, the warmth, the comfort of being safe. Or maybe she didn't want to be so small and be comforted. Maybe instead she wanted him to hold her like a man held a woman and teach her about the fires of desire without pain.

Chapter 19

The storm broke the moment Nick got into his apartment. He stood at his front window and watched the wind lash the trees as the rain fell in slanted sheets. Thunder boomed overhead and lightning snapped and crackled through the black sky.

Nick hated storms. He'd hated them since he'd been a young boy. When he'd been ten his family had lost all their possessions to the fury of a tornado. As he and Tony and their mother and father had huddled together in a corner of their basement, they'd listened to the roar of nature's wrath destroy everything aboveground.

It had been Nick's first taste of nature at its worst but no more frightening than human nature at its worst. Just as in nature, most of the time before a perp exploded, electricity crackled in the air, and thunder pulsed through his veins. And the destruction, when it came, wreaked havoc on lives, as well as property.

Nick's family had survived the tornado. With the help of insurance they'd been able to replace most of what had been lost. What they hadn't been able to replace was just things. Some held sentimental value, but they were all basically replaceable.

But when a murderer exploded, no insurance policy in the world could assess a financial gain equal to the loss. That loss was paid in burning tears, in aching memories, and in an emptiness impossible to fill.

That's what David Blankenship dealt in, the worst kind of destruction. And what pissed Nick off was that he had no idea how to preempt a new strike, how to anticipate the next move. There were no forecasters warning of impending danger, no sirens whistling to take cover.

Blankenship had broadsided him with his attack at the motel and Nick now knew there was no more need to stake out Juliette's apartment. They apparently hadn't fooled Blankenship at all.

Nick moved away from the window and went into the kitchen and grabbed a beer from the fridge. He popped the top then returned to the living room where he plopped down on the sofa and stared at the darkened television screen.

He hadn't hung around next door much longer than to make quick introductions and he now wondered how the two women were getting along.

He took a deep swallow of his beer and checked his watch. It was almost ten. He knew Diane was usually early to bed so he imagined she'd shown Billy and Juliette to the room that used to be Miranda's, then had gone to bed herself.

He wondered how Diane would do with virtual strangers in the house. Certainly she hadn't invested anything emotionally in anyone for the past two years. How would she react to having a child in the house again? He hoped Billy's presence didn't push her further into her world of darkness.

After making the initial introductions between Diane and Juliette, he'd left, needing to think about their next move. By finding Juliette in the motel room, David had proven himself to be more than a worthy adversary.

In order to protect Juliette and Billy, Nick had to enter the dark recesses of David's mind, he had to allow himself to be pulled into the storm.

He closed his eyes and tried to imagine a love so intense, so twisted that it would drive a man to do anything to sustain it. He tried to imagine a love so all-consuming that it occupied every thought and every breath you drew. He attempted to understand the depth of controlling love that would make it okay to own a woman so completely that you felt the right to cut her, to beat her, but he couldn't.

There was no way Nick could imagine that kind of perverted love. And now it seemed David's love for his wife had turned to a murderous hatred.

He finished the last of his beer, then walked back to the window in the living room and stared out where the storm still raged.

Directly overhead, the storm created thunder and lightning simultaneously as the wind howled like a banshee. Where was Blankenship now? Was he already plotting his next attack?

If Nick was going to help Juliette, then he needed to learn more about David Blankenship. He needed to find out what made him tick. Part of what made Nick a successful negotiator had always been his ability to get into the minds of the men he negotiated with.

He realized now that during those hours he'd negotiated with David to try to get him out of the day care center he hadn't even scratched the surface of David's twisted brain. He had a feeling that David had known all along he was going to eventually walk out of there and Nick's negotiations had been nothing more than white noise in his ears.

If David knew where Nick lived, then Nick would have to be careful about going next door. He didn't want the man to have a clue where his ex-wife and son were hidden, nor did he want David's attention drawn to Diane.

The phone rang, the shrill sound piercing the silence of his apartment. It was almost ten thirty. Normally a call at this late hour would portend trouble. Many times in the past he'd been called out of his bed at all hours of the morning. Criminals didn't respect the nighttime hours.

But he was officially on vacation and nobody from the station would be trying to get hold of him. He hurried into the kitchen and grabbed the cordless from the counter.

"Nick, what's up?" Tony's voice filled the line.

"Not much. How's my baby brother?" Pleasure swept through Nick as he walked back into the living room and sat on the sofa. Tony called about once a week and it wasn't unusual for their conversation to last an hour or longer.

As the two brothers caught up on each other's lives, Nick found himself telling Tony about Blankenship and Juliette and Billy.

"I can't get a handle on this one, Tony. He's already surprised me, and that worries me." Nick walked back into the kitchen with the intention of grabbing another beer, then changed his mind.

He had no idea when or how Blankenship might make a move, and he certainly didn't want to be muddleheaded from one too many beers when it happened.

"Nicky, what have you gotten yourself into? Tell me more about this helpless female who has manipulated you into helping her."

"It's not like that," he protested. He thought of the steely strength she'd shown on the day of the hostage situation at the day care. No cries, not a single tear had left her eyes despite the danger to her son.

"She's strong. She might have been a victim in the past, but there's nothing of the victim in her now and manipulation definitely isn't in her makeup."

"So what's going on, Nick? It isn't like you to get personally involved."

"I know, but something about this one has gotten to me. I've got to figure out a safe place to keep the two of them until this man goes to trial in December." Nick stood from the sofa and once again moved to the front window and peered out. "I don't dare put her in a motel room again. I don't know how he did it, but Blankenship found them there."

"You'll think of something . . . and I'll try to think of something from this end. You know the three of you could get on a plane and fly here."

"Thanks, but no. I don't want to take them out of the city." Nick frowned thoughtfully. He was afraid if he got them settled in another city they wouldn't come back here for the trial and the only way she would ever be free was to face him in a courtroom and hope for a judge having a bad day.

There was a long pause. "How is she?"

It was the same with every conversation with Tony. The two brothers would chat about all kinds of topics, but at the end of the conversation his question was always this one.

"The same." Nick wished he had something different to say about Diane. "Juliette and her son are over there now. I didn't know where else to take them after the attempted break-in at the motel."

"They'll be fine," Tony replied. "I know you, bro. You've never met a bad guy you couldn't beat."

Nick touched the rock in his pocket. "That's not true. I got beat once by a bad guy."

Again there was a long moment of silence and when Tony spoke again his voice was soft. "That wasn't your fault, man."

"I know. I just don't want to get beat again. I'm in too deep on this one, Tony. I can't walk away now."

Tony laughed. "I knew that from the moment you said her name . . . Juliette. Listen, I'll be in touch over the next day or two."

"All right . . . and Tony, I miss you, brother."

"Back at ya."

Without saying good-bye, Tony disconnected. Nick hung up and carried the phone back into the kitchen to place it on the base.

It was after eleven and he knew he needed to get some sleep, but a restless energy surged inside him. The brunt of the storm had passed. The wind no longer howled and only a light rain pattered gently against the windows.

Nick wasn't fooled. This particular storm had passed, but he had a feeling that for Juliette and Billy, the mother of all storms was yet to come.

* * *

It was just after seven the next morning when Diane stood at the door of the bedroom and watched the young boy sleep in the same twin bed where her daughter had once slept.

It was odd, seeing another child in her bed, his pale blond hair on her pillow. She'd had no interaction with the child the night before. Nick had carried the sleeping boy in and placed him in bed, and the boy had slept through the night.

She wondered if his eyes were brown like Miranda's. Miranda had had big brown eyes that had always shone with an inner light, a rich brown that had usually been filled with laughter. She'd been laughing that morning in the bank, dancing in her frilly pink dress and laughing at whatever it was seven-year-old girls found funny.

Diane closed her eyes and leaned against the doorjamb, for a moment her head filled with the sound of that sweet laughter. It echoed in every fiber of her being, ringing through every chamber of her heart and she wanted to listen to that memory forever.

A sharp crack stopped the laughter and Diane reeled backward, as if the force of a bullet had ripped through her chest. She bumped into something and whirled around, for a moment lost in the frantic horror of that day so long ago.

Juliette's eyes were wide with alarm. "Diane, are you okay?"

In that instant Diane left the past behind and returned to the present. She flushed with embarrassment and backed further away from the bedroom door. "I'm fine . . . just fine. I was just going to tell you that I'm putting the coffee on."

"Okay . . . thanks." Juliette frowned. "We didn't have much of a chance to talk last night. I can't tell you how much we appreciate you letting us stay here."

"It's no problem." Diane forced a smile to her lips. "It will be nice to have some company in the place. Coffee will be ready in just a few minutes."

She turned and escaped into the kitchen, needing some time alone to get her feet back under her. The memory of Miranda's last day on earth had shaken her. She rarely allowed herself to go back there.

As she busied herself making coffee she thought of her new houseguest. She and Juliette hadn't talked much the night before. It had been obvious that Juliette was exhausted and after a few minutes of general small talk, the two women had called it a night.

Now Diane was intrigued to find out more about the woman who had managed to get Nick to forget his creed of never getting involved with a case and become so devoted to keeping her safe.

It had been over two years since Nick had dated. Diane poured herself a cup of the fresh brewed coffee and tried to remember the name of the woman Nick had last dated. Shelly or Sheila or Sherri. That was it. Sherri. She'd been a nice woman, attractive and pleasant. The five of them, Nick and Sherri, Tony and Diane and Miranda had spent many evenings together.

Tony had told Diane over and over again that he thought Sherri was the one for Nick, but Diane hadn't agreed. There had been no signs of passion between the two, no sparkle of magic. Then the tragedy had happened and Nick hadn't seen Sherri after that.

Diane carried her coffee cup to the table and sat down. She stared at the closed blinds and thought of the world outside. The sun would be just peeking up over the horizon and the air would smell of that special fresh autumn scent.

In thousands of homes all over the area people were seated at their kitchen tables looking out the windows and enjoying the beauty of a perfect fall morning. And every morning for the past twenty-two months Diane had drunk her coffee staring at the hunter green blinds that kept the mornings out.

"That coffee smells wonderful."

Diane smiled at Juliette and motioned toward the counter. "Help yourself. Cups are in the cabinet just above the pot."

"Thanks."

Diane watched as the tall blonde poured herself a cup, then joined her at the table. Nicky had indicated the woman was attractive, but in truth she was nothing short of beautiful.

Without a drop of makeup, her skin was clear and creamy. Her eyes were the blue of an azure sea and her features were dainty and classically drawn. "Again, I want to thank you for letting us stay here," she said.

"Please, stop thanking me. It's not a problem. I'd do anything to help Nicky and because he wants to help you, then so do I."

Juliette smiled. "Nicky? I never thought of him as a Nicky. In my mind, he's Nick."

Diane returned the smile. "He's Nick when he's being a cop, but he's Nicky when he's being my friend."

"You've known him a long time?"

"For years. I met his brother Tony when I was twenty, so that was almost ten years ago. Tony and I dated and both Tony and Nick were my family. He's a good man." Diane took a sip of her coffee, her gaze still focused on Juliette. She'd rather focus on Juliette than thoughts of Tony, which merely brought more pain into her heart.

"I'm guessing Nick told you what brings us here?" Those blue eyes of hers gave nothing away.

"I know about the day care mess and the only other thing he told me was that you and your son have been running from an abusive ex-husband."

"That's it in a nutshell." Juliette paused to take a drink of her coffee and stared toward the window at the blinds pulled tightly closed.

"I hope it doesn't drive you crazy." A sweeping shame swept through Diane.

"What?" Juliette refocused on her. "Oh, you mean the blinds being closed? No, it won't make me crazy. It makes me feel safe."

Safe. Yes, if only Diane had been agoraphobic before that day at the bank. If only she'd been a shut-in and done her banking online and hadn't been out in the sunshine of the day, then Miranda would still be with her, laughing and singing silly ditties to make Diane laugh.

The ring of the phone forced Diane up and out of her chair. It had to be Nick. Diane never got any other phone calls except his. It was. He told her to unlock her back door, that he was coming over.

She hung up the phone and did as he asked, unlocking the sliding door that led out to a small enclosed patio. There was a connecting gate between her patio and Nick's.

She'd just sat back down at the table when Nick appeared at her back door. "Good morning," he said first to Juliette, then to Diane. In the space of those two words, Diane recognized the depth of Nicky's commitment to the blonde seated across from her.

There was a dark flicker in his eyes as he looked at her, a sudden tension in the air that snapped with energy. He helped himself to the coffee, then joined them at the table.

"How's everyone doing this morning?" he asked.

"Fine. Billy is still sleeping," Juliette offered.

Nick nodded and looked at Diane. "You doing okay?"

"I'm okay," she replied. And she was. When he'd first appeared on her doorstep last night asking for help, she'd been nervous about having strangers in the house. But she could do this. She could.

"Whenever I come over here from my place, I'll use the back door," he said. "I don't want anyone who might be watching my place to see me coming and going from here." He took a drink of his coffee, then continued, "Diane, it's going to take me a couple of days to figure out a safe place for Juliette and Billy. Is it okay if they stay here until I find an alternative?"

"It's fine." She smiled at Juliette. "They're welcome here for as long as they need to be here."

"Mom?" The little voice came from the doorway of the kitchen. Billy stood there, apparently hesitant to interrupt the grown-ups.

"Hey sport." Nick got up and walked over to the boy. "How did you sleep?" He reached out a hand and Billy took it. "From the looks of your bed head I'd say you slept like a log."

Billy swiped his free hand over his hair and

grinned. The blond strands spiked up on half of his head and out on the other half.

He's beautiful, Diane thought as Billy sat in the chair between her and his mother. His eyes were so like his mother's and thankfully so unlike Miranda's.

Diane wanted to pull him into her lap, smell that sleepy child scent that smelled of childhood dreams and tousled hair and warmth.

"I'll bet Diane has some sugar-loaded cereal for you for breakfast." Nick grabbed a box of cereal from the cabinet, then carried a bowl, the cereal, and the milk to the table.

"I could have done that," Juliette said.

"We men, we take care of ourselves, don't we, buddy?" Nick tousled Billy's hair as he sat down once again.

While Billy ate his cereal, they all small-talked, discussing the weather, football, and Diane's work building Web pages for companies.

When Billy was finished with his meal, Nick looked pointedly at Diane. "Maybe you could show Billy around the place?" It was obvious he wanted to speak to Juliette alone.

"Sure." Diane got up and smiled at the child, but a flurry of nervous butterflies took flight in her stomach.

"Billy, make your bed before you do anything," Juliette instructed.

Together Diane and Billy went into the room where he and his mother had slept. Juliette's twin bed was already neatly made and Diane sat at the foot of the bed and watched while Billy began to make his.

It had been so long since she'd had any interaction

at all with a child. She wasn't even sure where to begin.

"We didn't get much of a chance to visit last night," she finally ventured. "You can call me Diane."

"Okay. You can call me Billy." He pulled the sheet up and carefully swept his hands over the material to smooth out the wrinkles. So grown-up to be so little.

"Your mother told me you're five years old?"

"Almost six." He worked on the bedspread to get it neatly in place.

Diane smiled inwardly. Children and teenagers were the only ones who ever added to their age. Juliette had told Diane last night that Billy had just turned five and he was already trying to add an extra year. "Tell me something about yourself, Billy." Diane frowned. She sounded so stilted, as if she were trying too hard. "What kinds of things do you like to do?"

He sat on the foot of the perfectly made bed and shrugged. "I dunno. I like to color and I like to draw."

"I've got a computer program that lets you draw and make designs. Later I'll show you how to do it."

His eyes lit. "Wow, that would be fun."

She had no idea how long she was supposed to keep him occupied and searched for something else to say. "What do you want to be when you grow up?"

The light that had shone in his eyes dimmed and he cocked his head as if giving her question great thought. "I never thought about it before. Maybe a policeman like Nick. Yeah, that's what I want to be if I grow up."

Diane's heart constricted as she realized what he'd

said. Not *when* I grow up—but *if*. Five years old and he'd already faced his own mortality.

If this was the world today, she wasn't at all sure she wanted to return to it.

Chapter 20

She smelled of freshly showered woman. Nick had noticed her scent the first moment he'd walked into Diane's kitchen. Now as the two of them remained at the table alone, that dizzying scent once again filled his head and conjured up visions of her naked beneath a steamy spray of water.

The vision sprang unbidden to his mind, a voyeuristic pleasure that both shocked and stimulated him. He got up and refilled his cup with more coffee. By the time he rejoined her at the table the vision was gone although her clean, sweet fragrance still swirled in his senses.

"You sleep well?"

She nodded. Once again this morning she had her hair pulled back at the nape of her neck, although a beige turtleneck hid the scar he knew decorated her skin.

"You and Diane getting along okay?"

"We really haven't had much of an opportunity to chat. I went to bed almost immediately after you dropped us here, but I'm sure we'll be fine."

He wanted to reach out to touch her, not necessarily

in a sexual way, but as a connection, as a way to breach the distance he saw in her eyes.

"I'm going back to work," he said. Her eyes widened with surprise. "Just for a few days until I figure out what we do next. I think it's a good idea if I go back to my usual routine, the routine I had before I met you."

She wrapped her slender fingers around her coffee mug, a furrow digging into the center of her forehead. "He won't be fooled."

"We can't know that for sure," Nick replied. "If he's watching me in hopes of finding you, then all he'll see is that I've gone back to my life before you. Maybe he'll think you and Billy ran once again and have left the city . . . the state."

"Maybe." Her gaze still held a distance and he wondered if that's exactly what she was contemplating—running.

"Juliette." He finally did what he'd wanted to do since he'd walked in. He reached out and touched her cheek with two fingers. It was a quick touch, just a sweeping caress. Just as he'd imagined, her skin was like silk.

He sensed she would tolerate nothing more and he dropped his hand back to the table. "I know you don't like to feel as if you're disrupting others' lives and I swear the time here is only temporary. In the next day or two we'll figure out somewhere to stash you two where you'll be safe and won't feel like you're an intruder."

She nodded, but he could tell she didn't believe him, probably had long ago given up the idea of believing anyone. Before he could say anything else his cell phone rang. He grabbed it from his pocket.

"Corelli."

"Nick, got something going on here and thought you might be interested." Sammy's deep voice boomed over the line.

"Where's here?" Nick asked.

Sammy gave him an address and Nick clicked off and looked at Juliette. "That was Sammy. I've got to go." He stood.

"Is it about David?"

"I don't know. He didn't say. Tell Diane I'll call later."

He left her sitting at the table staring at the closed blinds and he wondered if she'd still be at Diane's when he returned or if she'd succumb to habit and run.

A few minutes later he was in his car and headed to the address Sammy had given him. The storm the night before had brought cooler temperatures and the trees had lost some of their colorful leaves to the wind.

Still, the sun shone brightly and the sky was an electric blue that would be a challenge for even the most talented artist to duplicate.

As he drove he replayed in his head the conversation he'd shared with his brother the night before. Nick was so proud of him. Tony had done well for himself and had managed over the last several years to amass a small fortune. He'd always been an idea man while Nick had always been the action man.

It had been that way from the time they'd been young. Even as a child Tony had been able to dream up schemes and plots for trouble and Nick had implemented them.

It would stand to reason that Nick would be the child most punished, but their mother had been a woman who knew her two boys and whenever Nick got into trouble for something he did, Tony shared the punishment for thinking up the idea in the first place.

In the eighteen months since Tony had left Riverton and moved to California, not a day had passed that Nick hadn't missed his brother. Despite the three years' age difference, the two had been best friends when growing up and their closeness had followed them into adulthood.

Nick liked to believe that they would have been good friends even if they hadn't been connected by blood. They complemented each other perfectly.

Thoughts of his brother faded as he approached the building holding the address that Sammy had given him. It had once been a Kmart store and the big red K sign still remained even though the storefront had been empty for some time. Patrol cars were parked at both sides, blocking off the back area. Nick parked his car on the side of the building next to a banged-up pickup truck. A young patrolman stood guard in front of a barrier of yellow crime scene tape. At the moment the officer was involved in a conversation with two young punks.

The officer held up a hand to quiet the two as Nick approached. "What's up," Nick asked and showed his badge.

"A stiff in a car. Officer Bellows said to let you on through when you arrived." He held up the crime scene tape so Nick could go underneath.

A stiff in a car. Why would Sammy think he'd have any interest in a stiff in a car unless the stiff was David Blankenship?

He couldn't be so lucky. Juliette and Billy couldn't be so lucky that David, in a fit of despair, had sucked on his car exhaust and solved their problems.

The fragile surge of hope died a quick death when he saw the car and the dark hair of the victim. Blankenship had a full head of sandy-colored hair.

Apparently the crime scene was still fresh as technicians worked the scene. Nick spied Sammy standing nearby and hurried over to him.

"It might be nothing," Sammy said in greeting. He left the small group he'd been standing with and pulled Nick to the side. "I might have called you out here on a wild-goose chase, but on the off chance there's a connection, I figured I'd better call you."

"Okay, now you want to tell me what you're talking about?" Nick shot a glance toward the car. "Who's the stiff and a connection to what?"

"His name is Byron Camp. Morgan has ruled it death by strangulation." Morgan was a Kansas City medical examiner who moonlighted for the Riverton Police Department when needed. "Somebody used a thin cord or rope and wrapped it around Camp's neck while standing outside the driver's door. Poor bastard never had a fighting chance."

Nick frowned. "Am I supposed to know him? Name doesn't sound familiar. Maybe if I get a look at his face—"

"Probably won't help. You know how it is with strangulation deaths."

Yeah, Nick knew. The face would be contorted,

tongue protruding, eyes bulged and red. Insect infestation would have begun seconds after death—the final heartbeat a dinner call to every fly in the area.

"Besides," Sammy continued, "I doubt if you knew him. He was an ex-con, hasn't been in trouble with the law since his last stint in Leavenworth."

"Then why am I here?" Nick tried to keep the impatience out of his voice. It was the one thing that had driven Nick crazy when he and Sammy had been partners—the man's seeming inability to think in a linear path.

"Like I said before, it's a long shot, but I thought maybe you'd want to hear about this because of her . . . you know . . . Juliette."

"Sammy, for God's sake, you're killing me here," Nick complained.

"Time of death has been established between three and six p.m. yesterday afternoon."

Sammy stuck his big hands into his bigger pockets. "I just thought it was weird, you know, that Byron Camp is found murdered within an hour or two and not more than a ten minute drive from where Blankenship found his ex-wife at the Twilight Time Motel."

"Who are the two punks?" Nick asked and pointed a finger to where the two young men remained next to the police officer.

"Now that's when all this gets even more interesting," Sammy replied. "They found the body. Apparently they're friends of Byron and saw his car and wondered why he was parked here. They also said that for the last week they'd been helping Byron find a woman."

Nick's muscles tensed. "A woman?"

"Yeah, Camp paid them each two hundred bucks with the promise of more to come if they could locate a blond-haired, blue-eyed woman who might be staying in one of the local motels."

Was it possible? Nick looked at the car where the victim was being placed in a body bag and being readied for transport to the morgue. "Then we got him," Nick said.

"No we don't," Sammy countered. "Seems Camp told the boys that he was looking for his ex-girlfriend. We got nothing tying any of this specifically to Blankenship and his ex-wife."

Nick sighed in frustration, knowing he was right. "It's not a coincidence," he said. "Blankenship is behind this. I know it. He hired Camp to find Juliette, then he killed him."

"Slokem gave me the okay to check out Camp's home. Thought you might like to tag along," Sammy said.

"My car or yours?"

"Let's make it official and take mine."

Minutes later the two were once again riding as partners and a healthy flood of adrenaline ripped through Nick. If they could find one connection, a single piece of evidence that tied Blankenship to Camp, then they would be on their way to seeing the man behind bars for the rest of his life.

"If he left anything behind in that car, the techs will find it," Sammy said as if reading Nick's mind.

"And then we'll have the bastard by his short hairs," he replied.

"Of course, that's only if there's a connection. It is possible it's just coincidence that Camp got on the wrong side of somebody at about the same time Blankenship found his ex. Camp wasn't exactly an upstanding citizen."

"Yeah, could be coincidence." But Nick knew it wasn't. He had no reason on earth to be certain that somehow Camp and Blankenship were tied together, but he was certain.

Blankenship had to have had help to find Juliette and it made sense that he would have hired a low-life ex-con. Nick had no idea how Blankenship would have hooked up with Camp, but he had no doubt he had. It just proved to Nick again that Blankenship was resourceful and would stop at nothing to find his ex-wife and son.

Hopefully they would find something at Camp's home that would tie him to Blankenship.

Byron Camp's current residence was at the Skylark Motel, a seedy little five-unit motel turned apartment building that rented by the hour, day, or week. It had a reputation for being a haven for prostitutes, meth labs, and lowlifes.

In the small office they found the manager, who informed them that Camp had been living there for the past four months and had given his notice to move the day before. "Said he was coming into an inheritance and was taking off for sunny California," he informed them as he handed Sammy a key.

"An inheritance or a payoff?" Nick said a moment later as he and Sammy walked to unit three.

"Hell of a coincidence, isn't it?" Sammy said dryly.

"The man was a filthy pig," Sammy pronounced as they walked into the front door of the small unit. He looked around with obvious distaste on his features. "I mean, I'm a pig, but Camp was a filthy pig."

Nick had to agree as he gazed around the sparsely furnished living room. Without the trash, there would be little left in the place. Fast food wrappers, take-out cartons and empty scotch bottles littered the coffee table. Long blond cat hair covered the threadbare sofa and wafted in the air.

The whole place smelled like a mixture of a dirty litter box and the sloppy spills of a tavern floor. The living room was just the tip of the proverbial iceberg. The kitchen was nothing more than a room for more trash and dirty dishes.

In the tiny bedroom a long-haired blond cat stared balefully from its resting place in the center of dirty sheets on the bed. The smell of nasty litter was stronger in here and Nick followed his nose to the bathroom, where the overflowing litter box and a filthy bathtub and sink greeted him.

He returned to the living room, where Sammy had begun to pick through papers that littered one end of the sofa. "I guess this means I toss the bedroom?"

Sammy snorted. "I'm not going any further into this little stink hole."

It took nearly two hours to look at every scrap of paper, go through every dresser drawer and check out all the closets. In the bedroom closet Nick found a shoebox full of old photos and personal papers. The pictures chronicled the highlights of Camp's miserable life.

He'd been a sullen teenager who'd grown into a dangerous man. The photos showed Camp on a motorcycle with a scantily clad woman on the back, in a bar raising a drink in mock salute and leaving prison with a cocky grin on his face. Hell of a scrapbook, Nick thought.

The paperwork included a marriage certificate and a divorce decree, and several newspaper clippings reporting a variety of crimes Nick could only assume Camp had been responsible for. But there was nothing to connect him to David Blankenship.

"Forensics should pick up something," Sammy said as they drove back toward the old Kmart store where Nick had left his car.

"Yeah, maybe." In Nick's pocket was a fairly recent photo of Camp. He pulled it out now and gazed at it thoughtfully. "If Juliette can ID him as the man who came by her motel room, then I'll have the connection I need."

"But not one you can use," Sammy countered. "Face it, Nick. You can't prove that Blankenship was even at the motel. Even if she does ID him as the man at her door, that doesn't prove anything. It could be argued that Camp really was looking for his own girlfriend, somebody he called his bunny."

"Yeah right. He was looking for the fucking Easter bunny and got lost along the way." Frustration gnawed at Nick.

"Come on, Nicky. We'll know more after the guys get done going over that car and the crime scene area. I told you from the very beginning this might just be a wild-goose chase."

"But if it isn't, then we've learned something very important," Nick said.

"And what's that?"

"I thought David Blankenship might be capable of

murder. If he killed Byron Camp, then I know he's not only capable of murder, he's already committed the crime." Despite the warmth of the sun shining through the car window, a wintry chill swept through Nick.

Chapter 21

It was just after noon, but in Diane's apartment it was always twilight. Juliette and Diane sat at the kitchen table lingering over cups of hot chocolate. They'd just finished eating lunch and Billy had left the table to return to the television in the living room.

"He's a sweet little boy," Diane said when he'd left the room.

"He's an amazing child," Juliette replied. "And I'm not just saying that because he's mine. He has an inner strength that most adults could only wish to possess."

"I guess it's been hard on you both."

Juliette smiled at the pretty young woman seated across from her. "Yeah, it's tough." Her smile faltered. "I don't worry about myself so much, but I do worry about him. No child should have to live the way Billy has."

Diane looked at the blinds at the window, then gazed at Juliette. "There's danger out there everywhere." She reached across the table and grabbed Juliette's hand in a painfully tight grip. Her eyes lit with fervency. "Hold tight to him. Keep him safe. He's so precious . . . they're all so precious . . . the children . . . he could be gone in the blink of an eyelash."

Diane gasped, as if startled by her own actions. She released Juliette's hand and sat back in her chair. "I'm sorry. I didn't mean—"

"It's all right," Juliette replied, although she wasn't sure exactly what had just happened.

An awkward silence fell between them. Juliette wanted to ask a hundred questions. It was obvious that the room where she and Billy slept had once been a child's room and yet neither Diane nor Nick had mentioned a child.

She wondered what had happened to Diane that had driven her to this life of isolation and fear. But she was a guest in Diane's home. It was enough that she and Billy were intruding on her physical space. Juliette wouldn't attempt to trespass into Diane's psyche.

"Nick mentioned that you did computer work," she said to break the silence before it grew too big to bear.

"Yes, I build and maintain Web pages for companies. It's work I can do from home. I don't know what I'd do without the Internet. For the past twenty months everything I've needed I've bought online."

It was an opening and Juliette took it. "So that's how long you've been agoraphobic? For twenty months?"

Diane nodded. "Give or take a month or so." She reached up and grabbed a strand of her brown hair and twisted it between two fingers. "My work is perfect for a shut-in, but I don't know how I would have survived without Nicky's friendship. He's been my only link to the outside world, my comfort and support. You probably don't realize how lucky you are to have him on your side."

"Trust me," Juliette said dryly, "I realize. In the past

year I've had a lot of contact with a lot of policemen and police departments, but nobody seemed to care about our situation until Nick."

"He's a great guy. He and I have plans to skate on Tanglewood Lake on Christmas Eve." There was a wistfulness in her voice, as if she desperately wanted to fulfill that plan, but wasn't sure she would be capable.

Juliette hoped she achieved her goal. This was no way for a pretty young woman to live. "That sounds wonderful. My parents used to take me ice skating when I was little at a skating rink. I was never very good at it."

"Me either. Nicky is okay, but his younger brother, Tony, is a wonderful skater." Diane stood abruptly. "I'd better get back to work." She carried her cup to the sink and rinsed it and put it in the dishwasher.

Juliette remained at the table and Diane left the kitchen. She sipped the last of her hot chocolate slowly, her thoughts on the woman who had just left the room. It had been obvious in her tone of voice when she'd said Nick's brother's name that there was still a wealth of feelings for the man.

Nick had said that his brother and Diane had dated. What had happened between the two and why did the shadows in Diane's eyes remind Juliette of the shadows she occasionally saw in Nick's?

She sensed a tragedy that bound the three of them together, and she had a definite idea that whatever had happened had involved a child. But she didn't want to know.

She had enough problems of her own and had too much fear for her own son to speculate about what had happened to somebody else's child. She had no energy left to deal with somebody else's tragedy while trying to prevent her own.

A soft knock fell on the back door and she got up from the table and moved the curtain aside to see Nick. She unlocked the door.

She knew instantly that something had happened. Raw energy poured from him as he stepped inside. "What happened?" she asked.

"Could be something, could be nothing," he replied. He walked over to the doorway that separated the living room from the kitchen, apparently checking to make certain that Billy was occupied and couldn't hear their conversation.

When he turned back to look at her his features were taut, his eyes somber. "An ex-con who told his landlord he was coming into a large sum of money was murdered sometime late yesterday afternoon. Byron Camp . . . ever heard of him?"

"No, but there's no reason I would have," she replied. Her heart ticked an accelerated beat as if to mirror the pulse of his energy in the air.

She wasn't a stupid woman and instantly she understood the ramifications and the timing of the murder. "Tell me the truth, he was working for David, wasn't he?"

"So far we haven't been able to make the connection between the two."

"But you know it was him. He probably hired the man to find me and when he did and David had what he needed, then David killed him." Juliette clenched her hands at her sides and tried to gain control of the trembling that had seemed to have taken possession of her limbs. She'd always sensed deep in her heart that David was capable of unspeakable sins. But, sensing and knowing were two different things and the actuality of a man's death swept a new kind of horror through her.

Nick pulled a photograph from his pocket and held it out toward her. "Is this the man that showed up at the motel yesterday?"

Her hand trembled slightly as she reached for the photo. She gripped it tightly and closed her eyes for a long moment, then looked at it. "Yes . . . yes, it's him." She looked back at Nick. "This is proof, isn't it? Now they can arrest David and put him away for the rest of his life."

The hope that had swept through her died when she saw the look on Nick's face. He looked dangerous. A dark anger simmered in his gray eyes and a muscle ticked in his taut jaw. "I wish to hell it was that easy. Unfortunately what we know and what we can prove are two different things."

"And so a man is dead because of me," she said bitterly. "I told you it would have been best if we would have just left town." She threw the photo on the table. "If we'd done that, then this man would still be alive."

She gasped as Nick grabbed her by the shoulders and backed her up against the refrigerator. "That man is dead because of David, not because you decided to stay in town. Whether you would have been here or not he would have been dead. You didn't do it. David did." The last couple of words shot out of him like bullets from a gun, sharp staccatos in a harsh voice.

"Everything all right in here?" Diane spoke from the doorway.

Nick flushed and dropped his hands from Juliette's shoulders. "Everything is fine." Diane turned to leave them alone once again, but Nick stopped her. "Diane, I want you to do something for me."

"What's that?"

"I want you to work your computer magic and get me anything and everything you can find on David Blankenship. Juliette can give you any personal information you might need." He looked at her for confirmation and she nodded.

Her chest still trapped her breath from the close physical contact she'd had with Nick. His grip on her shoulders hadn't hurt, but she felt as if his touch was burned deep into her flesh.

She didn't have to worry about David killing her. The stress of everything was apparently making her lose her mind, for in those moments when Nick's eyes had burned into hers, with his body so close she could feel the heat emanating from it, she'd wanted him to kiss her.

She'd wanted him to pull her into his arms and feel his wild energy coursing through her. She'd wanted to be swept up with desire, lost in passion and removed, even for a short time, from reality.

"So, you want background, financial, health info?" Diane asked.

"Everything. Every single piece of information you can find on him from the moment he was born until now," Nick replied. He looked at Juliette, his eyes still blazing with emotion. "Byron Camp's murder was neat and clean, not the sloppiness we normally see from a first time offender. I think David killed Byron Camp and I don't think it was his first murder."

As his words sank into her heart, into her soul, a cold wind blew through Juliette and she leaned back against the refrigerator. If what Nick said was right, then she'd not only married, lived with, and slept with an abusive man. She'd married, lived with, and slept with a murderer.

"And now I need to get back to the station. I need to tell Chief Slokem that I want to go back on duty for the next couple of days. Although I'm relatively sure you're all safe here, make sure you keep the doors locked and call me if there's any problems."

Diane locked the door when he left then turned back to Juliette. "It looks like you and I have work to do, girlfriend."

Billy stared at the television, but he wasn't watching it. It was a dumb cartoon he'd seen before. Billy didn't like cartoons very much. He'd rather watch shows about animals, especially dogs.

At the moment the only thing he could find on TV for kids was cartoons, so instead of watching, he was thinking. He thought a lot, probably more than his mom knew. He knew a lot, probably more than his mom knew he did.

Like he knew that David was a very bad man. He'd known it before what happened at the day care. Sometimes he thought he'd known it before he was born.

Billy wasn't scared of the dark and he wasn't scared of bugs or thunder. He was scared of David. David made his stomach hurt like he was sick.

One time when they'd still lived in David's house Billy had woke up in the middle of the night and he'd smelled David in his room. David always smelled like what Billy thought a dark forest might smell like. He'd cracked open his eyes and had seen David standing next to his bed. Billy had squeezed his eyes tightly closed and pretended to be asleep and when he'd finally opened his eyes once again to take a peek, David had been gone.

For several nights after that Billy had stayed awake all night long, afraid to close his eyes, afraid that David might sneak into his room and do something bad.

As he sat on Diane's sofa and stared at the television he knew something bad had happened. He always knew when something bad had happened. His mom's mouth looked different. Her lips were straight and her eyes looked so sad it made Billy feel sad.

He knew David was his daddy, but he didn't want him to be. When he was at day care other kids talked about their daddies. They said stuff like how their daddies took them places and played ball with them. And when the other kids said stuff like that Billy made up stories about his daddy.

He'd tell them that his daddy was big and strong and took him fishing and colored pictures with him. He boasted about a daddy who made him breakfast and told him fun stories and loved him more than anything else.

Billy didn't think he'd ever get a daddy like that, but he hoped that someday he could at least get a puppy. That's if David didn't make him dead first.

He thought maybe David would make him dead, maybe even before he turned six. Billy thought a lot about being dead. Billy had seen a dead squirrel once. It had been hit by a car and was all squishy. He hoped if David made him dead that at least he wouldn't be squishy.

The worst part about being dead was that he'd miss his mom. The best part would be that maybe in Heaven God would let him pick a new daddy, and have a puppy.

Chapter 22

Nick wanted Blankenship to believe that he was back at his regular schedule and it was his normal habit on Tuesday evenings to eat at The Corner Cafe. Although he wanted to be at Diane's to check out how things were going and what information Diane had gotten from her Internet search, at five o'clock he pulled into the parking lot of the cafe.

The Corner Cafe was something of an anomaly. Dressed like a gaudy whore the establishment boasted a bright red brick facade with purple shutters and a neon sign that flashed like a traffic light.

The exterior should have kept out the families and conservatives the neighborhood boasted, but it didn't. Instead the cafe, with its excellent food and friendly waitresses, had garnered an almost cultlike following among the members of the community.

Mothers met for midmorning coffee after dropping kids at school, business was conducted during lunch hours, and in the evenings friends and families met at The Corner Cafe for a night of good food and company.

"Hey Nick." Sally, one of the waitresses, greeted

him as he walked in the door. "Where you been? We haven't seen you for a while."

"I took a little vacation time last week." He slid onto a stool at the long counter and breathed in the scent of fried potatoes and onions and fresh baked pastries. The smell welcomed him like an old, familiar lover.

"Do anything exciting?" She grabbed the coffeepot and poured him a cup.

"No, nothing exciting. So, what's the special today?"

Sally grinned at him. She'd been around for as long as Nick had been coming to the cafe and she was the waitress who always served him. "What difference does it make? No matter what it is you always order the special."

Nick laughed. "You're right. Give me the special."

As he sat and waited for his meal, his thoughts went over the day's events. At the time he'd left the station for the day none of the results from Camp's car had come in. However, no fingerprints had been found anywhere in the car except for Camp's around the driver area.

There was an additional complication of contamination. Both the driver and the passenger window had been down throughout the night, allowing the passing thunderstorm to sling rain and wind into the interior of the car. If there had been hair or fibers tying Blankenship to the scene, they had probably been blown to hell overnight.

He knew the two detectives who had been assigned to the case had spent much of the afternoon hours poking through Camp's room and, like Sammy and Nick, hadn't come up with any leads.

He sipped his coffee and wondered how the women were getting along. And Billy. How was he doing in the dark apartment without sunshine and fresh air?

The kid got to him. From the moment Billy had told Nick that he didn't pee the bed, the kid had managed to grasp hold of a corner of Nick's heart.

He had a dignity that far exceeded his age, a calm acceptance of a life twisted and complicated by powers far beyond his control. He was an amazing child and Nick feared for him. How could a father hate his own child? How could a father want to destroy his own flesh and blood?

David Blankenship was evil.

He motioned for a second cup of coffee, then tried to empty his mind of disturbing thoughts. He swiveled on his stool and looked around. The cafe felt like a second home. For years Nick had eaten his Tuesday night meal here. Before Tony had left town the two brothers had often met here to eat together. Often on those nights they had been four: Nick, Tony, Diane, and Miranda.

He absently touched the rock in his pocket. Those had been happy, innocent days. None of them had known how fragile their happiness had been.

Within a few minutes Sally had served him the special of beef stew and cornbread and he emptied his mind as he filled his stomach. The stew was hearty, with thick chunks of vegetables in a savory gravy and the sweet cornbread was a favorite of Nick's.

He hadn't realized how hungry he was until he began to eat. He'd skipped lunch and had run all day on the cup of coffee he'd had at Diane's early that morning.

He was halfway through the meal when a young woman entered the cafe. Directly behind her was David Blankenship. Every muscle in Nick's body tensed. The mouthful of stew turned to mud. His blood began a slow boil at the audacity of the man.

They were seated at a booth on the opposite side of the cafe and Nick turned on his stool to watch them. There were dozens of eating establishments in Riverton and Nick knew it was no coincidence that the man had chosen this particular place at this particular time.

If he'd needed proof that Blankenship was watching him, following him, he now had it. The fact that Blankenship had entered the cafe showed Nick that he didn't care if Nick knew that he was following him.

As Nick's gaze met David's, he tipped an imaginary hat at Nick and smiled. Nick's blood boiled hot. The bastard was enjoying this. Cat and mouse. It was all an amusing game to him. But, Nick didn't find it amusing at all.

He turned his attention to the companion with Blankenship. The mousy young woman must be SuEllen Maynard, the woman who had provided an alibi for him during the time David was at the motel terrorizing his family. She looked like a baby, her gaze lingering on David with adoration. Did she have any idea about the nature of the man she was involved with? Nick didn't think so.

He turned back around on his stool and stared at the last of his stew. His appetite had fled the moment he'd seen his nemesis. The fact that the bastard was flaunting his presence here in one of Nick's zones of comfort only pissed him off more.

Nick was surprised that nobody else in the place

seemed to recognize David. He told himself he shouldn't be surprised, the day care situation had been on the news almost two weeks before. Even though Blankenship's face had been flashed on the television screen a number of times during the ordeal, it hadn't been shown again since and the viewing public had short attention spans.

He forced himself to finish his stew, refusing to allow the presence of Blankenship to make the rest of his meal go to waste. Finally, unable to eat any more, he got up from his stool and headed to the restroom.

In the privacy of the bathroom Nick swiped his face with a cool paper towel and tried to halt the rising anger that stirred in his stomach like a bad case of flu. What did Blankenship hope to gain by exposing himself like this?

He tossed the paper towel in the wastebasket, then left the bathroom. He met David at the mouth of the narrow hallway that led to the restrooms.

"Hello Nick," David said. Nick had no intention of speaking to the man. He started to sweep past him. "Are you fucking her, Nick?"

Nick stopped in his tracks and turned back to face the creep. The blood that had pounded hot now went icy cold and he was aware of a pulsing vein in his forehead. "What do you want, Blankenship?"

"I wanna know if you're fucking my wife."

"Ex-wife," Nick replied. "And she's none of your business."

David laughed, an unpleasant deep rumble. "You think you're something special to her? She fucks a different cop every time she moves to a new city. She's nothing but a loose whore . . ."

David's nose spurted blood and it took a second for Nick to realize his own fist had been the cause of it. He sure hadn't planned it, but felt more than a little satisfaction as he saw the result.

A female scream rent the air as David staggered backward and grabbed a handkerchief from his back pocket. "You stay away from Juliette," Nick said, then turned.

Fists slammed into his chest and he grabbed the arms attached to the fists. SuEllen Maynard tried to attack him again, her features twisted with rage. "Leave him alone! Don't you dare hurt him again. This is the worst kind of police brutality."

Nick released her and she ran to David's side. Nick didn't wait around for more words or fists to fly. He turned and walked back to his stool, where he pulled out enough money for his meal and a tip, then left the cafe.

He slid into his car and flexed his right hand. His middle knuckle ached just a bit, but it was a satisfying ache. It had been pure instinct that had driven the punch out of him, no thought, no premeditation, just the instinct of a man protecting his own.

His sole desire had been to stop the filth that had spewed from Blankenship's mouth. He wasn't going to hear derogatory remarks about Juliette from her stalker.

He started his car engine and looked in his rearview mirror to see if David and his young girlfriend had left the cafe. Apparently not.

Just to be on the safe side, when Nick left the cafe he didn't head directly home. He drove aimlessly, simmering from the brief encounter. Blankenship had come into the cafe for one reason and one reason alone: to taunt Nick.

If what Nick believed was true, then yesterday David had murdered a man and gone after his ex-wife and child. And today he'd stalked Nick and had come into the cafe to play a game of cat and mouse and there was nothing Nick could do about it.

As satisfying as the fist in the face had been, it had accomplished nothing and in fact might have only served to exacerbate the situation. In truth it pissed Nick off that David had managed to push his buttons and get a violent response from him.

He found himself on the dirt road that paralleled the Missouri River. Ahead there was a small riverfront park where teenagers came to make out and drink.

It was too early for the teenagers and late enough that the families who enjoyed the park had left for the day. Nick parked his car and walked toward the river, hands shoved in his pockets and forehead puckered in thought.

He knew he was in trouble. Never in his life had a perp managed to push him into any kind of display of physical violence. Yet with a few words, Blankenship had managed to shove him over the edge.

He stared at the river, a dirty rush of water that claimed at least two or three lives a year in its watery depths. His problem wasn't so much Blankenship, it was Juliette.

Somehow, someway with her cool blue eyes and her ice cold hands, with her champagne hair and rigid set of her slender shoulders, she'd managed to get under his skin. She'd shared so little about herself, about her life before and with David.

He didn't know anything about her beyond her past with David, and yet it didn't matter. What he did know about her was that she was a wonderful mother, passionate about the safety and well-being of her son. She asked for nothing, but deserved so much.

Drawing a deep breath as the last of day's light snuffed out, he turned and went back to his car and headed home.

It was just after eight when he pulled into the driveway of his apartment. He didn't even glance at the apartment next door as he headed into his own.

Once inside he turned on the lights against the approaching darkness outside the windows, then closed his blinds so nobody could peek inside and see what he was doing. He went out the back door, through the connecting gate in the privacy fence, and onto Diane's small patio.

He knocked on the back door and it was opened by Juliette. In the instant of seeing her, the smile that curved her lips, he decided not to share with her the events of his night and his run-in with David. He didn't want her to lose the smile she wore on her face as she let him in.

"Hi," he said as he walked in the door. "How did your day go?" She looked more relaxed than he'd ever seen her.

"Fine. What about yours? Anything new on that man's murder?"

"Nothing." For a moment he wanted to do nothing but stand there and look at her. She cocked her head and looked at him quizzically.

"Everything all right?"

She was so beautiful. He nodded. "Fine. Where are Diane and Billy?"

She took him by the arm and led him into the living room where Diane and Billy sat side by side in front of one of Diane's computer monitors.

Diane had some sort of action game pulled up on the screen and Billy was using the mouse to play. He showed more animation than Nick had ever seen as Diane guided him to find hidden treasures amid the program landscape.

As Billy pointed and clicked on a treasure chest a little animated creature with purple hair and an orange face popped out. Billy giggled.

Nick had never heard him laugh before and the sound hung in the semidarkness of the room like the echo of a half-remembered happy melody. He shot a glance at Juliette and the soft, loving smile on her face punched him in the gut like the kick of a mule. Damn, but he wanted her, and nothing good could come of it.

"Did you get something for me today?" he asked Diane.

"As a matter of fact I did." She stood and motioned Juliette into the chair she'd just vacated. "Why don't you watch your son play for a few minutes and let me talk with Nick."

"All right," Juliette agreed. As she sat next to Billy Diane grabbed a folder thick with papers and motioned Nick back into the kitchen.

When they got into the kitchen Diane set the folder on the table. "There are reams of papers in there," she explained. "I got plenty of information not only on David, but also on his parents. I thought you might want to know what kind of people raised him."

"Thanks, I really appreciate it." Nick picked up the folder and gazed at his friend. "You doing okay? I know having Billy around can't be easy on you."

She smiled but he saw the shadow of pain in the gesture. "I'll admit, it was a little tough this morning, but as the day has gone on it's become easier." She hesitated a moment, holding Nick's gaze. "It helps that he's nothing like her." It was the first time in two years that Diane had alluded to the child she'd lost, and Nick placed an arm around her thin shoulders. "He's much more somber and quiet than she was."

"I know I threw this all on you without warning. I can't tell you how much I appreciate you taking them in. I didn't know what else to do."

"It's all right." She reached up and kissed his cheek. "We're doing just fine."

"It's only going to be for another day or two, then I need to get her out of here."

"As far as I'm concerned there's no hurry."

Nick frowned. "Maybe not from your end, but I don't want them staying any one place for too long a time." What he didn't tell Diane was that he was concerned for her safety. He didn't trust that Blankenship wouldn't eventually figure out that Juliette and Billy were near and this would be a logical place for him to look.

Nick needed to move them before that happened. He released his hold on her and clutched the folder to his chest. "Guess I'll get back home. Looks like I've got some reading to catch up on."

"I think you'll find it interesting. I didn't show a lot of it to Juliette. There didn't seem to be any point."

"I'll check in tomorrow." With these final words, Nick left and returned to his own apartment.

The evening had turned into a nightmare and the nightmare hadn't ended yet. SuEllen sat on the sofa in David's apartment and cast a surreptitious glance at David. He sat at the dining room table in the dark, his laptop monitor providing the only light in the room.

Although he'd told her in curt tones that he had work to do, he wasn't working. He was staring . . . just sitting and staring blankly at the screen saver that danced geometric designs across the monitor.

When they'd gotten home from the cafe she'd tried to fuss over him, worried about his nose, which had bled for the entire way home. She'd raged against the man who'd hit him, telling him he should press charges.

David had told her to shut up, that he needed to think, and both the look in his eyes and the tone of his voice had frightened her.

It wasn't the first time in the days she'd been with him that he'd frightened her. There were moments when he drew into himself, got lost in a blackness that shone from his eyes as he stared unseeing at some point or another.

She'd quickly learned not to bother him when he disappeared into that darkness. Tonight he'd been lost longer than usual and even though she sat some twenty feet away from him she could feel the sick tension that rolled off him.

Nervous tension jangled in her stomach and anxiously she picked at a fingernail cuticle and wondered what the rest of the night would bring.

It was all the fault of that cop who had hit him. She had no idea what conversation had been exchanged between the two men, but she knew the cop had no right to punch David in the nose.

The punch had done more than made David's nose bleed, it had put him in a mood SuEllen had never seen before, a black mood that filled not only the orbs of his eyes, but the entire apartment.

She shot him another glance. He looked as if he were in a trance with the bright colors from the monitor bleeding onto his still features.

How long could he sit like that? It was freaking unnatural for anybody to be so still for so long. What was he thinking? She shut off the television. It was impossible for her to concentrate on anything on the screen when she was so focused on David.

She wondered if it was time to leave, time to go back to the trailer, back to the life she'd led before David. If she begged and pleaded she knew she could probably get her job back at the Dairy Shack and her mother probably wouldn't have even noticed she'd been gone.

Yes, it was probably time for her to leave, but the very idea of returning to her previous life shot dread through her. No more champagne, no more scented sheets and candlelit meals. She'd be back to fighting off creeps and trailer trash life.

It wasn't just the amenities of wealth she'd miss. Even though there were moments when he frightened her, she'd miss David. Nobody had ever taken the interest in her that he had. Nobody had ever treated her so well.

She'd written several long letters to her dad in

prison telling him about David, about how good he'd been to her and how he talked to her like she had more than half a brain.

No, she wasn't going anywhere. David had never done anything to hurt her, and even if he had she'd rather be beaten to death living here than die a slow death in her old, miserable life.

She cocked her head as she heard a strange sound. It took her a moment to realize it was the sound of David whistling. She looked back toward the dining room. He still sat perfectly still, but his lips were pursed to produce a familiar melody.

SuEllen recognized the song. Her mother had loved old songs and SuEllen had cut her teeth on Big Band music and old standards. This particular song had never affected her on an emotional level, but as the melodic whistling of "Ain't Misbehavin'" filled the apartment a shiver of inexplicable horror swept through her.

Chapter 23

"Ever hear of a man named Jeffrey Beacham?" Richard Slokem was pissed. The moment Nick had entered the station house that morning he'd been told that Slokem wanted to see him in his office.

Slokem was furious. His face was red, and his voice held a clipped politeness. He pointed to a chair and gestured for Nick to sit down.

"Jeffrey Beacham? No, I don't think I know anyone by that name," Nick said.

"I didn't know the man until this morning, when I got a phone call from him." Slokem turned his back on Nick and straightened a picture hanging on the wall. "It seems Mr. Beacham is a lawyer."

Instantly Nick knew where this was going. Blankenship had whined to his lawyer.

Slokem turned back to face Nick. "Jesus Christ, Nick, what were you thinking? Beacham is threatening a lawsuit on Blankenship's behalf not only against you personally, but against the department. He said you punched the man without provocation."

"It wasn't without provocation," Nick said thinly. "He followed me into the cafe with the distinct intention of provoking me."

"I don't give a damn if he danced naked on your lawn and winked at your mother." The hot spots that had decorated Slokem's cheeks spread all over his face. "My cops don't go around punching people, especially assholes out on bail."

"I made a mistake." The words stuck in his craw, but he knew it was what the chief wanted to hear. "It won't happen again."

"Damn right it won't happen again. I want you to stay miles away from David Blankenship. If you see him coming, then you go the other direction. And I'm telling you right now, you keep out of the Camp murder investigation. Do we understand each other?"

"Perfectly."

Slokem turned his back to straighten another framed photo, this one of him and the mayor on a golf course, and Nick knew he'd been dismissed.

He left the office with a burn in his gut. If Slokem thought he was going to stay out of the Camp murder investigation, he was crazy. Officially he would do as his chief asked: unofficially he intended to follow every step of that investigation.

What had begun as a simple desire to keep a woman and her child safe had somehow grown into something much more complex. He wanted Juliette and Billy safe and now he wanted David Blankenship put away in prison for the rest of his life.

Back at his desk, Nick opened the folder that had kept him up reading late the night before. Diane had managed to get into records she had no legal right to be in and the picture those records drew was one familiar to Nick.

Juvenile records indicated a troubled child with a

penchant for setting fires, bullying, and cruelty to animals. Although the young David's parents' money had kept him from serving any time in a facility, it was obvious that the pattern of offenses was one of a sociopath.

After the age of sixteen there were no more records of any run-ins with the law. Nick had to assume that David hadn't quit his bad behavior but had gotten smarter and crafty enough to avoid getting caught.

He'd excelled in college and afterward had been appointed by his father as President of Blankenship Enterprises, a company that dealt in computer software. According to news clippings, over the next several years under David's management, the company had grown by leaps and bounds and David spent much of his time conducting business seminars on college campuses.

Nick now pulled out one of the papers from the folder and stared at the photo. It was the marriage announcement of David Blankenship to Juliette Monroe. In the photo David looked the epitome of a handsome wealthy entrepreneur and a younger Juliette looked softer, her eyes shining with hope and her lips curved into a sweet smile.

It was a Juliette Nick had yet to see—a young woman with the promise of the future on her face, with untold possibilities before her.

Nick touched her paper cheek, wishing he could bring back this woman and erase the devastation of David from her life. He pulled out another piece of paper, this one with a photo of an older couple— David's parents, John and Rachel Blankenship. The article that accompanied the photo indicated that the two had just celebrated their fortieth wedding anniversary. John's accomplishments as a businessman were listed, as was Rachel's charity work, but there was no mention of a son.

Nick wanted to talk to them. He wasn't sure what would be served by talking to them, but any information he could get on Blankenship might prove useful.

Diane had found their address and unlisted phone number and the phone number was already burned into Nick's brain. Nick stared at the phone on his desk.

These people, according to Juliette, had disowned and disconnected with their son the moment he'd married. What the hell kind of people were they to let Juliette marry their insane son and not warn her of trouble?

Nick picked up the phone and dialed the number. As a cop, as a person who had dealt with all kinds of criminals in all kinds of situations, Nick knew that knowledge could be power. He needed to find David's weakness.

He dialed the number and waited for a connection. A woman with a Hispanic accent answered the phone. "Blankenship Residence."

"Yes, I'd like to speak with John Blankenship."

"May I tell him who is calling?"

For just a moment Nick thought about using some ploy to get the man to the phone, but he decided against it. "Tell him this is Detective Nick Corelli of the Riverton Police Department in Kansas and I could use his assistance with a personal matter."

"One moment and I'll see if Mr. Blankenship is available."

It was much longer than a moment before a deep

male voice filled the line. "Detective Corelli . . . this is John Blankenship. I can only assume that the personal matter is something to do with my son." There was a heavy weariness, a defeated resignation in the voice.

Nick shoved aside the unexpected pity that attempted to grab hold of him. "I'm sorry to bother you, sir, but we have a bit of a situation here."

"Yes, we saw the news reports. It isn't every day your son makes the national news. Is there something more?"

Nick wasn't even sure where to begin. "You know your son married some time ago."

"Almost eight years ago. Unfortunately my wife and I couldn't attend the wedding."

Nick noted the use of the word *couldn't* instead of *wouldn't*. "David married a woman named Juliette and a year ago she divorced your son."

"We weren't aware of that, we lost contact with our son years ago. We'd hoped that the marriage would be good for him. He seemed to have settled down, seemed to have found peace when he met her. We hoped he'd become a better man." Measured tones, but with just enough curtness to hint at stress.

As a hostage negotiator, Nick had to analyze voice patterns and inflection. Often the only interplay Nick had with a hostage taker was over a phone line. "Did you know you have a grandchild?"

The silence Nick's words brought wasn't quiet, but rather screamed with surprise . . . and with the weightiness of grief. "His name is Billy and he's five years old. He's a hell of a kid, Mr. Blankenship."

"What do you want from me . . . from us?" Again the resignation and just a touch of fear.

"Information," Nick replied. "I just need some information about David. It might save the life of your former daughter-in-law. It might just save the life of your grandson."

"We haven't seen him in almost eight years, what kind of information can I possibly give you?"

Nick tensed as Slokem came out of his office. If the chief found out who Nick was talking to Nick had no doubt that he'd be suspended on the spot. He breathed a sigh of relief as Slokem headed out of squad room, then he returned his attention to the phone conversation.

"I understand David was a difficult child."

A small bark of bitter laughter. "That's an understatement. You have no idea. Do you have children, Detective Corelli?"

"No, sir."

"We thought we'd been blessed when David was born, but right from the start he was a difficult child. He didn't sleep and cried a lot. I know, lots of children are colicky or have sleepless nights. But, that was just the beginning of our problems. By the time he was two we knew we had a real problem." It was as if a dam had burst in John Blankenship. The words tumbled from him as if he'd been waiting all his life to speak on the phone to a stranger about his son.

"He had uncontrollable temper tantrums, would tear apart his room, destroy his toys and hurt himself. The doctors kept telling us it was just a severe case of the terrible twos, but my wife and I, we knew it was something much worse. And he just kept getting worse with every year that passed." There was another long, pregnant pause.

"When David was twelve, we got a dog, a cute little terrier. David professed to love that dog and my wife and I hoped that maybe by caring for an animal he'd learn about empathy and responsibility."

Nick frowned, easily able to guess what came next. It was textbook.

"David would disappear with the dog for hours at a time and when they returned he always had a story about how the dog got hurt—a dog fight with a neighboring dog, a broken leg from jumping off the bed—that poor dog was always in pain. It got so whenever David approached the dog, the little fellow would pee himself. It was then I realized if I didn't do something that dog was going to die. So, one night while David slept, I took the dog to the pound. I wish we would have kept the dog and taken David to the pound," he said bitterly. "Terrible thing for a parent to say, isn't it?"

"I'm certainly not in a position to judge you," Nick replied.

John Blankenship laughed, a half-desperate, sad kind of sound. "Trust me, my wife and I judged ourselves, wondering what we had done wrong, what we might have done differently. We studied the nature versus nurture argument and saw psychologists and psychiatrists throughout David's childhood and adolescence. There was a period of time when we thought he'd gotten better. He worked for my company and he'd met the woman he was going to marry. He seemed kinder, better centered, and we hoped he'd finally outgrown all his problems. Of course, we know now that didn't happen. I'll tell you what I believe, Detective Corelli. I believe David was born bad. He was an evil little boy who grew up to be an evil man. There's nothing redeeming inside him."

"What's he afraid of? I need to know his weaknesses."

"He has no weaknesses and he's afraid of nothing. I don't know what he's done now or what he's done in the past eight years. I don't want to know. And if you call again, I won't speak with you. My wife and I don't have a son named David." There was a soft click as the man hung up.

Nick hung up and leaned back in his chair. The sounds of the squad room created a white noise hum that did little to distract him from his thoughts.

From what he'd read about John Blankenship, the man had been a success in the business world and a respected member of the community where he and his wife lived. What must it be like to have on your life résumé a failure in parenting?

Nature versus nurture. Nick had read enough profiles and case studies of criminals to believe in the bad seed theory. Children of abominable parents often became respectable, hard-working adults, and children of good parents sometimes became monsters.

He knew that people could do horrible things to their children and in those childhood traumas mental illness, dysfunction and antisocial behavior could be born. But he also believed that there was a thing such as true evil and nothing, not even the best, most loving parents in the world, could change the path of destruction of such a being.

He had his answer now, on why they hadn't warned Juliette of their son's problems. They'd convinced themselves, through desperate hope, that his sickness was behind him, that for her he would be a good man. What they'd really done was serve her up as a sacrificial lamb to a madman.

"Nick." Adam Burton, a fellow officer, motioned to him from the doorway.

Nick left his desk and joined him. "What's up?"

"A call just came in, a man barricaded in his apartment with his infant son. Two officers are on the scene, but they want you there as well."

"Address?"

Seconds later Nick was in his car headed to the scene, grateful to have something, anything to take his mind off David Blankenship.

It was almost two in the afternoon and Billy had fallen asleep on the sofa. Diane had spent the morning at her computer and Juliette had spent much of the day seated at the kitchen table thinking.

She was constantly playing games of What if? and What might have been?, predicting future disaster while trying to make sense of the here and now.

The moment she'd married David the world had become a smaller place and in time had shrunk to contain just David, their home, and her son.

It hadn't always been so. There had been a time when she'd had lots of friends and a head full of dreams and the world had seemed a huge place of possibility. Now it had been reduced to just this dark apartment and fear.

"How about a cup of hot chocolate and some girl talk," Diane said as she entered the kitchen.

Juliette smiled. "That sounds good. I'd welcome

anything that takes my mind off myself. I'm feeling quite self-involved these days."

"It's understandable with everything you've been through. I've been living inside myself for the past two years." Diane fixed the mugs of hot chocolate, then joined her at the table. "Fear can be so crippling. Trust me, I know."

Juliette wrapped her fingers around the warm mug. "I have no right to ask this and I understand if you tell me to mind my own business, but what happened, Diane? Did you just wake up one morning and were afraid?"

Diane stared into her mug for a long time and Juliette was afraid she'd offended the woman with the question. "No, it wasn't like that." She looked at Juliette, her eyes filled with pain.

"I'm sorry, I shouldn't have pried."

"No, it's all right." She leaned back in the chair and worried a hand through her hair. "My therapist keeps telling me I need to talk about what happened." She smiled ruefully. "But it's hard to talk about it when you're the only one home." She took a sip of the hot drink as if needing it to fortify her.

"It was a beautiful November morning that day," she began, her voice soft. "The sun was shining and the air smelled of that woodsmoke scent of autumn. Life was perfect. I was working at a computer software company here in town and Tony and I were planning our wedding. My daughter, Miranda, adored Tony and couldn't wait for the wedding, when he'd officially be her daddy."

"How old was she?" Juliette asked softly.

"Seven." Diane raised her mug to her lips once

again, this time her hands trembled visibly. It took both her hands to set the mug back on the table. "She was the brightest, most beautiful, happiest child I'd ever seen. Always laughing and always singing, she drew people to her with her happiness."

She closed her eyes for a long moment and when she finally opened them tears glimmered. "I needed to cash a check, such a simple thing. People do it every day. So, Miranda and I got into the car and drove to the bank. Miranda always liked to go inside instead of doing the drive-through. She had a favorite teller she liked to visit with on trips to the bank."

Juliette reached out and took her hand, wanting to stop the story, halt the pain that filled Diane's eyes. "You don't have to finish," she said and squeezed her hand.

Diane shook her head. "No, I want to. I want to talk about it." She drew a deep breath. "We were at the teller window when a man came in with a mask on his face and guns in his hands. It was crazy. People were screaming and the gunman ordered us all up against a wall. Somebody must have pushed an alarm or something because within minutes the police were outside. Squad cars were everywhere. We realized it wasn't just a bank robbery anymore but we were all hostages."

Juliette saw what was coming. It would have been just like that day at the day care center. "And so Nick was called to negotiate?"

Diane nodded and pulled her hand from Juliette's. "I found out later that Nick had no idea Miranda and I were inside. He'd been at our place that morning for coffee and I hadn't mentioned going to the bank to him. Anyway, for the next four hours Nick talked to the man and tried to get him to release all of us."

She rose abruptly from the table and stood next to the window. She ran her fingers down the closed venetian blinds. "Nick thought he'd talked the man into giving up. We all thought he was going to give up. He threw his guns out the door just as Nick had told him to do, but before the police could get to him, he pulled another gun from his pocket and just fired wildly."

Her hand moved faster up and down the blinds. "People were screaming and the police burst in—it was chaos. Miranda was on the floor and I was on top of her, covering her. It took me several minutes to realize one of the bullets had hit her. She was . . . gone." Diane shuddered and stepped away from the window.

Juliette could well imagine the horror of that day. Living with David had given her a keen understanding of terror, and the hours she had stood outside the day care while David held her son hostage had been a fear unlike any she'd ever known before. But still, she couldn't imagine, refused to allow herself to imagine, losing Billy.

She rose from her chair and went to Diane. Without hesitation she wrapped her arms around her. Diane remained rigid for a long moment, then yielded to the embrace. Together the two women wept.

It was some time later that they once again sat at the table, a bond forged through tears and the universal fear of mothers everywhere.

"I got through making all the arrangements that needed to be made. I went to the funeral and said my good-byes, then came back here, pulled the shades all shut and I haven't left since." She sighed and twirled a strand of her hair between two fingers.

"It wasn't just me who was devastated by Miranda's loss. Tony loved her, too. But Nick and Miranda had a special kind of relationship and he took it really bad."

"How do you mean?"

"Nick felt so responsible and he's been doing penance ever since—being my nursemaid, seeing to my needs . . ."

"Diane, I think Nick does that because he loves you, because you're his friend."

"Yes, I know that's true, but I see it sometimes in his eyes—the guilt—and it's as killing to him as this life of mine was to my relationship with Tony. Nick hasn't had a date since that day, he hasn't opened himself to anyone."

Diane sighed, obviously spent from the cathartic release of the past. "He's a good man, Juliette, and it's important that you let him help you and Billy. I think you might just be his redemption and it would be so nice if one of the three of us could heal from this mess."

"At the moment I have few options other than to let Nick help us," Juliette said. She wasn't sure she wanted to be part of a man's redemption. She just wanted to keep her son safe. "What about you, Diane? I'm sure Miranda wouldn't have wanted to see you like this. Are you working with a therapist regularly?"

"I'm trying. I'm just so afraid."

"Of what? It would seem to me that the absolute worst has already happened."

Diane stared at her for a long moment, then got up from the table once again. "You know, I think maybe

Billy has the right idea. A little nap sounds good right now. I'll see you later."

When she disappeared from the room, Juliette wondered if maybe she'd pushed too hard, said too much. But Diane had seemed adamant about telling her what had happened. She now understood the shadows she occasionally saw in Nick's eyes, the shadows of loss and of guilt.

If Nick hadn't felt responsible for Miranda's death would he be here now helping her and Billy? It didn't matter. She didn't care what forces drove him to help them, she cared only that he was helping them.

Diane's grief still clung to the room, fresh and raw. Two years ago Diane's daughter had died and had been buried. Diane had died at that time too, the only difference was instead of being placed in a coffin in the ground, she'd buried herself in this dark apartment.

Juliette washed out the cups from their hot chocolate, then went into the living room where Billy still slept soundly sprawled on the sofa.

Careful not to wake him, she eased herself down at his feet and stared at him. What frightened her more than a little bit was the fact that she understood Diane's mental illness. If anything happened to Billy, Juliette knew she wouldn't want to go on with her life.

Diane lay on her back on her bed, playing and replaying their conversation in her mind. Juliette was the only person other than her therapist that she'd told about Miranda and the day of her death.

She'd never even discussed it with Nick, although silently they shared the grief, the despair of loss. Tears burned her eyes and ran down the sides of her face.

What was she afraid of? Juliette's statement that the worst had already happened was true, even though Diane had never really thought about it before.

There was absolutely nothing that could happen to Diane that was worse than losing Miranda. So what was she afraid of? She didn't know. The fear was irrational, but that didn't make it less real.

She swiped angrily at her tears and rolled over to her side to stare at the blinds at the window. She wondered if Juliette had any idea that Nick was falling in love with her.

If what she believed was true, if Nicky did finally find self-forgiveness through helping Juliette and Billy, if he really was falling in love with Juliette, then there was a good chance that Diane would lose him.

Then she would really, truly be alone in the dark.

Chapter 24

It had been easy to talk the man out of his apartment and into releasing his infant son to his wife. The situation had been a domestic dispute that had gotten ugly but had been successfully resolved. No one had gotten hurt and Nick was grateful it had gone smoothly.

As he drove home he thought again about what to do with Juliette and Billy. If Nick were a wealthy man, then keeping them in motel rooms wouldn't be a problem. He could move them from motel to motel every couple of days and probably keep them under the radar.

But Nick lived on a cop's salary and nobody on the Riverton Police Department was getting rich. Unfortunately, what little savings Nick might have once had he'd spent on the renovations at the fishing cabin.

The cabin was always an option, although he hated to think of them there. Although the place had running water and electricity, it still needed lots of work and there was no furniture except a cot in one of the small bedrooms.

He had enough money and a credit card that might keep them for another couple of weeks in different motel rooms, but what then? They were still looking at almost two months before David went to trial.

One thing was certain, he was only willing to keep them at Diane's for another day or two. He didn't trust that Blankenship couldn't figure out the neighbor connection. David appearing in the cafe had shaken him up more than he'd realized.

When he entered his apartment his first impulse was to head out the back door and over to Diane's, but he didn't. Instead he made sure his curtains were open, allowing anyone who might peer in to see him as he went about his usual evening activities.

There was no reason to go next door. He knew the women were fine. Had there been any problems he would have gotten a phone call on his cell phone. It was better that he stay home and if Blankenship was into window peeping he'd see nothing amiss with Nick.

He went into the kitchen and searched the refrigerator for something for dinner and tried not to think about Juliette. He found a TV dinner in the freezer and shoved it into the microwave.

He then wandered back into the living room, turned on the television and channel surfed until the microwave dinged, announcing his dinner cooked.

He was in the process of taking it out of the microwave when his home phone rang. With his hands full he ignored the phone and let the answering machine pick up.

"Nicky . . . I heard you come home. Are you coming over?" Diane's voice filled the room. "If you are I'll unlock the back door."

He wasn't surprised that she knew he was home.

The walls between the two apartments were paper thin. Nick set the dinner on the counter and grabbed the phone receiver.

"I'm here, but I'm not going to come over. Is everything all right there?"

"It's fine, everything is fine." He heard no stress in her voice to indicate anything different. "I just wanted to see if you were going to stop over. If you were I'd put some coffee on."

"No, I think it's best if I keep my visits over there to a minimum."

"Has something else happened? Do you think he's watching?" Diane's voice was soft and he guessed that Billy or Juliette must be nearby.

"I think it's very possible. But I'm also relatively certain that at the moment there's nothing to worry about. There's no way Blankenship can know about our friendship, no way he can tie me to you. I just want to make sure we keep it that way."

"Do you want to speak to Juliette?"

Nick hesitated. Yes, he wanted to speak to her, he wanted to see her. He wanted to do more than that, he wanted to glide his fingers through her silky hair. He wanted to kiss those lips of hers and take her to his bed. "Nah, I've got nothing to report so there's no point. Just tell her I'll check in with her tomorrow."

"Will do."

They disconnected and Nick carried his meal into the living room and set it on the coffee table. He fought the impulse to go to his front window and peer out and see if there were any suspicious cars parked next to the curb.

Instead he found the local station with a rerun of *Law & Order* playing and settled back to eat.

For the next two days he adhered to this schedule, working at the station during the days, coming home and eating alone in the evenings. He stayed away from Diane's, but checked in with them by phone each night.

Slokem seemed to have forgiven him for punching Blankenship, especially since there had been no further action from Blankenship's lawyer. Things had been relatively quiet at the station and most of the cops figured a new cold front that had moved through the area was keeping people inside and out of trouble. As the holidays approached and stress levels rose, the police would have plenty of work on their hands.

Thursday night was Halloween, and as Nick dispensed candy to the neighbor kids who knocked on his door, his head was filled with thoughts of Billy.

Had Billy ever had the pleasure of dressing like a ghoul and going door-to-door to collect candy? Had he ever tasted the nip of frost in the air as he ran down a sidewalk filled, for the night, with creatures from a dark and stormy night? Had he ever waited impatiently, mouth watering while his mom checked the candy to make sure it was all safe to eat?

Nick knew the kid had never had a chance to indulge in such childish tradition and the thought only made him more determined to see that Billy's future was different than his past.

It was close to ten p.m. when the doorbell rang yet again and Nick opened the door, his candy nearly depleted and his joy of the holiday wearied. The trick-ortreater on his porch was no kid. Tony, wearing a big red plastic nose, grinned at his brother.

"Trick or treat . . . smell my feet."

"No thanks, I smelled them when we were kids and that was enough to give me nightmares for years." He yanked his brother through the door and into a bear hug. "What the hell are you doing here?" He released his hold on Tony and closed the front door.

Tony popped off the plastic nose. "When we spoke on the phone the other night you sounded stressed. I thought you could use a little moral support."

Nick hugged his brother once again. "I could definitely use a little moral support," he replied.

He gestured his brother to the sofa, then joined him there. God, the kid looked great, tanned and clad in a pair of jeans and shirt that probably cost half of Nick's last paycheck.

"So, tell me again about this woman who has you twisted up in knots," Tony said.

For the next two hours the brothers visited, talking not only about Juliette and her son, but also about Tony's life in California, Diane, and old times when they'd been younger.

Although Nick encouraged Tony to stay in his spare bedroom, Tony declined. He'd already booked a room for the night and had things he still needed to take care of before calling it a night.

By the time Tony left, Nick was warmed by the hours spent in his brother's company. He also felt a new optimism about Juliette and Billy's situation. Between Tony and Nick, they'd make certain that Juliette and her son were safe.

His optimism lasted until the next morning when

he stood at his front window drinking a cup of coffee and saw Blankenship's car parked across the street.

Blankenship sat in the driver's seat, his gaze riveted to Nick's apartment. Bold as could be, he wasn't even attempting to hide his presence.

Nick's blood boiled, but it was tempered with a new worry. He had to move Juliette and Billy. There was absolutely no doubt now that Blankenship was watching his place. All it would take was for Billy to peek out a blind or Blankenship to somehow find the closed blinds next door odd.

Next door was too close. They had to be moved, sooner rather than later.

Sooner came later that afternoon. Blankenship had remained parked on the opposite side of the street in front of Nick's apartment complex for about half an hour, then had left.

Nick had gone to the station as usual, but he'd spent the hours there trying to figure out what to do. At two he called Diane with his plan. It was risky, but he knew it was necessary to get them as far away from his apartment as possible.

There was no sign of Blankenship anywhere in the neighborhood and so Nick pulled into his garage, closing the door behind him. Inside the garage, Billy and Juliette waited with their bags. Lines of stress creased Juliette's brow.

"All set?" he asked as he got out of his car. He wanted to reach out and stroke the lines out of her forehead, take the worry out of her beautiful eyes.

"I guess. Where are we going?" she asked.

He put their suitcases into the trunk, then turned

back to her. "We'll talk as we drive. I want to get out of here now."

Within minutes Juliette and Billy were crouched down on the floor in the backseat and Nick pulled out of his driveway. He breathed a sigh of relief as he looked around. There was still no sign of Blankenship.

He just hoped his plan worked. Their lives were depending on it.

Chapter 25

He'd found them. He couldn't believe he hadn't thought of it before. It had been so easy. David tapped his fingers on his steering wheel and hummed beneath his breath as he drove to the destination where he suspected she would be.

It had been six days since she'd left the motel, six days that David hadn't known their location. He'd followed Corelli to and from his work, watched his apartment off and on, but had seen no trace of his wife. With each day that passed his anger had grown deeper, richer, and his frustration level had reached explosive proportions.

The answer had been in his computer all along. One of the first things David had done when checking into Corelli's background was to check county records to see if he owned any property. That search had yielded nothing.

It was late that morning that David realized he hadn't checked the real estate records for the counties surrounding the small town of Riverton. That search had yielded an address. Nick Corelli owned a place two and a half hours' drive from Riverton.

He now traveled in the dark of night, tools of destruction in the back of his car. He'd doped SuEllen so heavily she'd be lucky to wake up in eight to ten hours. But he hadn't wanted her with him. He was sick to death of her.

If he had to hear one more word about Big John Maynard who ruled his prison block, David might puke. How bright could the man be? He was serving a life sentence, for Christ's sake.

David would never see prison time. The court date that loomed closer and closer didn't worry him. He didn't intend to appear.

His passport was ready and he had enough money in a bank in the Cayman Islands to live the rest of his life quite comfortably.

He'd kiss the good old USA good-bye before he'd ever spend another day in a jail or in prison. He'd find some nice place without extradition and build a life there. However, at the moment his plans for the distant future were the last thing on his mind.

His focus was solely fixed on what was to come, on finding Juliette and making her pay for her betrayal. While he was at it, he intended the bastard cop to pay as well. He hoped Nick Corelli had enjoyed fucking Juliette because she was the last woman he'd ever fuck.

He took his foot off the gas to slow down. The night would make it more difficult for him to find the exact location, but he liked the poetic sense of it, that death came in the darkness of night. It just seemed appropriate.

Tension ached in his veins. Adrenaline scorched through him. He could smell her, the hint of the floral of her perfume, the musky woman scent of her sex and the coppery odor of her blood.

Logically, he knew he couldn't possibly be smelling those scents now, but whether logical or not, the car interior was filled with the exciting smells.

He'd have her one last time before he killed her. It was a vow he made to himself. He'd touch that sweet, silky skin of hers, smell the musk of her womanhood and carve her so that her blood flowed as he pounded into her one final time.

And he'd make the cop watch. And as he pounded into sweet Juliette, he'd whisper all the details of exactly how he'd killed that kid.

He shifted in the seat, his pants tightening across his crotch with the image. Knowing he was close, he pulled over to the side of the road and parked the car. At this time of night and in this area there was next to no traffic, so the odds were good nobody would pay any attention to a parked car.

He got out of the car and reached into the backseat to get the items he'd brought with him. Rope, duct tape, surgical gloves and two different kinds of knives, all the accoutrements of revenge and death. He placed the items in a plastic grocer's bag.

He'd never owned a gun, had always believed guns were for pussies who needed to distance themselves from their crime. David preferred something more intimate than the kind of death a gun delivered.

The night embraced him as if a coconspirator in his plot. Thick clouds obscured the moon and any star that might have had the audacity to shine. Insects clicked and buzzed and a dog bayed in the distance, a plaintive cry that fed the hollowness David had been left with when Juliette had gone.

Nothing had been right since she'd left him. Nothing would ever be right as long as she lived a life separate from his. He knew now that she would never come back to him, that the promise she'd made at the day care had been nothing but a lie. He could go on and find happiness as long as he knew she didn't.

He pulled out a penlight from his pocket and clicked it on and used the tiny beam of light to guide his way through the overgrown brush.

As he walked, his thoughts drifted back in time, back to when Juliette had been his, body, mind, and soul. He'd owned her every thought, her every wish, her every smile and pain, until the kid had been born.

David hadn't shared well when he'd been a child and he sure as hell hadn't shared well as an adult. Once the boy had been born, he'd known Juliette was split in half and that was unacceptable to David.

He picked his way through the brush, irritated that he hadn't taken a pillow and smothered the baby when it had first been born. Then Juliette would still be his.

He crouched down as the place came into view, the windows all darkened. Sleeping. David didn't require sleep like other people did. A couple of hours at night and he was good to go. It used to drive his parents crazy.

Good. He wanted them asleep and vulnerable. He wanted Juliette to be pulled abruptly from serene dreams and into the mouth of terror.

He clicked off his penlight and approached the place. He had no idea what the layout was and so crept around the perimeter and tried to peek into darkened windows.

It was impossible to see inside, but he found a window at the back of the house that opened easily. Poking his head inside, he discovered it entered into the kitchen. Perfect.

With the stealth of an experienced B and E man, he slid the plastic bag to the floor inside, then slithered through the window after it.

It was the smell of dust that assailed him first. Not just the dust that might gather during a single day that floated in the sun and fell on surfaces. This was the smell of old dust, of thick dust. A sense of disquiet swept through him.

Once again he used the penlight and shone it around the tiny kitchen. The room was in the midst of remodeling. Two cans of paint thinner sat on the countertop and the old wooden cabinets were half stripped of puke green paint.

There was no sign of recent habitation, not a dish or plate in the sink, not a lingering scent of a recently cooked meal. It doesn't mean anything, he told himself as he clenched and unclenched his hands at his sides.

They could be eating their meals out, going into restaurants and pretending to be a happy family. He closed his eyes and drew a measured breath in through his nose. He could just see them: Nick, Juliette, and the pissy boy seated around a table in a restaurant, eating chicken fingers and fries, laughing and smug in their sense of safety.

Now they were probably snug as bugs in sleeping bags. Spying a hammer on the counter, he picked it up and hefted it in his hand, testing the weight of the tool. Perfect for incapacitating sleeping bugs.

With the hammer in one hand and the plastic bag in his other, he went in search of his lovely wife, the pissy boy, and the cop who played hero and didn't know how to mind his own business.

The place was silent—too silent—and with every step David took the certainty that he'd finally found them began to fade. Adrenaline seeped away, being replaced by the white-hot fire of frustration.

A can of paint and a handful of brushes were the only things in the first tiny bedroom he came to. Drop cloths covered the floor, but there was no sleeping Juliette, no vulnerable Nick Corelli, and no sniveling kid.

He didn't even have to check the other bedroom.

He knew.

They weren't here. Just to be sure, he went into the last bedroom, another tiny room that held only a cot and more paint and cans of varnish.

They weren't here. By the look of things they had never been here. His ears buzzed and the white-hot frustration exploded and David's mind went blank.

He had no idea how much time had passed when he found himself seated on the floor in the living room, the hammer in his hand. Gasping to catch his breath he looked around, satisfied by the destruction around him.

There wasn't a single wall that hadn't been bashed in. Shattered windows allowed in the cold night air and paint spattered every surface visible.

He'd been so sure. He'd been so fucking sure they'd

be here. The minute he'd discovered that Corelli owned this little fishing shack, he'd been so certain.

Now he had no idea where they might be.

Still, there was this. Again satisfaction filled him as he gazed around. It had been obvious that the cop had been working here, renovating the shanty. He probably looked forward to the day when he would come here and spend weekends far from the maddening crowd.

The maddening crowd had come here.

David pulled himself up off the floor and flung the hammer away. He went into the kitchen and picked up the container of paint thinner. On the label was the HIGHLY FLAMMABLE warning.

He opened the lid and began to pour it over the floor, across the counters, then into the other rooms. Beneath the sink he found an old stack of newspapers.

He'd come in through the kitchen window, but he left by the front door. He'd taken only three steps when he heard the whoosh of the flames finding the puddle of fuel and the crumpled newspapers.

Within an hour there would be no more retreat for the bastard cop. David didn't wait around to watch the flames lick up the walls and toward the roof.

As he drove back to Riverton, the car no longer smelled of Juliette. It smelled of crackling, burning wood and acrid smoke and the odor of his own fiery rage.

Chapter 26

For the second time in two days Juliette and Billy scrunched down on the floor of Nick's backseat as they drove down the streets of Riverton. Juliette tried to ignore the fact that her legs had gone numb at least fifteen minutes ago.

It had been surprisingly difficult yesterday to say good-bye to Diane. Over the last couple of days Juliette had remembered what it had been like to have a girlfriend. The two had stayed up long after Billy went to bed each night and had talked and laughed and shared portions of their lives they hadn't shared before.

For a few hours on each of those nights Juliette had actually managed to forget her fear, forget that her life and her son's life were in danger. And she thought that perhaps for several hours on those same nights Diane had managed to forget her loss.

They'd talked about old fashion and new, high school traumas and embarrassments. They'd gotten giddy from lack of sleep and had laughed until they cried.

Before they'd left Diane's, Juliette had promised that she'd stay in touch, that perhaps she'd even be there Christmas Eve at Tanglewood Lake to skate.

Juliette had no idea where Nick was taking them. He'd taken them from Diane's to another motel room where she and Billy had slept the night before. Nick had returned to the motel room half an hour before and had once again hustled them into the back of his car.

It seemed as if they'd been driving forever. The only sound in the car was Billy's video game beeping and buzzing as he played games to pass the time in the car.

"Won't be too much longer now," Nick said from the driver's seat. "I just want to make sure we aren't followed."

"Can you tell me where we're going?"

"Yeah, now I can. I wasn't sure things would be ready until an hour ago when my brother called me."

"Your brother from California?" she asked.

"He isn't in California anymore. He's here in town. He bought a house and that's where we're going."

Juliette winced and tried to find a position of comfort. Another ten or fifteen minutes in this crouched position and she was afraid her legs might fall off. "Won't David be able to find us? Corelli isn't exactly a usual name."

"Tony thought of that. The house isn't in his name, it's in the name of one of his co-workers in California. Look, David might be crafty and he can access all the records he can find, but he isn't omnipotent and I can't imagine that he'll be able to find us in this house."

The car slowed and made a right turn. "Tony has the garage door up. I'll pull in, close the garage door, then you two can get out."

When the car finally came to a stop, Juliette almost wept in relief. The rumble of the garage door closing was her cue to pull herself up and out of the car on legs that shot pins and needles from toes to hips.

With a child's agility, Billy got out, no worse for the wear, and smiled at Nick. "So, we're going to stay here?" He looked around the empty garage.

"Not in here, buddy," Nick said affectionately. "We're going to stay inside the house and I have a feeling you're even going to have your own room."

Before Billy could respond the door between the house and the garage opened and a young man who could only be Nick's brother stepped out. Although he was taller and thinner than Nick, the two looked remarkably alike. "Hi, you must be Juliette." He approached her with a smile and an outstretched hand. "I'm Tony, Nick's younger, more handsome, more charming brother."

Juliette found herself smiling as he took her hand in his. "I'm Juliette and it's nice to meet you." Her smile faltered as she saw the friendly warmth that shone from his eyes and emotion welled up inside her. "I don't know how to thank you—"

"Then don't," he said simply. He dropped her hand and walked over to Billy, who stood by Nick. He crouched down in front of the boy. "And you must be Billy. Nick has told me all about you, that you're smart and strong and one heck of a kid."

Billy nodded. "Did he tell you I don't pee the bed?"

"Yeah, I think he mentioned that, too." He straightened. "Well, let's go inside and get settled in."

Juliette followed Tony through the door and into a fully furnished kitchen complete with table and chairs in the small breakfast nook. The living room held a sofa and a love seat, a huge television, and coffee table.

The entire place was decorated in warm shades of burgundy and navy blue and instantly felt warm and homey. "Did you buy it furnished?" she asked.

"Nah, I just ran through a couple of furniture stores yesterday and insisted they get it all delivered and set up this morning," Tony replied. A lump of emotion formed in the back of her throat. What kind of people had raised such wonderful sons? She kept her gaze averted from Nick, afraid she might cry if she looked at him.

He led them up the stairs to the three bedrooms. The first bedroom was apparently the space Nick would occupy. A navy spread covered a double bed and a dresser stood against one wall. "Nick, I figured this would be good for you," Tony said, confirming her thoughts.

When Tony led them into the next bedroom, tears burned at Juliette's eyes. Bunk beds in a fire engine red frame stood against one wall and Billy's eyes widened as he stared first at the bed, then at the rest of the room. A desk stood in one corner and atop the desk was a container holding crayons and colored pencils and chalk. "This will be your room, Billy. Is it okay with you?"

Billy nodded. "Can I sleep in the top bunk?"

"You can sleep wherever you want," Nick replied. "You can spend one night up top, then the next night down in the bottom or whatever you want to do."

"One more to go," Tony said and walked across the hall and opened the last bedroom door. He smiled at Juliette. "I don't know much about what women like . . . I figured I couldn't go wrong with pink."

Juliette stepped into the room with its lacy pink

bedspread across a double bed and a pink lamp on the nightstand and emotion choked up inside her. A sob escaped her.

"If you don't like pink we can get something green—or blue—whatever you want," Tony said hurriedly.

Juliette shook her head as sobs continued to swell in her chest and burst out of her. Tears blurred her vision as she sank down to sit on the edge of the bed.

"I think she's happy," Billy said.

Juliette nodded, feeling like a fool but unable to halt the tears. She couldn't believe that these two men had done so much for them. It had been so long since a hand of kindness had been extended to her and this house and Nick and his brother were all too much.

Somewhere along the line she had stopped believing in the kindness of people, had given up on believing in charity and mercy. This evidence of such traits left her weak with gratefulness.

"Come on, champ, let's go check out your room and let your mom and Nick have a few minutes to themselves." As Tony and Billy left the room, Nick sat down next to her on the foot of the bed.

"I'll never be able to repay you and your brother for everything," she said as she swiped at her cheeks with the back of one hand.

"I don't recall either of us mentioning any sort of repayment necessary," Nick said. "Tony was just waiting for a reason to come back to Riverton, and our problem gave him that reason. Long after David is in prison and you and Billy are living a life without fear, Tony will remain in this house filling the rooms with kids of his own."

"Has he come back for Diane?"

"Maybe. I'm not sure the end of that story has been all written, but I'm also not sure that story has a happy ending."

"It would be nice if every story had a happy ending, wouldn't it?" she said wistfully.

"Yeah, but they call that fairy tales, not real life."

She was aware of his woodsy cologne and a hint of shaving cream. A strand of his dark hair teased his forehead, and she fought an impulse to reach up and push it back with her fingertips. He awed her, this man who had not only given up his life to protect her, but who also treated her son with care and affection.

"Tony and I did some talking this morning and we think it best if we pretend that you and I are married and Billy is our son. You know, as a cover story for neighbors or whatever. I think it's a good idea if both you and Billy change your hair color from blond to dark brown. Tony picked up a couple of boxes of hair color this morning. What do you think about Burnt Almond?"

"Sounds good to eat. We'll see what it does to my hair."

"It seems a shame," he murmured, more to himself than to her. He leaned closer to her and reached a hand up and touched a strand of her light blond hair. "I've wanted to do that since the first time I saw you. I wanted to see if it was as soft, as silky as it looked."

His breath was warm on her face as his hand continued to stroke through her hair. "Is it as soft?" she asked, surprised to discover her voice breathy.

"It is," he replied. For a moment time seemed to stand still. In his eyes she saw the hint of heat simmering and she wanted to fall into his heat. She leaned forward, not clear exactly what she wanted from him but desperately wanting something.

"Mom!" Billy's voice shattered the moment and Nick dropped his hand back to his side as Billy appeared in the doorway. "Tony said there's a park right down the street and he bought me a ball glove and is going to teach me how to play baseball."

She cleared her throat and stood. "We'll have to talk about the possibility of playing ball in a park," she said. "But right now you and I are going to have some fun with hair color."

"Huh?" Billy looked at her blankly.

"We're going to make your hair look like mine and Tony's," Nick explained. He also rose from the bed.

"Cool . . . hey Tony, I'm going to have hair like yours and Nick's." Billy disappeared down the hall.

"It appears your brother had made a hit with my son," she said.

Nick smiled. "Tony's good with kids. Hell, he's nothing but an oversized one himself."

"Will we be safe here, Nick?"

"I can't make any promises, but I think you're as safe here as we can get."

"Just please help me protect Billy. I need to know that whatever happens, he'll be safe."

Nick took her by the shoulders, a different kind of fire burning in his eyes. "In order for him to get to you or Billy, he's going to have to come through not just me, but my brother as well. And we Corellis are a tough breed. I promise you, we will be here protecting you both until David is back in jail."

She wanted to believe him. God, how she wanted to

believe. But she knew all about promises. David had promised to love and honor her when they had married. She had promised him when he'd been in the day care center that she would go back with him, be a wife to him again.

David's promise had been perverted and hers to him had been intentionally broken. She didn't think Nick would intentionally break his promise or twist it to mean something else, but she knew that sometimes in life promises went unfulfilled. She hoped this wasn't one of those times.

She was betting her life and that of her son on the promise of a man she'd known for mere weeks—on a man who had already suffered one terrible tragedy in his life. She didn't want to be his second tragedy.

Chapter 27

As Juliette and Billy disappeared into the bathroom to color their hair, Nick stood at the kitchen window and stared outside.

Mature trees and overgrown brush comprised the bulk of the backyard. It was a good news–bad news kind of deal. The good news was that it would be difficult to see into the house windows. The bad news was that the thick tree trunks and brush provided plenty of hiding places.

"So, what do you think?" Tony came to stand just behind Nick.

Nick turned to face his brother. "I still can't believe you did all this."

"Ah hell, Nick. Don't thank me too much. I did it as much for myself as for anyone." He moved next to Nick and peered out the window. "I can't get past it. I can't forget her. I should have never allowed her to shove me out of her life. I should have stayed here and fought for her . . . for us." He turned his head to look at Nick. "Do you think it's too late?"

Nick smiled ruefully. "You're asking the wrong guy. I'm not the person to ask anything about women. I haven't exactly been real successful in that arena myself."

"That's because you quit trying." He paused a beat. "You like her, don't you. I mean, this is about more than just a cop trying to stop a crime from happening. This isn't about just doing your job anymore."

Nick returned his gaze to the window. "I don't know what's going on or exactly what I feel. I don't think about how I feel very often," he replied. The conversation made him uncomfortable. He wasn't accustomed to talking about feelings with anyone.

"That's your problem, bro." Tony shook his head. "We're a fine bunch. We lost Miranda and everything fell apart. Diane crawled into a cave, I moved to La-La land, and you shut off all your emotions. Yeah, we're one hell of a fine bunch."

"All I can tell you is to call Diane," Nick said, wanting nothing more than for the conversation to end. "Either she'll talk to you or she won't. And now, I'd like to check out the neighborhood a bit. Can I have the keys to your car?"

They had already agreed that Nick's car should remain parked in the garage. It wasn't a stretch to believe that Blankenship had the plate numbers and would be looking for him on the streets of Riverton.

A few minutes later Nick backed Tony's rental car out of the driveway and headed down the tree-lined street. The neighborhood was an older one, the houses no longer holding the brassy sheen of newness, but rather the stately elegance of permanence.

Ranches and trilevels, no house stuck out from the others. An occasional bicycle littered a yard, or a ball and bat lay abandoned, but for the most parts the yards were neat and tidy, tended by people who obviously took pride in their homes.

The park that Billy had mentioned was just down the road from the house. It was an empty lot between two other houses that sported a swing set, a slide, and a basketball hoop. More thick woods lined the back of the lot, and in the distance Nick could see a couple of picnic tables beneath big trees.

It looked safe, like a place where kids would come to play ball and swing and just be kids. It looked like a place where families kicked back and enjoyed the last of good weather before winter set in.

This neighborhood was like a dozen others in Riverton filled with middle-class people working hard to get ahead and take care of their families.

He turned the car around and headed back to the house. The house that Tony had chosen looked just like the rest of the homes on the block, nothing unusual to differentiate it from the others. A white split-level with black shutters and a neatly trimmed yard.

It was a good place to hide.

Even if Blankenship hired another thug, or two more or ten, it would take time for them to check out every motel and hotel in the general area. No matter how good they were, no matter how good Blankenship was, Nick knew there was no way they could conduct any kind of a house-to-house search and find the prey.

As far as the police department was concerned, Nick was on an extended leave of absence. He hadn't told anyone, not even Sammy, where they were going.

Everything had been done to assure their safety. The house wasn't in their name . . . had never even had a FOR SALE sign in the yard. The utilities were also in the name of Tony's co-worker in California. Nick had no acquaintances in the neighborhood. Surely Juliette and Billy would be safe here until David's court date.

He pulled back into the driveway and cut the engine. And what happened if Blankenship went to trial and got probation? What if he never had to serve a day in jail? Surely that would never happen. The man had held children at gunpoint, for crying out loud. Nick still couldn't understand how the bastard had gotten bail. The judge who'd granted it should be arrested.

Surely the pressure from the parents of the children who had been hostages that day would weigh heavily on the side of justice. Surely no sane judge in the world would just let him walk without serving any time at all.

Back in the house, he found Tony seated at the kitchen table, staring at the phone on the counter. Apparently Juliette and Billy were still in the bathroom.

"I called her," Tony said.

"And?" Nick sat in the chair opposite him.

"The good news is she didn't hang up on me. The bad news is she says she doesn't want to see me." Tony sighed and raked a hand through his thick dark hair, then smiled with his natural boyish charm. "I'm going to keep calling her and I'm going to e-mail her every day. Sooner or later she'll see me. She still cares about me. I know it."

"I've been telling you that for months," Nick said.

"Ta da!"

Both men looked toward the doorway, where Juliette and Billy stood, dark hair gleaming.

Nick's breath clogged his throat. She was just as

stunning with dark brown hair as she'd been as a blonde. Her eyes appeared even more blue against the contrast of the darker hair and her skin looked like the clearest porcelain ever made.

Billy walked toward Nick and stopped just before him. "Now I look more like you," he said. "Now I don't look like him."

It was the first time Billy had alluded in any way to his father, the first time Nick had seen the hint of real, deep scarring on the little boy's soul.

He reached out and drew Billy into an awkward embrace. He came willingly, as if hungry for Nick's arms around him. So small, and already such a big man, Nick thought.

"You look mighty fine with that dark hair, but I like your blond hair, too, and in a couple of weeks you'll have your nice blond hair back. Besides, when you have blond hair you don't look like him. You look like your mother." The last thing Nick wanted was for Billy to harbor a bad self-image because he looked like his father.

Billy looked at his mom at the same time he leaned closer to Nick. The warmth of his little body brought back memories of another child, memories of neck hugs and sweet cheek kisses and laughter. Loss swelled inside Nick, along with a well of protectiveness for the little boy.

"If I look like my mom, then I must be pretty," Billy said.

Juliette blushed and Nick and Tony laughed. "I think it's time we do something about dinner," she said.

"The refrigerator and freezer are stocked," Tony

said. "I'll be glad to help you but I recommend we keep Nick as far away from food preparation as possible. All he knows how to do is heat up things in a microwave."

"There's a package of steak in the fridge," Nick offered, ignoring his brother's derogatory remark about his cooking skills.

Juliette went to the refrigerator and opened it. "How about I broil the steaks and make a salad?"

"Sounds good to me," Nick agreed.

As Juliette prepared the steaks and Tony cut up vegetables for the salad, Billy and Nick sat at the kitchen table and played a game of Go Fish.

Although Nick tried to keep his attention completely on the game of cards, he couldn't help but be distracted by Juliette. She moved with an elegant grace, as if she'd once been a dancer, and even though Nick didn't consider himself much of a dancer he wanted to take her into his arms and glide her across the floor.

Romantic music would play and the top of her head would fit neatly beneath his chin. Their bodies would mold against each other and he would be able to feel her heartbeat against his own.

Billy beat him at three games of Go Fish.

By the time they finished the meal, twilight painted the backyard in amber tones. The trees, with their dresses of multicolored leaves, sashayed in an evening breeze and Nick could tell Juliette was more relaxed than he'd ever seen her.

"I helped cook, so Nick gets cleanup," Tony said as he rose from the table. "And Billy, you and I are going to set up my laptop and I'll show you a couple of games you can play."

"Cool." Together they left the room.

"More coffee?" Juliette asked Nick as she got up and grabbed the coffeepot.

"Sure, thanks." She filled his cup, then her own, then returned to the chair next to him at the table. She gazed out the window as he gazed at her.

With her frost-white blond hair and ice blue eyes, he'd thought her a winter kind of woman. But, with the darker hair and her eyes momentarily without any fear, she was warm, beautiful autumn.

"Your brother is nice," she said as her gaze found his. "Billy likes him."

Nick smiled. "Yeah, he's a good guy."

"Billy likes you, too," she said. "It was very nice, what you said to him about his blond hair."

He shrugged. "We don't want him to grow up with a complex."

Her gaze held his for a long moment and every one of his nerve endings seemed to take flame. "Diane told me Miranda thought you and Tony were pretty special."

Nick straightened in surprise. "Diane told you about Miranda?"

Juliette nodded. "Does that surprise you?"

"It stuns me," he admitted. "Other than her therapist, I don't think Diane has mentioned her daughter's name since that day." And neither had Nick. He stared down into his coffee cup. Thoughts of the little girl lost would always pierce him with pain.

"She told me that you and Miranda were quite close."

"Tony was her father figure and I was like a favorite uncle to her. I'd take her to McDonald's and occasionally to the movies." He stood abruptly. "We'd better get these dishes cleaned off." He didn't want to talk about Miranda. Thinking about her, talking about her, made the weight of the rock in his pocket too immense to bear.

They worked side by side to clear the table, then Juliette insisted they hand wash and dry the dishes rather than use the dishwasher. "My mother used to tell me that the worst invention in the world was the automatic dishwasher," she said as she filled the sink with soapy water.

Nick stood at the ready with dish towel in hand. "Why is that?"

She began with the water glasses, swishing a sponge inside and out of the first one. "Mom said that the dishwasher took away one of the most important social times people could share. She insisted that it was during the act of washing and drying dishes by hand that real conversations between people took place. Husbands and wives shared dreams and plans, children talked about their day at school and whatever scared or excited them and friends shared secrets that forged deeper bonds of trust."

"Your mother sounds like she was a smart woman." Nick took the glass she held out to him and carefully dried it.

"She was wonderful and so was my father. I lost them both in a car accident three months before I met David. My mother died instantly in the accident and my father died three weeks later from his injuries."

He wondered if she had any idea how much information she'd given him in that simple statement. It was obvious she'd been close to her parents and had probably still been reeling with grief when she'd met the handsome, dynamic David Blankenship.

"How did you meet him?" They'd moved from the glasses to the silverware. The steamy hot water she stood above seemed to intensify the scent of her.

She began on the plates. "I was one semester away from getting my teaching degree when I met David on the University of Pennsylvania campus." She slowed the sponge working across the top of a plate. "I was sitting under a tree studying and he'd just finished giving a seminar." She handed him the plate to dry. "Diane told me you and Tony were pretty good at ice skating."

He blinked at the abrupt change of subject and realized she'd shared as much as she'd intended to on the topic of David Blankenship.

As they finished the dishes, they talked about skating and winter and Christmases past. They kept the conversation light, nonthreatening, and painless, but Nick found it anything but. Her nearness made it difficult for him to think. The scent of her threatened to push his self-control over the limit. His need to touch her, to kiss her was torturous.

After dinner, the four of them played Go Fish at the kitchen table. Billy won two games and Nick won one, then Juliette announced that it was bath- and bedtime for Billy.

"Hey Tony, if you want to sleep in my bottom bunk you can," Billy said before he left the kitchen. "I mean, if you don't wanna sleep on the sofa I wouldn't mind if you wanted to stay in my room with me."

Apparently Tony heard the same edge of anxiety in Billy's voice that Nick heard. "Hey, that would be great. Do you snore?"

Billy frowned and looked at his mom. "Do I?" She shook her head negatively. "I don't snore. Do you?"

Tony laughed. "I might just a little, but you can throw something at me if I get too noisy."

Juliette went with her son to start his bathwater and Nick got up to put away the cards. "I think Billy might be just a little anxious about his first night in a new place," he said to his brother.

"I don't mind bunking in there," Tony replied. "He's a little heartbreaker, isn't he? I get the feeling he hasn't had much of a chance to be a kid. I see why you wanted to help them."

He was definitely a little heartbreaker and Nick had a feeling if he allowed himself to get too close to Juliette, he'd discover she was a heartbreaker as well.

It had been a long day with the move to the new place and by nine p.m. everyone had decided to call it a night. Tony and Billy disappeared into their room and Juliette went into hers while Nick checked all the doors and windows to make sure they were locked.

He went into his bedroom and unpacked the suitcase he'd brought with him. As he hung his clothes in the closet and placed underwear and socks in the dresser, he realized that spending twenty-four hours a day under the same roof as Juliette and not becoming intimately involved with her might just be the most difficult thing he'd ever done in his life.

Although he'd thought himself tired when he finally got into the bed, sleep remained elusive. His mind whirled with possibilities, looking for ways they could be found here by one deviant bastard.

He hadn't checked in with Sammy all day to see what, if anything, was new on the Camp murder case. He made a mental note to check in with his buddy first thing in the morning, although he knew if anything had been discovered that tied Blankenship to the murder, Sammy would have called him already.

He drifted asleep, feeling as if things had gone too smoothly, too easily, and certain that David Blankenship wasn't finished with them yet.

Sleep shattered in a single instant. Nick sat up, for a moment disoriented. Gazing at the nightstand he saw that it was just after midnight. He knew instantly that something had pulled him from his sleep.

He reached for his gun on the nightstand at the same time shoving aside the covers to ease himself up and out of bed. Muscles tense, adrenaline pumping, he made his way to the door of the bedroom. The gun was a familiar weight in his hand as he crept out into the hallway.

He stood in the hall, trying to discern what had awakened him. A whisper of sound rose to his ears, the faint sound of footsteps against carpeting. He eased the safety off his gun and started down the seven steps that led to the living room.

She stood silhouetted against the windows and for a moment he froze and simply watched her. She stood with her back to him and wore a gauzy nightgown. The moonlight from the full moon outside filtered through the cloth, making it almost transparent.

Her slender curves were visible beneath the pale gown, the indentation of her waistline, the curve of her hips and the outline of bikini panties. Nick's hand grew slick on the gun and he quickly clicked the safety back on.

She whirled around at the audible click. "Nick!"

He saw her eyes widen as she saw the gun in his hand. What a picture he must make, naked save for a pair of navy boxers and a gun. "I heard a noise."

"I'm sorry. I didn't mean to wake you."

He placed the gun on the end table and stepped closer to where she stood. "Couldn't sleep?"

She shook her head, her dark hair whispering around her head like a soft cloud. "Maybe it's the full moon." She turned back to face the window and Nick moved to stand right next to her.

He followed her gaze to the back lawn, where the overripe moon spilled down shimmering cascades of illumination that danced on the tree tops and filtered through the leaves to the ground below.

"You know, it's true what they say about a full moon. It does affect people."

"I know," he replied. "Down at the station we call it a crazy moon." He felt half crazy at this very moment. Her scent, the unmistakable scent of a woman, filled his head.

"A crazy moon . . . yes, that seems appropriate. I feel a little crazy right now. Do you feel it?" She turned away from the window and faced him.

Her nipples showed through the gossamer fabric, dark circles with pebble-hard centers. A swell of heat suffused him as blood pumped thick and hot through him. His boxer shorts got smaller as he began to grow hard.

He took a step backward, afraid that if he didn't distance himself from her he'd do something stupid, something that he might regret.

But she didn't allow him distance. Her blue eyes shone like those of a wild animal as she moved toward him, standing so close to him he could feel her nipples brushing his bare chest, felt her warm breath fanning his face.

"Nick." His name fell from her lips as a soft plea. He wasn't sure what she wanted, but knew his own desire. He grabbed her to him and crushed his lips to hers.

Her response was immediate. Her arms wound around his neck and she pressed herself against him as his tongue swirled into her hot and eager mouth.

He could feel her breasts against his chest, the warmth of her long legs and hips molded to his own. His hands tangled in her hair, then caressed down her back and came to rest on either side of her slender hips.

Crazy, crazy that her mouth tasted every bit as sweet, as inviting as he'd imagined it would. Crazy that the feel of her hands on his bare skin drove him half mindless with the need to pick her up in his arms and carry her to that pink lace bed of hers.

He had no idea how long the kiss lasted. It felt like both a moment and an eternity. But when their lips finally parted, she pulled back from him and he instantly released her.

"I'm sorry . . . I . . ." She ruffled a hand through her newly darkened hair and he could see the deep color of her cheeks.

"No, I apologize." It was one of those awkward moments Nick remembered from his youth. "Let's just blame it on the moon and leave it at that." He picked up his gun from the end table. "Good night, Juliette."

"Good night, Nick."

He left her standing by the windows and went back to his room. It was a very long time before he finally fell back asleep.

As Juliette and Nick shared their first kiss, David pummeled into SuEllen. He didn't know or care whether her cries were from pain or from passion. All he knew was that the rage that always simmered inside of him threatened to explode if he didn't do something physical.

He knew better than to indulge himself in beating the hell out of somebody, so screwing SuEllen without mercy, without pity or emotion, was the second best way to alleviate the roar that resounded in his head.

He had to find her. He had to find her. The mantra screamed in his head and through his pounding, throbbing veins. He opened his eyes and stared down into SuEllen's face.

If he looked at her long enough, he knew he'd lose his hard-on, and he needed to do this, he needed to relieve the stress, pound out the fury.

He withdrew from her and motioned her to turn over on her stomach. He grabbed her by the hips and raised her up to her hands and knees so he could take her like a dog, without looking at her.

Closing his eyes, he imagined that it was Juliette he was driving into the mattress, Juliette who cried out as her face burrowed deeper and deeper into the pillow beneath her. He drove deep and fast, frantic to possess, to destroy.

When he reached his climax, it was explosive and there was no way to mistake the cry that came from SuEllen, the mewl of a woman grateful that the act was finally complete.

Chapter 28

She awakened to early morning sunshine streaming through the window. She felt surrounded by pink ruffles and more at peace than she could ever remember. She had a madman hunting her down, desperate to kill not only her, but Billy as well, and yet for the moment she was utterly at peace.

The source of that peace was simple. Nick. The steely determination in the set of his jaw comforted her. The strength that radiated from his eyes made her believe that he could handle whatever David threw their way.

She could tell from the faint sun that slanted through the window that it was still early, but she knew further sleep was impossible. She got out of bed and dressed quickly, then left the bedroom, intent on exploring the rest of the house before anyone else was up.

To her surprise the minute she stepped into the hallway, she smelled the scent of fresh-brewed coffee and realized she wasn't the first one up.

The moment she saw Nick standing at the kitchen window with his back to her, desire struck her like a punch to the stomach. Nobody wore jeans better than

Nick did and his gray sweater clung to him, stretched across his broad back. She wanted to run her fingers across his muscles, wrap her arms around him, and hold tight.

He turned at the sound of her feet against the floor. "Good morning," he said. "Coffee's ready if you are."

"I am." She walked over to the cabinet, aware of his gaze on her. She poured herself a cup of coffee, then walked over to the table. "What's all this?" she asked. On the table were several gold frames and pictures that Billy had colored.

He walked over to the table. "I thought I'd frame a couple pieces of artwork to hang in the living room."

She stared at him, for a moment her heart too full to speak. How many other men would even think of doing such a thing? "Billy will be pleased," she finally managed to say.

He shrugged and pulled out a chair to sit. She sat across from him and noticed that he looked stressed. Lines creased the sides of his face and his shoulders looked rigid with tension.

"Something has happened," she said. "What is it, Nick? What's wrong?"

He hesitated a moment, as if contemplating if he wanted to tell her. He shrugged. "It's no big deal."

"Tell me. It's about David, isn't it?"

He frowned and directed his gaze out the nearby window. "I don't know if it's about David or not. I got a call on my cell phone about an hour ago. I own a little fishing cabin about two hours' drive from here. The deputy sheriff called me to tell me sometime within the past forty-eight hours it burned to the ground."

"Oh, Nick."

He raised a hand and waved it as if to dismiss any sorrow she might feel. "It needed a lot of work and I'd only just begun the renovations."

"He did it, didn't he?" Weariness swept over her. When would this all be over?

He smiled dryly and took the back off one of the frames. "I don't think it's a stretch to believe that David was involved."

"Involved in what?" Tony shuffled into the kitchen, dark hair holding evidence of losing a battle with a pillow. As he poured himself a cup of coffee Nick filled him in on the latest.

"He must have found the place through tax records and probably thought we would be there," Nick said.

The ring of his cell phone interrupted the conversation. Nick pulled the instrument out of his pocket and answered.

He shot upright in the chair and gripped the receiver closer against his ear as he listened to whatever the caller was saying.

Juliette looked at Tony, who shrugged, then back at Nick, who wouldn't meet her gaze. It was him. Juliette knew with certainty that the person on the other end of the phone was David.

"You torched my cabin," Nick said, a muscle ticking ominously in his jaw. His gunmetal gray eyes were hard and distant. "I don't need proof to know you're responsible."

With one swift movement, Tony reached out, grabbed the phone and disconnected the call.

"What the hell did you do that for?" Nick demanded.

"There's equipment out there that can pinpoint the

exact location where a cell phone signal is coming from," Tony said. He held the phone back out to his brother. "I find it odd that he decided to call and have a nice long chat with you."

"I didn't realize . . . I didn't think, but you're right. It is odd that he would call."

"He's hunting," Juliette said. "He's going to use every tool at his disposal to find us. He's relentless."

"Just don't let him tie you up on your cell phone," Tony said. "That's the only way I can see that he might be able to find us."

The words barely left his mouth when the cell phone rang again. Nick looked at the caller ID readout. "It's coming from a pay phone."

"Then it's him," she said.

Nick pressed a button and the phone stopped ringing. "I'll just have it go directly to voice mail."

At that moment Billy came into the kitchen. "Hey, buddy." Tony jumped up. "Before we get you breakfast why don't we go make our beds?"

"Is everything all right?" Billy's gaze sought his mother's, his blue eyes worried.

She smiled and nodded. "Everything is fine, honey," she assured him. "Run along and see that Tony makes his bed right, then we'll see about getting some breakfast."

The worry disappeared from his eyes as he smiled up at Tony. "Come on, I'll show you how to make your bed so you don't have all those wrinkles in it."

When they had gone she turned back to Nick. "I'm so sorry about your cabin."

"Don't be. I'm just grateful none of us were there. I

thought about it, but was afraid he might find out I owned it."

"And he did." She watched for a moment as he placed one of Billy's drawings into one of the gold frames, then carefully placed the frame back together. "Promise me something, Nick."

He looked up at her. "What?"

"If by some chance David finds us, you have to promise me that if it comes down to it and you can only save one person, you'll save Billy."

"Juliette." He winced.

She'd wanted to touch him when she'd first entered the kitchen and she did so now. "I'm serious, Nick." She reached out and took his hand and squeezed it tightly. "I need to know that whatever happens, Billy will have a chance to grow from a wonderful, loving boy into a wonderful, loving man."

"It's not going to come to that," he protested and squeezed her hand back. "I won't make a choice. I'll see to it that we all get out of this all right. He can't find us. His phone calls smack of desperation. We're going to be all right, Juliette."

She wanted to believe him. God, how desperately she wanted to believe him. But David had always won in the past and she had a fear deep inside her that he would win this time, as well.

Chapter 29

David spent two days trying to engage Nick in a phone conversation, hoping to keep him on the line long enough to trace where the call was coming from. But after the first initial brief contact, his calls were going directly to voice mail.

Throughout the years David had, at times in his life, felt the gnaw of frustration, but nothing like what burned inside him now. He'd never before known the kind of soul sickness that plagued him.

He couldn't eat. He couldn't sleep. All he wanted, all he needed to do was to find them and destroy them. Their life was an abomination, an affront to him on every level.

It was on the morning of the third day after the fire that he stood in front of the bathroom mirror and checked out his reflection.

Gone was the sandy hair that had photographed well, making him appear the handsome, successful golden boy. Through the magic of Clairol, his sandy strands had been transformed to a near black. A tube of SuEllen's mascara had turned his brows into matching black bushes.

He was pleased with the results. It was amazing

how changed a person could look with different hair coloring. The dark hair and brows made his face look more slender and with a pair of dark sunglasses obscuring his brown eyes he didn't think his own mother would be able to immediately recognize him.

He left the bathroom and walked into the bedroom. "What do you think?"

Sprawled on the bed in front of him, SuEllen snored off the effects of the latest dose of tranquilizers. A rivulet of drool ran down her chin. Disgusted, David turned and left the bedroom.

He grabbed a pair of sunglasses, along with his car keys from the kitchen countertop, then left the apartment. For the past two days he'd been staking out Nick Corelli's apartment. During the past forty-eight hours there had been no sign of the cop anywhere in the area.

Today David intended to begin the hunt in earnest. He had a gut feeling that they were still in town, holed up someplace like mice hiding from a cat. David would find them, it was just a matter of time.

In the apartment garage he got into the rental car that would be his hunt vehicle. He hadn't really thought about disguising his looks or changing his car until yesterday. He'd gone to the grocery store and had been confronted by a woman who recognized him.

She'd screamed and cursed him, her plump face red with hatred. He'd tried to walk away, but she'd followed him up and down the aisles until he'd wanted to kill her. Instead he'd left the store empty-handed. That's when he decided it was time for an appearance change.

He started the engine and pulled out of the parking

garage. Riverton wasn't that big of a town. It might take him several days, but he was going to drive up and down the streets and work it like a grid search until he spotted one of them.

Sooner or later one of them would have to buy groceries. Sooner or later one of them would have to leave their hiding place for one reason or another. He'd begin on the south side of town, one street at a time.

He'd already checked all the motels and hotels. He'd spent all day yesterday making phone calls. He'd asked each operator at each place to be connected to Juliette Monroe's room, but had come up empty-handed.

He'd then called back each place and asked for Angela Corelli's room. His research had told him that Angela had been Nick Corelli's mother's name and he thought the cop might have checked in using that name, but there had been no results.

Whistling absently, he tapped his fingers on the steering wheel. He knew it might be days before he found them, but he was a patient man.

"Bye, baby bunting, Daddy's gone a hunting," he murmured, then laughed. Yes, indeed. Daddy was hunting.

Chapter 30

They had been seven days in the safe house. They had been seven days of laughter and fun, and a feeling of security Juliette hadn't felt since the chilly autumn afternoon she'd finally gotten the opportunity to leave David.

However, the air held something more than peace and laughter. It shimmered with possibility, with an energy that ached inside her. The kiss she'd shared with Nick had stirred a tension inside her she couldn't ignore.

She would have loved to blame that kiss on the full moon of that night, but she knew it had come from something far different. She'd felt a physical pull toward Nick since the moment she'd first seen him, and the kind of man she'd come to know him to be had only intensified that pull.

It was the healthy reawakening of herself as a woman that shimmered in her veins when she looked at him, tingled through her body when they happened to have any kind of accidental physical contact.

And accidental physical contact was all there had been in the seven days since the kiss. Nick seemed to be consciously keeping his distance from her, but she wasn't fooled.

He felt the pull, too. She saw it in his eyes when he looked at her when he thought she didn't see. She felt it simmering from him whenever they were in the same room, seated at the same table, sitting on the same sofa.

It wasn't just her acute attraction to Nick that haunted her. It was also the fact that for the past seven days she'd seen what life should have been like for her and for Billy.

Pleasant evenings filled with warmth and laughter, conversations without fear of saying the wrong thing, and best of all Billy shared in the warmth and the laughter instead of being hidden away in a bedroom and awaiting for the time his mommy could slip in to spend time with him.

The longer she was away from her past with David, the deeper her guilt and shame over how twisted, how utterly defeated and submissive she'd become while with him.

On the eighth morning in the house, she awakened to a cloudy, gray day. She remained in bed, snuggly warm beneath the pink sheets and bedspread and stared out the open curtains to the backyard. The trees, like winsome strippers, had begun to shed their clothes—pools of gold, red, and orange leaves at their feet instead of covering their limbs.

If not for Nick and his brother and the extreme measures they had taken to assure her safety and Billy's, she was certain that she and her son would be dead. They would have never survived to see the leaves shedding from the trees this year.

She was pushed out of bed on a wave of anger and self-hatred, a fairly new companion. In the first weeks and months after leaving David, there had been little room for any emotion except fear. The act of simple survival had left no energy for thoughts of anything other than their next move.

But, in the past couple of weeks, Juliette had a burning anger inside her. She knew that David deserved her hatred and fury, but lately she'd found the anger turned inward toward herself. How had she let her life spiral so out of her control? How had she allowed David to threaten not only her own life, but Billy's?

She pulled on a robe and headed for the private bath the room afforded, a luxury in a house filled with two men and a boy. Beneath the spray of a warm shower, she ran her hands over her badges of shame and wished that she'd had the strength, the knowledge to have made better choices.

Minutes later, dressed in a white button-down shirt and a blue floral long skirt, she left her bedroom. As she headed down the stairs she heard the laughter coming from the kitchen.

It was easy to distinguish between the three— Tony's boyish chuckling, Billy's childish giggles, and Nick's deep, melodious laughter. The chorus of happiness shoved away, for the moment, any anger that might have festered inside her.

She found the three of them at the kitchen table eating bowls of oatmeal. "Good morning," she greeted.

"Hey, Mom, Nick makes oatmeal even better than yours," Billy announced.

"Contrary to what my brother has been saying about me for the last week, I do have a few culinary tricks up my sleeve." Nick's handsome smile took her breath away.

"Yeah, instant oatmeal—he has a special thing he does with the microwave buttons," Tony said wryly.

"Don't listen to him," Nick protested. "I went to great lengths to make that oatmeal special just for my buddy here." He leaned over and ruffled Billy's dark hair.

As Juliette saw the smile that lit her son's face, she took back all the regrets she might have had about meeting and marrying David. If there hadn't been a David, there wouldn't be a Billy. All that she had suffered at David's hands was worth it for having Billy in her life, in her heart.

At the moment her heart was not only filled with Billy, but with Nick as well. As she saw Nick interacting with Billy, once again she felt a dizzying desire for Nick well up inside her.

It was a desire built on more than the power of his beautiful smile and sexy physique. Over the past seven days he'd carefully framed each and every picture that Billy drew and colored for him. The pictures hung on the living room wall, a charming array of boyhood artwork. How could she not want a man who so obviously cared about her son, who could make the sun shine in Billy's eyes?

She padded over to the coffeemaker and poured herself a cup, then joined the others at the table, intently aware of Nick's gaze lingering on her.

"Hey Mom, Tony doesn't believe it that I've never been to the movies," Billy said.

Just like that her anger came back. Damn David for all he'd taken from her. And damn herself for allowing it to happen, for allowing her son to be deprived of ordinary pleasures.

"He said there's a movie theater close by and we could go see a movie if you'd let us." Billy's voice held a quiet, desperate plea.

Tony smiled apologetically. "Actually, I meant to bring this up with you privately, but Billy sort of jumped the gun here. The theater is five blocks from here and it's playing a Disney movie. I thought maybe if you agreed he and I could catch a matinee this afternoon."

Juliette looked at Nick. "You know there's only one thing that concerns me—the safety issue."

"I can't think of any reason that would prompt David to look in a movie theater," Tony said. "Especially one playing a Disney movie."

Nick nodded, his eyes dark with thought. "The theater is close and Billy's hair is certainly different. He won't be in my company or yours," he said to Juliette. "I think it would be fine."

"Besides," Tony added, "Nick showed me a picture of David's mugshot. I'd recognize him if he was within a mile of us."

Billy looked from Nick to his mother and there was no mistaking the deep yearning in his eyes, the need to be a normal child for just one afternoon, to eat buttery popcorn and watch the magic of Disney unfold on a huge screen. How could she deny him this?

"Looks like you're going to a movie this afternoon," she said.

Billy whooped with excitement and jumped up from the table.

"Where are you going?" Juliette asked.

"I got to go get ready. I'm gonna wear the new shirt Nick bought me." Before anyone could explain to him that the movie was still several hours away, he flew out of the room and up the stairs.

"That's pathetic." Juliette took a sip of her coffee and slammed her mug down on the table with more force than she'd intended.

"What?"

"Five years old and he's never been to a movie. Five years old and he's never been trick-or-treating, never played a game of baseball." She got up from the table, negative energy making it impossible for her to sit still. She moved to the window and stared out, for a moment lost in thoughts, lost in regrets.

"Juliette. It's not too late," Nick said, his voice soft in an obvious attempt to soothe.

Tony murmured something about checking on Billy and left the kitchen. She turned to face Nick. "You're right. It isn't too late, but five years of normal, healthy life he's lost because I was stupid and afraid."

"And now you aren't stupid anymore and hopefully after the court date you won't have to know fear again. Stop beating yourself up. Today he'll eat candy and popcorn until his belly aches and he'll laugh at the cartoon antics on-screen and he'll be fine."

"For today," she said, refusing to relinquish her anger.

"For today. And the only way to deal with things is one day at a time."

"Is that the way you deal with your loss?"

"What do you mean?"

"Miranda."

His eyes darkened and a hand went to his pocket in

a gesture she'd come to recognize as some kind of nervous habit. "Your situation has nothing to do with what happened to Miranda."

"No? You just told me to stop beating myself up and yet Diane seems to think you're still beating yourself up over Miranda's death." Somewhere in the back of her mind, she knew she was delving into personal issues, trying to pick a fight, stir up something between them besides her desire to fall into his arms.

Nick stood and crossed his arms over his chest. "What's going on?"

It was impossible for her to sustain her anger, her need to pick a fight with him so calm and patient. She suddenly felt small. "I don't know . . . bad morning." She picked up her coffee mug. "I think I'll take this out on the back porch and get a little fresh air."

"Here, take my coat. It's chilly out." He pulled his coat from the back of his chair and handed it to her.

Once outside she sank down into one of the chairs on the back porch and stared at the woods. Nick's coat wrapped around her with warmth and his familiar scent. As she sipped her coffee she began to relax.

She'd spent so many years living in an emotionless void, afraid to feel, afraid to display any emotion that might be used against her, might be used to punish her.

In the last seven days of being in the house, she'd battled the birth of emotions, afraid to embrace the feelings she'd almost forgotten were normal.

She sipped her coffee and stared at the woods, aware that in the past seven days she had come alive again after years of being dead with David.

*   *   *

Tony and Billy had been gone only about fifteen minutes when Juliette wandered into the living room, where Nick sat reading the morning paper.

She sat in the chair opposite the sofa and even though he kept his gaze focused on the paper he was aware of her gaze lingering on him. He waited for her to say something and when she didn't, he kept his own silence and continued to try to read.

"This is the first time since I met you that the two of us are completely alone."

His fingers tightened on the paper at her words. "Yeah, I guess that's true." He finally looked at her. Desire punched him in the gut, drove all thought of any news article he'd just read straight out of his head, and forced his pulse to rise just a bit. It was a reaction he'd grown accustomed to, one he lived with every single time he looked at her.

She stood and he watched as she moved to the window. Was it just his imagination or had her hips swayed a little more sensually than usual?

For a long moment she remained with her back to him. She turned to look at him once again. "You remember the night of the full moon when I told you I couldn't sleep, that the moon made me feel a little crazy?"

He nodded, unable to make an audible sound.

"I'm feeling that way again."

He placed the paper next to him on the sofa and cleared his throat. "You mean, crazy?"

She reached a slender hand up and touched her lips, then nodded. "Yes, I'm crazy for wanting another kiss from you."

Nick didn't even realize he'd risen until he stood

mere inches in front of her. It was like a rerun of the night in the moonlight, only this time there was no moonlight, only the gray of the clouds outside. Nick didn't need the romance of moonlight to want to kiss her again.

"I feel like if you kiss me again I'll shatter and if you don't kiss me again I'll shatter." Her voice was whisper soft.

"Then I'm not sure what you want me to do."

The tip of her tongue touched the bottom of her top lip and twisted Nick's stomach into a knot. "Kiss me, Nick."

He didn't wait for a second request. His mouth met hers in a kiss that held the hunger of weeks of want. There was something wild in the kiss, a carnal greed for more than the mere meeting of lips.

Her arms reached up and her fingers tangled in his hair as she urged him closer—closer against her. Nick knew he had only a tenuous hold on his control. As her hands moved from his head to his back, then to his lower back, she pulled his hips against hers.

She was effectively trapped between the surface of the window behind her and him and she didn't seem to mind. Her hips moved against his in an unmistakable rhythm and with a conscious effort he broke the kiss and stumbled a step back from her.

"Juliette, I'm not a saint." His voice was thick, husky with his need. "I want you. I've wanted you for a long time and I can't turn it on and shut it off at will."

"Then don't, don't shut it off."

He held her gaze for a long moment, needing to assure himself of exactly what she meant. He saw it in her eyes, that her need was as great as his own. He reached out a hand to her and she placed her hand in his. Cold. Her hands were always cold and he wanted to warm them, warm her.

Without speaking a word, he led her up the stairs and into his bedroom. Once there, he turned to look at her once again, giving her a second opportunity to call a halt to the force that drove them. The room was shrouded in shades of gray, but she was vibrant color, shimmering like a rainbow in hues of temptation.

She reached out and took the rock from his breast pocket and set it on the nightstand, then began to unbutton his shirt.

Button by button her slender fingers worked to undress him as he stood stock-still, allowing her to take the lead. When she'd finished with the buttons, she shoved the shirt off his shoulders and it fell to the floor behind him.

She stepped back from him and grabbed the bottom of her turtleneck in her hands, but hesitated. "I . . . I have scars." The words held a wealth of emotion—pain—shame—and the fear that disfigurement had turned her into something ugly and undesirable.

"Don't we all." He tucked a strand of her dark hair behind her ear and pressed his lips against her smooth neck. "You're beautiful, Juliette, and no scar you have on your body could make me want you less."

His words apparently soothed whatever fears she might have, for in one swift movement she pulled the turtleneck over her head and tossed it to the floor.

He saw the scar on her neck, the one she hid with tall-necked blouses. The angry pucker of skin did nothing to staunch his need. She reached behind her and unclasped her bra and when it fell he saw the second scar, a half-circle around her right nipple.

"He's a monster," he said, then he grabbed her to him and captured her mouth in a kiss that broke the thread of control he'd been desperately hanging on to.

They tumbled on the bed, mouths and limbs, sighs and moans and within minutes both were naked and indulging in the joy of discovery of each other. Their rapid breaths filled the room, the only sound in the house.

Nick kissed the scar on her throat, then moved down to kiss the old wound on her breast. Although his body yearned to go fast, to take complete possession and not waste time in foreplay, on some level he knew she needed the foreplay. She needed the assurance that nothing David had done to her body had ruined her.

When Nick moved to kiss the scar on her inner thigh, a scar in the shape of a letter D, he fought against a rage the likes of which he'd never known before.

The pain she must have suffered for those wounds to have left such scars. The thought of it made him want to hunt down David and beat him to a bloody pulp. But before his anger could take hold, Juliette issued a moan filled with such exquisite pleasure that he lost himself in it—in her.

He took her slowly, tenderly, like a longtime lover rather than hard and fast like a quickie after too many long, lonely nights. She gave as well as received, stroking his skin with hot hands and burning her lips into his flesh.

They moved together faster, frenzied with aching

need, tortured by days, weeks, years of unfulfillment. Even though Nick wanted to make love to her for hours, all too quickly he felt himself spinning out of control, climbing toward what he knew would be a shattering climax.

She seemed to sense his imminent explosion and a low moan ripped from her throat as she arched beneath him. Her eyes fluttered and he felt her convulsing around him as her fingernails bit into his back.

That was all it took for his release to rupture and he cried her name as wave after wave of pleasure crashed through him.

Later, she stirred against him. "Don't get up," he said, not ready to relinquish the warmth of her body next to his, the smell of her hair in his head, the sound of her breathing in sync with his own. "They won't be home for at least another hour."

She settled back against him, as if reluctant to leave his arms. He lay on his back with her in the curve of one arm and his fingers caressed her bare shoulder, loving the silk of her skin.

"Tell me why you stayed as long as you did." She stiffened and he hurriedly continued. "The question isn't an indictment, Juliette, I've often dealt with battered women and know about the syndrome of abuse. I'm just curious about you, if the story is the same."

She relaxed. "I'm sure it probably is." She sighed, her breath a sweet whisper of air across his chest. "I can tell you this, no matter how many stories you've heard from battered women, you can't really understand it until you live it."

She curled her fingers into the hair on his chest. "He wasn't always the monster you've seen. When I first met him he was so smooth, so charming. I was filled with such a sadness, an emptiness, due to my parents' deaths three months before."

She sat up abruptly, as if not wanting any closeness with Nick while she spoke of David. "He was more than charming. He was the most charismatic man I'd ever met. He had the ability to make me believe I was the most important person on the face of the earth. He swept me right off my feet and into marriage within two months. He talked me into putting the rest of my schooling on hold and I agreed, assuming that I'd skip a semester, then return. During the first year of our marriage we traveled abroad a lot." She frowned. "That's when the control began."

He sat up next to her and took her hand in his. Hers was cold again, as if the mere act of her memory could pull all the warmth from her body. "Control. What do you mean?"

"It was so insidious, that's the horror of it all. We were in countries where I didn't know the language but David did. I had to rely on David for everything. He loved it and I didn't see what was happening."

"And what was happening?"

"My world had become smaller and smaller, so that all that was in it was David. When we finally got back to the States and settled into his home, the pattern continued. I'd lost track of my school friends and had no other friends. David worked from home so I was never left alone and the mental abuse he'd begun was so subtle I didn't even realize it was happening."

"Like what?" Nick asked. He'd always been fascinated with the aspects of victimology and what made particular people victims.

"Little things, like he started picking out my clothing, implying that I had no taste and would be an embarrassment to him if I wore what I chose. He made sure I never had any money because I wasn't good with money. We didn't entertain because I wouldn't be able to pull together a party in the style he was accustomed to having. Even though he never told me I was unworthy and stupid, he made me feel that way." She squeezed Nick's hand. "But when you're in the middle of it, you don't see it happening."

"When did the physical stuff start?"

She reached her free hand up and touched the side of her neck. "Not until after Billy was born. David was controlling and I had begun to grow restless and unhappy, but he'd never hurt me physically until Billy was almost a year old."

She dropped her hand from her neck. "He cut my neck first. It all happened so fast and he was so apologetic afterward. I thought it was the adjustment of having Billy and the pressure of being a parent." She laughed bitterly. "But, of course, that was just the first of many times."

"When did you decide to leave him?"

"That night that I got the pizza order wrong and he cut my neck—that first night that he drew blood." Her features were bloodless now, the same pale gray as the sky outside the window. "After he cut my breast, I knew he'd kill me if I tried to leave him, but my main concern was for Billy. If I died, David would have custody and so I had to stay alive. And so I waited. It took almost three years before I finally got the chance to take Billy and run. Something happened at his business and he had to leave. For the first time he left me and Billy home alone. So, I ran."

"And you've been running ever since."

She drew his hand up to her lips. "Until I met you."

He pulled her against his chest and kissed the top of her head, knowing that he'd go to hell and back to make certain that nobody ever hurt this woman again.

"Tell me about the rock," she said.

His first instinct was the self-protective silence he always hid behind. Nobody knew about the importance of that rock. But he found that he wanted to tell her, wanted her to know why that rock was a part of him.

"It was Miranda's lucky rock." As always her name on his lips brought with it the bitter taste of regret, the hollowness of grief. "I don't know where she'd found it, but one day she had it and told me it was her lucky rock. She carried it everywhere for about a month. That particular morning, I stopped in for an early morning cup of coffee and Miranda had her lucky rock on the table next to her while she ate her breakfast."

He fought the impulse to get out of bed and pace while he spoke and instead stroked a hand through the silk of Juliette's hair. "I had my coffee, then had to leave to go to work. I had just gotten into my car when Miranda came running out the door to me."

He remembered that particular morning as clear as any memory he had ever, would ever possess. The sky was the piercing blue of a perfect autumn day and the air smelled of golden leaves and fresh apples.

Miranda's dress had been a splash of yellow as she'd raced to his car, her eyes lit with her usual laughter.

"Uncle Nick!" she'd shouted.

"What's up, peanut?" he'd asked as he stooped down to her level.

She'd smiled as she'd thrown a skinny arm around his neck. She'd smelled of strawberry bubble bath and sunshine and all the childhood dreams a little girl could possess.

"Nick?" Juliette's voice pulled him from the pain of that last memory of Miranda alive and well.

"She said she wanted me to take her lucky rock for the day, that she just had a feeling I might need it. So, I took her lucky rock." He sighed, the weary sigh of a man with a million regrets.

"Oh, Nick." She leaned against him, as if in her closeness he might find strength.

"You asked me one time if there was a single moment in time that if I could, I would take back, remember?" She nodded. "That was my moment. If I could go back there I'd let Miranda keep her lucky rock."

Together they lay back down and held each other close.

As the movie played on the big screen, Tony alternated his attention between watching Billy's joy and thoughts of Diane.

He'd spoken with her on the phone every day since he'd arrived back in town, but she continued to refuse to see him. Miranda's death had not only destroyed the three of them on a personal level, it had also destroyed the relationship that had made Tony feel like the luckiest man in the world.

He and Diane had been so happy, so much in love,

but within weeks of Miranda's funeral, Diane had crawled into a hole where there had been no space for anyone else.

She had consciously shoved Tony out of her life, unable to embrace both him and the mental illness that was taking over her life.

Diane had never been out of his thoughts, out of his mind, despite the time that had passed since that fateful day. He found it heartening that she was talking to him, and in her voice—unspoken in words but there in inflection and subtleties—was that fact that she still loved him.

Patience, he told himself. That's what he needed, and for Diane he could be as patient as necessary. His thoughts were interrupted by Billy's laughter.

Billy was a good kid, but that wasn't why Tony had agreed to take him here today. For the past seven days Tony had felt the energy simmering in the air between Billy's mom and Tony's brother. Nick's glances at Juliette were filled with a heat Tony had never seen in his brother's eyes before and she returned that heat with gazes of her own.

The two were sick for each other and the sexual tension between them was heavy enough to cut with a knife. Tony had decided to give the two a break and spend a little time out of the house with Billy, leaving Nick and Juliette alone.

When the movie ended, he and Billy walked to where he'd parked his car. Billy had laughed throughout the movie and had eaten enough popcorn and JuJu fruits to make him positively ill.

He was silent as they walked to the car. "You feeling sick to your stomach?" Tony asked. "You ate a lot of junk in there."

"It wasn't junk," Billy protested. He remained silent as they slid into the car and it wasn't until Tony started the engine that he spoke again.

"Tony, what's wrong with my dad? What makes him so mean?"

Tony thought for a moment, trying to come up with an answer a kid could swallow. "I'm not sure, Billy. I think something is broken inside your dad."

Billy nodded thoughtfully. "Is there anything broken in Nick?"

"No way," Tony replied. "Nick doesn't have anything broken in him at all."

"Good."

In that single word Tony recognized how deeply this little boy had grown to love, to look up to, to adore his brother. There had been only one other child who had felt the same way about Nick and she had ended up dead.

Chapter 31

David's hunt had yielded nothing so far. For the past three days he'd driven the streets of Riverton, writing down addresses, making notes of the houses where he couldn't discern who lived there. It was a torturously slow process and he was sick of it.

The rage inside him now hummed constantly, like the white noise of a television station that had gone off the air. He refused to accept that they might be smarter than him, that they might have found a place to hide where he'd never find them.

Failure was not an option.

He'd decided to give up his street-to-street search. He knew Corelli was no longer staying at his own apartment. A call to the police station had told him that Corelli was on vacation.

David was banking on the fact that even though Juliette and Billy weren't in Nick's apartment, the apartment might hold a clue as to exactly where they were holed up.

He'd decided he needed to get into that apartment and look around. He'd also decided to go in during the day.

It was an apartment complex of working-class people and he'd noticed there wasn't much activity during the day. Children caught the buses early in the morning and mothers disappeared either for a day of shopping, or work or whatever. People reappeared around three in the afternoon when the yellow buses appeared to drop off their daily burdens.

A calm cool descended through him as he drove toward the complex. He was aware that he was running out of options.

It had been so easy while she'd been out on her own, without support of any kind. There were times he'd lost track of her for weeks, months at a time, but always she made a mistake that brought him right to her doorstep.

This time she wasn't making mistakes and David knew it was because of the cop who helped her.

It was just after ten in the morning when he pulled into the parking lot of the apartment complex. Just as David had suspected, Nick's car wasn't anywhere in the lot.

He remained behind the wheel of his car, his gaze darting left and right. There was nobody around. The curtains at the windows of the apartment next to Nick's were tightly drawn, as they had been for the past week.

Even though there was nobody around, David knew better than to try to get into any of the front windows or door. He got out of his car, whistling just under his breath, and hit the sidewalk in front of Nick's place.

He walked at a leisurely pace, down the sidewalk and around the side of the building. He tried both windows on the side of the building, but found them locked tight. He moved to the backyard where a privacy fence surrounded the back door to Nick's apartment.

Looking around once again to make certain that there was nobody else around, David grabbed hold of the top of the fence and pulled himself up and over and to the ground on the other side.

Facing him was a sliding glass door and next to that was a small window. Probably the window above the kitchen sink, David thought. He tried the sliding doors first and found them locked, then moved to the window and tried to open it, unsurprised to discover it locked as well.

He wrapped his hand in a thick handkerchief and hit the glass with his fist. It took three hits before the glass crackled enough that he could pick it out and slide in through the frame.

Just as he'd suspected, the window led into the kitchen. No table, no chairs. Just a bare, plain kitchen. He looked in cabinets, in drawers, seeking something—a piece of paper, a motel room charge slip, a phone number—anything that would hint at a current location.

There had to be something here. He refused to consider he wouldn't find anything. He had to find them.

From the kitchen he moved into the living room, growing more frustrated with each passing moment. The cop lived like a freaking monk, with few possessions or personal belongings. The living room yielded nothing and David moved on to the bedroom.

In the nightstand he found paperwork neatly filed in manila folders—bills paid in full, a life insurance policy, a letter from social security informing Corelli how much his monthly pay would be if he retired at sixty-five.

What he didn't find was a scrap of paper, a matchbook cover, anything that would help him in his search.

The closet yielded nothing but cheap clothes and a shoe box full of old photographs. He threw the shoe box across the room in a fit of anger. The box hit the bedside lamp and it crashed to the floor.

The phone rang.

David froze.

The phone rang three times, then he heard the click of an answering machine pick up and a woman's voice filled the air. David followed the voice into the kitchen where the answering machine sat on the countertop.

"Nicky? Is that you? I thought I heard something over there. You know these paper-thin walls . . . if it's you, pick up the phone." There was a long pause. "Nicky?" Another pause. "Okay . . . then I'll talk to you later."

The voice winged through David. His blood pounded at his temples as energy built inside him. "Nicky" implied familiarity, a closeness that stoked David's excitement. He was certain the call had come from the nearest neighbor, where the curtains stayed closed day and night.

Were they there? Right next door? He didn't think so, but he had a feeling he might learn a lot by talking to the neighbor.

He left the apartment the way he had come in and headed to his car. He wanted to do a little research into the neighbor before he had a chat with her. It shouldn't take him longer than an hour or two to find out what he wanted, then he'd be back.

"You owe me big-time," Tony said to his brother. The two were alone at the kitchen table. Billy was in the living room watching television and Juliette had gone to her bedroom.

"Owe you for what?" Nick eyed him curiously.

"The movie time yesterday? Was it my imagination or did you and Juliette both look like you'd shared a canary when we got back home."

"Must have been your imagination," Nick replied.

"Ah, I remember a time when you weren't such a gentleman," Tony teased. "I was about ten and you were thirteen and in love with Stacy Worthington. You used to come home and tell me about trying to cop a feel from her beneath the bleachers at the football games."

Nick smiled. "Yeah, those were different times, weren't they." He sighed, the memory of those days washing over him. "Everything seemed so easy then. The biggest problems were passing English and making sure Dad didn't know we occasionally stole cigarettes from him."

All humor left Tony's features. "If Blankenship goes to trial, you know there's a good possibility he won't get a stiff sentence. These days you gotta kill somebody to get put away for longer than a couple of months. Have you and Juliette considered what happens next? What happens if he gets out in three months' or six months' time?"

These questions had haunted Nick over the past several weeks. "We haven't talked about it and I don't have any answers. Right now my goal is just to see to it that she and Billy get to trial date, then we'll figure out what comes next after that."

Nick's phone rang and he pulled it out and checked the ID. Sammy. He answered. "What's up?"

"What? You don't love me anymore? I haven't heard from you in a week. How's it going, Romeo?"

"It's going. We're keeping a low profile. What's new there?"

"I hate to be the bearer of bad news, but figured I'd let you know that Blankenship is off the suspect list for the Camp murder."

"Why?" Frustration raked through Nick. He got up from the table and moved to stand at the window, staring unseeing toward the backyard.

"Not a single shred of evidence tying him to the scene or Camp himself. Meanwhile, Camp is proving to have been something of a sleaze ball and potential suspects are popping up all over the place. You know how it goes, Nick."

"Yeah, all too well. Anything else going on?"

"Nah, Slokem is still an asshole and the criminal types of the city are kicking our ass."

"You trying to cheer me up?"

Sammy laughed. "Why should you be happy when the rest of mankind is so miserable. Anyway, just wanted to check in. I'm not going to ask you where you are, but is there anything I can do? Anything you need?"

"Thanks, Sammy, but no, we're fine."

Nick clicked off and turned to find himself alone in the kitchen. He looked back out the window. Although disappointed, he was unsurprised that Blankenship wasn't being considered a viable suspect in the Camp murder.

Tony's questions burned in his brain and blood pounded at his temples in the beginning drumbeat of a headache. This had probably been a study in futility from the very beginning. Nick had ridden in on a white horse to save the day like a hero cowboy in a sappy western. But he hadn't thought about what happened after the movie was over and the bad guy was still alive.

Maybe he'd been a fool to get involved in all this. His heart was getting all wrapped up in this and there were no guarantees for a happy ending.

He'd made love to Juliette and had no idea what it had meant to her other than an expression of gratitude, a stress-relieving physical workout.

He raked a hand through his hair, wondering why in the hell his head raced with this kind of crap. Tony was the mental guy. Nick was the action man. The problem was he had nothing to do but sit in this house, fall deeper in love with Juliette, and think of all the things that could go so terribly wrong.

It took David exactly one hour to discern all he needed to know about one Diane Borderman. Twenty-nine years old and a talented webmaster, she was also apparently a shut-in who ordered every necessity on her Mastercard and had it delivered to her apartment.

She had a dozen prescriptions for a variety of antianxiety medication. Fucking little fruitcake. She should be easy to rip apart and get the information he needed.

"I'm leaving now," he said to SuEllen.

She stared at him with eyes widened in surprise. He had a feeling her surprise had more to do with the fact that the sheets around her were soaked in blood and less to do with the fact that he was leaving.

She hadn't even fought. Maybe it had been all the tranquilizers he'd had her on. She'd just looked at him in surprise when he'd drawn the knife and then it had been done.

Now that she was gone, he kind of missed her. She'd been a sweet enough kid, useful when he'd needed her. But he was at war, and she was collateral damage.

He leaned down and kissed her cold, slightly blue cheek, then grabbed a suitcase he'd packed and left the apartment for the final time.

It was just after two as he got into his car and headed for Diane Borderman's apartment.

Diane Borderman felt better than she had in months and she knew it was because Tony was back. She didn't know where he was staying, had insisted that she wasn't ready to see him, but he called every morning and they talked.

They talked about everything and nothing and as she listened to him laugh, as he made her laugh, she remembered all the reasons she'd fallen in love with him.

Still, no matter how much she loved him, nothing had changed. She refused to allow him back in her life. At the moment it was enough that he was back in her life by phone.

As she sat at her computer and worked on a new

Web design, a smile curved her lips and a warmth that she hadn't felt for a very long time filled her heart.

Despite the fact that she'd forced Tony out of her life, despite the months and months that had passed, there was still a connection between them, a crazy connection that gave her hope.

A knock fell on her door and she got up from her chair, wondering who it might be. She wasn't expecting any deliveries, but that didn't mean much.

Nicky occasionally had things delivered to her. He'd be at the grocery store and see a sale on steaks, and that afternoon several packages of steaks would be delivered to her door.

"Who's there?" she asked through the door.

"Delivery from Scimeca's," a deep voice replied.

Scimeca's was a favorite Italian grocer where she occasionally bought pasta and fresh-ground sausage. It was one of Nicky's favorite stores.

She opened the door and stepped back. "Please, just bring it in and set it on the counter."

As the dark-haired man with dark sunglasses entered the apartment, she closed the door behind him, then pointed to the kitchen counter.

"I'm afraid there's a problem here," the man said and set the brown paper bag he carried onto the chair next to the sofa.

"A problem?"

"I'm afraid I've entered your residence under false pretenses. You should be more careful about who you let into your home." He pulled off his glasses and grinned, a cold, merciless smile.

In that smile, she knew him. She'd never seen a picture of him, but she knew the man who faced her was Juliette's demon.

Stone-cold fear crashed through her. With a speed she hadn't known she possessed, she dove for the phone. He was one step ahead of her. He grabbed the instrument and ripped it from the wall.

"Sit down," he commanded. He pointed to the sofa.

"What do you want? Why are you here?"

"I told you to sit down." He reached into the sack he'd carried in and pulled out a knife.

Diane sat, her knees too weak to do anything else. Heartbeats raced, crushing her chest with frantic palpitations.

"Where are they?"

"Wha— what do you mean? Wher— where is who?"

He laughed and put the knife back in the sack. Instead he walked over to the window, reached out and grabbed one of the wands that controlled the blinds. "Don't play dumb with me, it doesn't become you."

"No, please." Sheer terror swept through her. She was already breathless. If he opened the shade she would die. She wouldn't be able to take another breath.

"Please what?"

"Please don't—don't open the shades." Dizzy. Tears blurred her vision. The room shrank as the air disappeared. "I don't know anything. I— I don't know where they are."

"I think you're telling me stories, Diane." He whirled the wand and the outside flew in on shafts of sunlight.

Diane collapsed within herself, curling up in a ball

in the corner of the sofa. Her heart tried to burst out of her chest. She pressed her fists against her chest in an effort to keep it inside.

Through the blur of tears she saw him move to another window. "I'm not lying," she cried. "I swear, I'm telling you the truth. I don't know where they are. I don't know."

He flipped the blinds at the second window open and more sunshine poured into the room. Death walked cold, bony fingers up her spine and she wondered why he kept talking to her, asking her questions.

She could see his lips moving, but she couldn't hear him. All she could hear was the sound of death reaching out to embrace her. It whispered to her in the shallow gasp of her breath, it roared in her ears making all other noise impossible to hear.

She fell from the sofa and onto the floor, gasping like a fish out of water, unable to take in enough oxygen to sustain life.

Darkness edged in and she was barely conscious when he kicked her the first time. The kick crashed into her ribs, the sharp explosion of pain momentarily forcing the darkness away.

With perfect clarity of thought, she wondered what she'd been so afraid of, why she'd closed herself off. If death wanted you, it found you no matter where you hid, no matter how tightly closed you kept your blinds.

When he kicked her the second time she felt something dislodge and a new wave of pain brought the darkness back close enough that she could grasp it. She reached for it and by the time he kicked her a third time, she had disappeared into the darkness where there was no pain, no fear, and the possibility of seeing Miranda once again.

David had every intention of killing her. The bitch hadn't told him anything. Unfortunately the bitch hadn't known anything. He'd believed her. When he'd threatened to open the blinds and she hadn't told him, he'd realized she truly didn't know.

He walked over to the paper bag he'd carried in and pulled out the knife that had gutted SuEllen. Blood had dried on it, along with tiny shreds of tissue.

When he had the time and the opportunity, he liked a knife. He liked the weight of it in his hand, the intimate experience of pulling the blade across pale flesh and watching the crimson flow of blood.

Juliette had been terrified of knives. Even though she tried not to show him fear when he got his knife, it was there. He smelled it emanating from her, saw just a whisper of it glinting in her cold, blue eyes.

It would have been better if Ms. Borderman was conscious when he used the knife on her, but either his kicks, or her own mental state had rendered her unconscious.

He was about to thrust the blade into her stomach when he realized she was worth nothing to him dead, but alive she might still be the link he needed to Juliette.

He closed all the blinds and left her there on the floor in a puddle of shadowed darkness.

Death wasn't supposed to hurt. In everything Diane had ever read, in all that she believed, she'd always understood that death was a release from pain.

So she must be alive. Each breath she tried to draw

sent pain ripping through her. Her eyes were closed and she was afraid to open them, afraid to see that her body was nothing more than a mass of broken, bloody parts.

For a moment she couldn't remember what had happened, how she'd come to be in such pain. Had it been a car accident? No, that wasn't right. She hadn't been in a car in almost two years. What then? What had happened? Had she fallen? Broken a limb?

David Blankenship.

Memory came crashing down around her and she gasped, the intake of breath stabbing a knife through her chest. The kicks . . . vicious kicks. Broken ribs. Broken body. He'd beaten her then left her for dead.

She needed help—and she needed to tell Nicky.

She had no idea how long David had been gone, no idea how long she'd lain unconscious, she only knew she desperately needed medical attention.

Opening her eyes, she realized two things. The phone would do her no good. She vaguely remembered David ripping it out of the wall. If she wanted help, she had to go after it.

That meant going outside.

She closed her eyes, a sob ripping from her as the familiar terror gripped her.

Chapter 32

Diane Borderman managed to crawl outside of her apartment where a neighbor saw her lying on the sidewalk and called 911. Sammy Bellows, recognizing the name as that of Nick's neighbor, responded.

He arrived at the scene to find her unconscious and already loaded into an awaiting ambulance. He followed the ambulance to the Riverton Hospital where Diane was taken directly into x-ray and Sammy was left cooling his heels in the waiting room.

From x-ray she was whisked immediately into surgery to inflate one of her lungs that had been pierced by a section of broken rib.

Sammy considered calling Nick, but decided against it until he was able to speak with Diane and find out exactly what had happened in her apartment that afternoon.

Maybe it was a robbery gone bad. Maybe it had nothing to do with the fact that Diane was Nick's close friend and David Blankenship didn't know where Nick had taken Juliette and her son. He didn't want to jump to conclusions. He needed facts before he alerted Nick to what had happened.

It was three a.m. when Diane finally left the recov-

ery room and the doctor agreed to give Sammy five
minutes with the patient.

Her room was in semidarkness and as he walked in
she uttered a soft, whispered moan. Sammy hated this
invasion into her pain, the necessity of speaking with
her when he was certain she wanted nothing more
than her morphine pump and silence.

"Diane." He moved to stand next to her bed, so she
could see his face in the faint illumination. "It's
Sammy, Diane."

Her face was the color of the sheets except on one
cheekbone, where a bruise had blossomed in deep
purple hues. She moaned and reached out a hand to
him.

He took her hand. It was tiny and trembling. "Tell
Nicky . . ." She winced and licked her lips. "Tell Nicky
he's crazy."

"Who's crazy? Who did this to you, Diane?" He
asked the question even though he now had the answer.

She closed her eyes and for a moment he thought
he'd lost her to the sweet rush of the morphine. Her
eyes opened once again, bloodshot and drowsy.
"David." The name oozed out of her like a viscous
slime. "David Blankenship." She swallowed visibly
and licked her dry lips once again. "He thought I knew
where they were. I don't. I— I couldn't tell him anything."

Sammy squeezed her hand. "We'll get him, Diane."

She nodded, then pulled her hand from his and
closed her eyes once again. This time he was certain
she was lost to the drugs and that was fine with him.
He had things to do. He had a man to find and arrest.

Thank God Diane hadn't known where they were, for if she had, Sammy was certain she would have told. She was only human, and she'd have sold out her mother to make the pain stop. Sammy wouldn't have blamed her for doing so.

By five a.m. Sammy had what he needed. Six officers and an arrest warrant accompanied him to David Blankenship's high rent apartment.

Blankenship had fucked up by leaving Diane alive. They finally had the ammunition needed to put him behind bars. Sammy would call Nick with the good news once Blankenship was in custody.

The high-rise apartment building where Blankenship lived on the tenth floor was, for the most part, occupied by professionals.

At five in the morning the place radiated with predawn silence. Still too early for the yuppies to be having their morning lattes and smoothies.

Knowing Blankenship had a penchant for violence, Sammy hoped to find the fucker sleeping in his bed. He'd stationed one officer at the front door of the building and one at the back, not taking any chances that Blankenship might squeeze by them.

He'd awakened the manager to get a key. Rick Martinez, a clean cut Hispanic, had complied without question. As he got the key off a huge ring, he told Sammy that his brother was a Kansas City police officer. Sammy was glad for the cooperation. The last thing he wanted was to get in some sort of a pissing match with a proprietorial manager.

Sammy and the other four officers rode the elevator up in silence. The greasy burger smothered in onions and the chili fries Sammy had eaten for dinner sat heavy in the acidic juice of nerves. The key to Blankenship's apartment burned in his palm. He wanted this bust bad. He wanted it for Diane. He wanted it for Nick.

The elevator arrived on the tenth floor and the five of them exited and headed down the hall toward the apartment. Their silence was surprising for five big, burly men.

Sammy wanted to go in quietly. He knew Blankenship had a roommate, a young girl who had provided him an alibi for the day of Camp's murder, and he didn't want the girl to become a casualty or a hostage.

By the time they reached the apartment, Sammy's heart thundered with the hyped-up energy of excitement and fear. Any cop who didn't regularly taste fear eventually wound up as a dead cop.

He placed his ear next to the door, listening for the sound of anyone stirring on the other side. Silence. There was no indication that anyone was awake.

Checking that his fellow officers were ready, Sammy inserted the key into the lock. The door unlocked with a barely discernible click.

Sammy pushed the door open and two of the officers entered, guns drawn. The living room was semi-dark, lit in the preternatural light of the first gasp of dawn. Two of the officers went into the kitchen and the other two followed behind Sammy as he went down the hallway toward the bedrooms.

Step by step, room by room, they cleared the place until there was only one room left. The master bedroom lay ahead with the door closed.

We got the bastard, Sammy thought. We finally got the bastard and there was no way he'd wiggle out of this one. With all four of the officers behind him,

Sammy reached out and grabbed the doorknob. He turned it slowly, then crashed open the door.

"Freeze!" he shouted, at the same time he hit the light switch.

The overhead light shone like a spotlight on the bed. "Ah, Jesus." They were too late.

The girl stared at them from the king-size bed. The sheets around her were saturated with her blood and her organs and intestines had been yanked out. The room smelled of death, of too-sweet coppery blood and ruptured bowel.

"Dammit," Sammy exclaimed. "Call it in," he instructed one of the others. As the officer radioed the station, Sammy stepped out of his room and used his cell phone to try to reach Nick.

She'd come to his bed in the middle of the night. She'd worn only a robe that she dropped at the foot of the bed just before she crawled in next to him beneath the covers.

"I couldn't wait until Tony decided to take Billy to the movies again," she whispered against his neck.

With those simple words, he'd been lost to her. They'd made love in midnight silence, not needing words to flame their desire. For the first time in his life, Nick felt the utter rightness of sharing his bed with a woman, of knowing her scent would transfer to his sheets, that a strand or two of her hair might linger on his pillowcase.

After they made love, she remained in his arms, not sleeping but stroking his chest hair with warm, soft fingers. "Why haven't you married?" she asked, her voice a mere whisper in the darkness of the room.

"I got close once, before Miranda's death."

"What happened?"

Nick stroked the soft skin of her bare shoulder. "I was a mess after Miranda was killed. I was drinking and miserable. Sherri, that was her name, she tried to be there for me, but I needed to grieve alone. I pushed her away when I was feeling my worst, but even when things started to turn around a little I realized that I really didn't miss Sherri. She was a terrific woman and I liked being with her, but it was almost as much about being with Tony and Diane and Miranda as it was about being with her. I knew then that the relationship wasn't meant to last."

She snuggled closer against him. "Anyway," he continued, "by that time I realized Diane was getting in a bad way. I moved into the apartment next door to her and since then there just hasn't been time for much of anything but work and keeping her company."

"Miranda's death left a lot of holes in a lot of people." Her hand stopped moving across his chest, coming to rest directly above his heart.

"Yeah, it did."

She was silent for another moment. He heard her deep intake of breath and her hand seemed to cool slightly on his skin. "Sometimes, in the darkest place of my mind, where all the horrible thoughts live, what hurts me more than anything is the knowledge that if something happened to Billy, I'd be the only person on this earth to mourn."

He wanted to say something, but knew from the stiffening of her shoulders she wasn't finished. "Nobody else has gotten the opportunity to love him. He hasn't even had a chance to make friends, and meet people."

She raised her head and in the moonlight he saw the glimmer of tears that shone in her eyes. "I know it's crazy, but my biggest fear is that if David somehow succeeds in killing me . . . in killing Billy, then who will mourn for my son?"

"Juliette," he began.

"I know . . . I know, it's a morbid, horrid thought." She laid her head back against his shoulder.

Nick suspected she didn't want another platitude, didn't need another promise that they'd all be safe from David's wrath. For a long moment he watched the night shadows dance on the bedroom wall and thought about what she'd said.

"I would grieve for him," he finally said.

She said nothing in return, but rather seemed to melt closer to him. Within minutes he knew she'd fallen asleep and he allowed himself to drift off as well.

The ring of his cell phone awakened him at five forty-five. He grabbed the phone, eyed the illuminated caller ID, and recognized the number as Sammy's.

Juliette remained asleep and Nick slid out of bed at the same time he answered. "Yeah, Sammy. What's up?" He padded out of the bedroom and into the bathroom down the hall.

"Something's happened." Sammy's voice radiated with taut tension.

Nick closed the bathroom door and locked it. "What?"

"Blankenship has upped the stakes. Sometime late

yesterday afternoon he managed to get into Diane's apartment."

Nick's knees threatened to buckle and he threw out a hand to steady himself against the sink cabinet. "Is she . . .?"

"She's okay, Nick. She's in Riverton Memorial. He beat her up, broke a couple of her ribs, but she's going to be just fine."

Relief shuddered through Nick, a relief so intense it rendered him speechless.

"Anyway, we went to arrest Blankenship and found another surprise waiting for us at his apartment." The relief Nick had felt was short-lived. He sat on the edge of the bathtub as Sammy continued. "That girl Blankenship had moved in with him? He gutted her, Nick—gutted her like a fish."

"Jesus. What about him?"

"Apparently he flew the coop. His car is gone from the garage. They found an empty safe in the apartment. We're guessing he's got money, his passport and whatever he might need to jump the country. But, we've got every cop looking for him and we're checking airlines now. He's not getting out of the city. We'll get him, Nick and this time he won't walk away. Tell Juliette it's just a matter of time before he's behind bars and out of her life for good."

"You'll keep me updated?"

"You know it."

Nick remained sitting on the cold porcelain of the tub after disconnecting with Sammy. He leaned forward, head in his hands, assessing and digesting what Sammy had told him. He'd have to tell Tony about Diane. God, he hoped what Sammy had told him was true, that she was banged up, but okay. Poor SuEllen Maynard. She'd never had a chance against a madman like Blankenship. He pulled himself up and left the bathroom and returned to the bedroom. Knowing there was nothing he could do, unwilling to awaken Tony with the bad news about Diane, he slid back into bed.

He was still awake half an hour later when Juliette stirred next to him and opened her eyes. "Good morning," she said, her voice a hushed whisper in the semi-darkness of breaking dawn.

In that golden light seeping through the windows and with her sleepy scent and warmth in his arms, Nick told her what had happened.

She listened without emotion playing on her features. As he spoke, he watched her become the woman she'd been that day at the day care center, a winter woman without emotion, removed from everything.

When he was finished, she got up and silently pulled her robe around her. "Juliette," he said as she began to leave the room. "They'll get him."

A shadow raced across the surface of her eyes. "Too bad they couldn't get him before he beat the hell out of Diane and killed that poor girl." She turned and left the room.

Tony drove toward the hospital like a madman. Nobody was going to stop him from seeing Diane. Minutes earlier when Nick had told him what had happened, a million regrets had haunted him.

Regret that he'd allowed her to make him leave her years ago, regret that he hadn't just shown up on her doorstep when he'd gotten back to town and the regret that he hadn't been there to kill David Blankenship when he'd shown up to hurt Diane.

Anger and regret accompanied him as he roared down the streets of Riverton and toward Diane. When he reached the hospital he found a parking space and was out of the car before the engine had completely shut off.

He entered through the main doors where he knew the information desk would give him Diane's room number. There were several people seated in the lobby, which also served as a waiting room for the emergency department in the small hospital. Tony paid no attention to them, his focus solely on his need to see Diane.

An old woman who sat behind the information desk told him that Diane Borderman was in room 110 and pointed Tony toward a hallway to the left.

As soon as he turned down the hallway, he knew which room was Diane's. A police officer sat in a chair outside of the room. He rose from the chair as Tony approached. The door to the hospital room behind his chair was closed.

"I'm here to see Diane," Tony said.

"Sorry, no visitors," the officer replied.

"On whose orders?"

"Ms. Borderman has requested no visitors and the investigating officer left me here to see that her request was honored."

"She'll see me," Tony said. "Please, just tell her I'm here. Tony Corelli. Tell her and I'm sure she'll want to see me."

The officer hesitated. "Let me see some identification," he said. Tony dug into his back pocket for his wallet, then showed the cop his driver's license.

"Please, tell her I need to see her."

He nodded and disappeared into the hospital room, then closed the door behind him. Now that Tony was so close to her, knowing that she was hurt and in pain, his need to be with her overwhelmed him.

The door reopened and the officer stepped out. "She said it's okay."

Suddenly Tony was afraid to see her again, afraid to get caught up in loving her again, wanting to build a life with her again only to have it all lost to the illness he didn't know how to fight.

He opened the door and stepped into the room and saw again the woman he'd loved more than anyone else on earth for the first time in eighteen months. In that first look, he knew with certainty that nothing had changed. He still loved her more than anyone else on earth.

Her eyes filled with tears at the sight of him and she reached out a hand. "Tony." In the whispered sigh of his name, he knew that nothing had changed for her, either.

He grabbed her hand and sat in the chair next to her bed. Her hair was smoothed back from her pale face, her petite features looking smaller, younger than ever. A bruise darkened one of her cheeks and it was obvious she was in pain.

"If I knew where he was, I'd hunt him down and kill him for hurting you," he said with passion.

"I'm just glad you're here now, with me."

"I'm telling you right now, you're not going to force me out of your life again, Diane." He leaned toward her and pressed his lips against the back of her hand. "Diane, we belong together. We've always belonged together. I love you, and I'm not leaving you again."

A sob escaped her and she squeezed his hand. "I don't want you to leave me ever again. Nicky and Juliette and Billy . . . they're safe?"

"Safe and sound."

"Thank God." She closed her eyes and was still for a long moment.

He didn't speak, although he had a million and one things he wanted to say to her. But, if she had fallen asleep, he didn't want to disturb her. She looked so achingly frail. She opened her eyes once again and smiled at him.

"Diane, I'll live in whatever world you need to be in. If that's a world of darkness, of being shut-in and away from others, then that's fine."

She tried to sit up against the pillows and Tony jumped up to raise the head of her bed. "Better?" he asked.

She nodded and he returned to his chair and grabbed her hand once again. "I should thank David Blankenship," she said.

"For what?"

"For saving me years of additional therapy that wasn't working because I didn't want to get well. A couple of broken ribs seems like a small price to pay for getting back the rest of my life."

"What do you mean?"

"I mean I want the light back in my life. I want to feel a winter wind on my face and smell the first snow in the air. I've been so afraid for so long." She licked dry lips and gestured toward a foam cup filled with ice chips.

Tony grabbed it and handed it to her. She drew several of the chips into her mouth, then continued. "When I came to, after David had left, I had two choices. I could stay in that apartment and I'd probably die, or I could crawl outside, out where my fear lived, and live. As I lay there trying to force up the nerve to inch out the door, I thought about Miranda."

Tony's heart constricted at her name. In the months immediately following her death, whenever he thought about the little girl he'd come to love as his own, a killing grief had assaulted him. Now, the sharp edge of that grief had dulled to a manageable ache he knew would always accompany thoughts of her.

"You thought about Miranda?"

"I kept seeing that smile of hers." Diane's lips curved into a soft smile of her own. "And her laughter. Remember, Tony, how she would laugh and we couldn't help but laugh along with her? She was so filled with life, and she would be so unhappy with me for being so sad for so long."

Her smile fell away and once again she reached out for his hand. "I want it back, Tony. For the first time since Miranda's death, I want my life back, our life together back."

"Then we'll get it back," he said. "Together we're going to get it back."

David Blankenship sat in the lobby of the hospital and waited for the dark-haired man to leave the hospital. For a moment when he'd first entered the lobby, David had thought it was Nick Corelli. It had taken another glance to realize it wasn't Nick, but it had to be Nick's brother.

David had been waiting for this, for somebody to show up to see the injured woman, for somebody to lead him back to where Juliette and Billy had hidden. He knew he was right when he heard the man ask at the information desk for Diane Borderman's room number.

He'd been busy since leaving Diane unconscious on her floor. He'd driven to the Kansas City International Airport and had parked his car in terminal C parking. He'd then taken a taxi back to Riverton and had the cabbie drop him down the street from a used car lot.

Thirty minutes later he left the lot driving a blue 1992 Ford Escort. He'd used tags he'd "borrowed" from a car parked in long-term parking at the airport and figured he was good to go for at least a couple of days.

He'd napped in the hospital parking lot for an hour just before dawn, then as he'd seen several people coming into the emergency waiting room, he'd come in as well. Thankfully it was a fairly busy morning in ER and nobody had questioned David's presence in the waiting room.

He waited patiently for the dark-haired man to finish his visit with Diane. It was nearly two hours later that the man returned to the lobby and left by the front door.

David followed.

Chapter 33

Nick sat at the kitchen table and spun the river rock as he stared out the back window and waited to hear that Blankenship had been found and arrested.

Tony had left for the hospital a little over an hour ago. Juliette had gone to her bedroom to shower and get dressed, and Billy was watching television in the living room.

Nick's cell phone sat on the table and he willed it to ring. They needed some good news. Surely he'd be picked up soon. They had all the information about him they needed to pick him up, description, license plate numbers, social security number.

He spun the rock and his thoughts shifted to Miranda. Somehow in the days and weeks of being with Juliette and Billy, the yoke of guilt that had weighed him down had lifted.

Maybe it was seeing Juliette blame herself for David's sins. Maybe in seeing the irrationality of her guilt he'd seen his own.

Miranda had been killed by a drug-crazed twenty-five-year-old man named Jackson Blalock. Nick hadn't killed her. He couldn't have known the man would draw a hidden weapon and fire indiscriminately. He couldn't have known that a single stray bullet would find Miranda. Just as Juliette hadn't known on the day she married David what evil she had invited into her life.

He looked up as Billy entered the kitchen. "Hey, slugger," he said.

"What are you doing?" Billy sidled up to Nick and leaned against his side. Nick put an arm around him, unable to stop from responding to the need he felt from Billy, the need for male affection.

"Just sitting here spinning a rock," Nick replied.

"Where did you get the rock from?" Billy asked as he leaned more heavily against Nick. He smelled different than Miranda had, and yet wonderfully similar, the smell of childhood and sunshine.

"A very special friend gave me the rock a long time ago." He spun it again. "It's been important to me for a long time. I always keep it here in my pocket."

"Why is it so important?" Billy asked.

"It's a lucky rock. And you know what I'd like to do with it?"

"What?"

"I'd like to give it to a special friend of mine." Nick spun it one last time and when it came to rest he picked it up and held it out to Billy. "I'd like to give it to you. Would you like to have a lucky rock?"

Billy's eyes lit up. Nick had never known a boy who didn't like rocks. "Really?"

"Really. Give me your hand." Nick placed the rock in the center of Billy's palm.

Billy curled his fingers over the rock and gazed at Nick for a long moment. Those big blue eyes of his held more emotion than Nick had ever seen.

"I love you, Nick," he said, then turned and ran from the room.

Nick sat unmoving, unsure that he even breathed as the sweetness of Billy's words rushed over him. He had known from the moment Billy had told him he wasn't a pissy boy that the kid was a heartbreaker.

He stood and walked to the window. He drew a deep breath and ran his hand over his pocket. *I love you, Nick.* The words warmed him as he felt his empty pocket.

It felt right not to have the rock weighing him down anymore and he had a feeling Miranda would have approved of him passing her lucky rock to Billy.

He still stood at the window a few minutes later when Juliette came into the kitchen. She smelled of fragrant soap and fruity shampoo and he realized that it was possible in the next minutes, hours, days their time together would come to an end. And what then?

"Billy told me you gave him your lucky rock." She stood just behind him, so close he could feel her body heat emanating from her. So close he felt himself responding like a teenage boy with out of control hormones.

"Yeah, every kid needs a lucky rock."

She placed her hand at the small of his back and took a step forward so she stood next to him. "I know what that rock meant to you."

"It was time to let it go." He smiled at her, wondering if she had any idea how beautiful she looked standing in the autumn sunlight. Her dark hair sparkled with strands of red and her blue eyes were as clear, as warm as he'd ever seen them. "I think

Miranda would like the idea of sharing her rock with a boy like Billy."

She stroked her hand across his back and returned his smile. "Sometimes, Nick, you take my breath away."

"If you keep rubbing my back like that, I'm going to want to do more than take your breath away," he warned.

She laughed and dropped her hand. "Has there been any more news from Sammy?"

"A little, but not much." He gestured her to the table and they both sat. "He called a little while ago and told me they found David's car parked at the airport."

"So, he got away?"

"Sammy didn't think so. They're checking with the airlines to see if he got on a flight. With all the security in place, he'd have to use his real name or have a damn good set of fake identification. They're showing a picture of him all around. Sammy feels certain they'll get him and so do I. It's just a matter of time."

She laced her fingers together on the top of the table. "The idea of waking up each morning and knowing David is in prison somewhere is almost too good to believe."

Her eyes took on a dreamy look, one Nick had never seen before. He'd never realized before that moment that a woman with dreams in her eyes was more beautiful than any creature on earth.

"Without David as a threat, I could go back to school to finish up my degree. Billy and I could get a place to live where he could have friends, and get a dog, and join the Cub Scouts. We could have a life, Nick. We could have a real life."

He reached out and covered her hands with one of his. "That will happen, Juliette. You and your son are going to have a wonderful life."

He pulled his hand away, afraid that if he touched her for too long he'd ask her questions that would only complicate things. He wanted to ask her where he fit into the picture of her life without David. Was there a place for him in the dream she'd spun?

What had begun for him as a bad feeling and a need to save lives had transformed into something far more personal. Her strength and dignity through adversity, her passionate desire to give her son something more than what life had brought him so far had touched him deeply.

The physical scars she bore spoke not of victimization, but rather of courage. Somewhere on the path of trying to save their lives and keep them safe from David, Nick had lost his heart.

Before they could say anything else, before Nick could say anything stupid, Tony returned home. He came into the kitchen and instantly Nick knew things had gone well between Tony and Diane.

"How's Diane?" Juliette asked as Tony joined them at the table.

"Banged up and sore, but okay. They're going to keep her another night for observation, then she'll be released tomorrow to go home." He paused a beat. "I'm going to go with her."

"Good for you," Nick said. His brother's happiness was evident and it warmed Nick. It was time to begin living again.

"Better than good," Tony said. "We're going to make it together. We talked for a long time before she finally kicked me out of the hospital so she could get some rest. But it's going to be fine."

"That's wonderful," Juliette said. "I'm so glad something good is going to come out of all of this."

Tony leaned back in the chair and smiled at her. "You know, as awful as it sounds, David Blankenship might have been the best thing that happened to Diane. She believed she was going to die, and in facing death, she found a will to live, the will that had been gone from her since Miranda's death."

Juliette smiled ruefully. "David would be absolutely miserable if he knew that something he did caused somebody to find happiness."

Tony's eyes darkened. "He just better hope the cops find him before I run into him. I'm not a violent person, but I could kill him for what he's done."

"At least he's finally done something that will put him away for a very long time," Juliette said.

She was right. Nick also knew that in killing SuEllen Maynard, in beating up Diane Borderman, David Blankenship had become a man who had nothing to lose.

They ate a leisurely lunch, still waiting for the phone call that Blankenship had been arrested. They spent the afternoon playing Go Fish, Crazy Eights, and Old Maid with Billy.

This was what Juliette had dreamed about before David had stolen those dreams. Lazy afternoons of card games and laughter, feeling safe and secure in the presence of people who cared.

It wasn't just the physical safety of her surroundings that soothed her. Nick had provided a mental safety for her, a place where she could have her thoughts, even speak those thoughts aloud and not feel judged or afraid.

Nick had given her back the pieces of herself that had been stolen through years of abuse. Self-respect, a sense of worthiness, and the knowledge that despite the disfigurements from David's knife, she was still a desirable woman.

If she lived a hundred years, she'd never be able to repay him for what he'd done for her.

He'd done as much for Billy, teaching the boy that men weren't all bad or needed to be feared. She'd watched her son blossom beneath the gentle love of Nick and the teasing camaraderie of Tony.

They halted the games for dinnertime. The four of them made homemade pizza and everyone participated. Juliette made the crust, Tony made the sauce and Billy and Nick topped it with cheese and a variety of other items. By the time they were finished, the kitchen was a disaster but the pizza was fantastic.

They all pitched in to clear up the mess and Juliette and Nick were washing the last of the dishes when Tony asked if it was all right if he and Billy went down to the park and shoot a few baskets.

"Just have him home before dark," Juliette said. "He definitely needs a bath before bedtime."

"No problem," Tony said and together he and Billy left the house.

Almost immediately Juliette felt the hunger to be in Nick's arms and feel his body next to hers.

It was so much more than a need for the act of love-making. It meant so much more than the physical release. She loved the feel of his heartbeat racing against her own and the smell of his skin, but more than anything she loved the intimacy of sharing pieces of herself, of him sharing with her long after the lovemaking was over.

Maybe it was because she felt an urgency of time running out that she reached out to him as the last dish was put away. David could be arrested at any moment then Nick would go back to his work, his life and she'd begin to build one of her own.

It took only a touch from her for his eyes to darken in that way that stole her breath. For a moment he did nothing, as if wanting to give her time to know her own mind. It was one of the things she'd grown to love about him, his careful consideration in letting her lead the way.

"Stolen moments alone," she said, already half breathless.

He grinned, a slow sexy spread of his lips that torched her from head to toe. He gathered her in his arms and their lips met in a kiss that spoke of urgency, of time running out and needy desperation.

When the kiss ended they climbed the short staircase but instead of going into his room, she led him to hers. They undressed quickly and fell amid her pink sheets.

Before Nick she hadn't realized what a selfish lover David had been. Even in the early months of their marriage when things had been pretty good, David had been the kind of lover who took his pleasure with little thought to hers.

Nick, on the other hand, seemed to love the foreplay as much as the final act itself. He wasn't satisfied, wouldn't take her until she was weak and trembling and half sated. Only then would he seek his own pleasure.

He stroked her now, his hands hot as they caressed her breasts. His thumbs razed across her nipples and with that simple touch she was ready for him.

But he wasn't ready for her. His mouth moved where his hands had been and closed around one of her hard nipples. His tongue teased and tormented as one of his hands smoothed down the flat of her stomach, then stroked up her inner thigh.

Magic. That's what she felt each time he touched her, a magical strand of white heat, a breathless magic of sweet unity.

As his hand moved between her legs and his fingers found the place where all the nerves of her body seemed to be centered, she arched up. His mouth took possession of hers in a frantic kiss and any further thought for her was impossible.

He loved her with his mouth, with his fingers, bringing her to a new height of pleasure and only then did he move on top of her and enter her.

She was more than ready for him, wet and welcoming. He stroked deep inside her, then halted. His gaze locked with hers. "It's never been like this for me." His husky voice splashed a greater heat through her.

"It's never been like this for me, either."

With his gaze still locked with hers, he moved his hips against hers once again, stroking in and out in a slow, measured rhythm.

When she could stand it no longer, she closed her eyes and allowed the sweet sensations to sweep over her and through her.

He increased the pace, moving faster as the room filled with the sounds of their breathlessness, their sighs and moans of pleasure.

When their climax came, it was a crashing disintegration of herself as she melted into Nick. They clung to each other afterward. She was reluctant to let him go knowing that this might be the last time she'd be in his arms.

She was almost sorry she was on the pill. She'd begun taking it after Billy's birth, knowing the worst thing that could happen would be that she'd have another child. But there was a small part of her that wouldn't have minded so much having Nick's baby.

She released her hold on him, disturbed by the thought. "We'd better get dressed before Tony and Billy come back home." She started to get up but he grabbed her arm and pulled her back down next to him.

"I just need one more second of this stolen moment," he murmured as she curled up against him once again.

She relaxed against him, confused by her own emotions where he was concerned. She thought she might be in love with him, but she was so afraid to trust that feeling.

There was no room in her life for a relationship. She had no idea what tomorrow would bring. Even if David was arrested in the next minute, she still had a long way to go before she'd feel ready to invite another man into her life. The next time she invited a man into her life she would be sure it was the right thing to do.

She loved so many things about Nick, and making

love with him felt utterly right. But she had to be cautious. If she'd learned any lesson at all so far in her life, it was to be cautious.

He leaned over and kissed her, a sweet, gentle kiss, then smiled ruefully. "Okay, you're right. We'd better get dressed before the kids get home."

She laughed and together they got up and dressed.

By the time they returned to the kitchen, shadows of night were beginning to steal across the western sky and Nick's phone still hadn't rung with the news of Blankenship's arrest.

David sat in his car and watched his son and the dark-haired man who looked like Nick play basketball. David had heard Billy call the man Tony.

He'd been watching them for thirty minutes, reveling in the taste of success that filled his mouth. He knew he could do it. He'd been certain that he could be smart enough to find them and he had.

He knew exactly which house they had come out of, the neat split-level up the street. Juliette and Nick were there, feeling all snug and safe in the nondescript house.

On the basketball court the bane of David's life dribbled the ball with surprising agility for a five-year-old. He'd ruined everything. The minute Billy had been born, David's life had changed for the worst.

Wearing his dark glasses and a baseball cap over his died hair, David got out of the car and walked toward a nearby picnic table. His presence hadn't so much as disrupted their game and David felt a flush of triumph. He could kill the two of them now, but he knew he must be patient.

There were still several people besides Tony and Billy in the park enjoying the last few minutes of light before sunset. David willed them to leave before Tony and Billy. At the same time he wished for sunset to fall completely. He wanted the dark. He couldn't wait for the night, for then he would finally get sweet revenge.

"Come on, kiddo, it's about time for us to head back to the house." Tony picked up the basketball and tossed it to Billy.

"Just a few more baskets?" Billy asked hopefully. "I know I can make one if I try just a few more times."

Tony smiled. "All right. Five more tries." He watched as Billy set up to try to sink the ball into the hoop. The kid dribbled a couple of times, then set his feet in place to throw.

The park had been filled with people when they'd first arrived, people enjoying what was probably one of the last warm days of the year.

In the last fifteen minutes or so the park had begun to empty as the sun began to sink and the air chilled by several degrees.

Billy pumped his arms and the ball went wide to the left of the hoop. He ran after it, then returned to the small court and once again dribbled.

Tony was anxious now to get back to the house and call Diane. He still couldn't believe they were finally getting it together. The promise of a life together, a future together sang in his heart.

Billy threw the ball again, this shot too short to make it through the hoop. Darkness was falling quickly and the last couple was walking away from the park, leaving only a dark-haired man seated at a picnic table not far from the basketball court.

"Come on, Billy. Three more throws—fast or your mom is going to be mad at me for keeping you out after dark."

Billy nodded and threw again, then chased after the ball as it rolled some distance away. Out of the corner of his eye Tony saw the man on the picnic table rise and head toward him, a pleasant smile on his lips.

"Michael Jordan, watch out," he said as he reached Tony.

Tony laughed. "I don't think the big guy has too much to worry about yet."

"No, but you do."

Before Tony could react to the words, the man punched him in the stomach. Tony's breath whooshed out of him as he stumbled backward.

Jeez, the man could definitely deliver a punch, he thought. It was the sight of the long, bloody knife in the man's hand that made him realize he hadn't been punched, he'd been stabbed.

At the same time that realization filled his head, the pain came. White-hot, it was like no pain Tony had ever experienced before. It seared through him. A gut pain like none other. He looked down and saw blood—blood everywhere—too much blood.

His knees buckled and he hit the ground. The last thing Tony saw was Billy frozen in place and the man Tony now knew was Billy's father advancing toward the boy.

Chapter 34

The basketball fell from Billy's hands as he stood and stared at the man who held the knife. The knife dripped blood and Tony didn't move at all.

Tony! He cried the name inside his head and shoved a hand in his pocket and grabbed the lucky rock Nick had given to him. At the moment he didn't feel so lucky. He felt like throwing up. *Tony!* He cried again although the name didn't reach his mouth, instead it cried out of his heart.

"Hey, pissy boy."

Billy knew that voice. He didn't know the black hair, but he knew that voice. He knew the man. His father. His mean father with the broken parts, his mean father who had just killed Tony.

As David rushed toward him, Billy pulled the rock out of his pocket and threw it at David with all his might. David raised his hands in an attempt to deflect the rock and in that instant, Billy turned and ran.

He ran faster than he'd ever run in his life toward the woods. He heard David roar from someplace behind him, but he didn't stop running or turn around.

He knew if he stopped, he'd die like Tony. Tears blurred his vision as he thought of Tony. Billy had liked Tony, who made him laugh and had taken him to the movies. Nick would be so sad, and his mother would be sad.

Billy tripped and fell to his hands and knees. A sob ripped from his throat. He sprang back up and kept running, deeper into the woods, deeper into the darkness of the night.

He heard David crashing through the brush behind him and he wanted his mom. He needed his mom. David was a grown-up and Billy was just a kid. He didn't know what to do except keep on running.

But David was a grown-up and Billy was just a kid and sooner or later Billy knew his father would catch him. Billy choked as if to throw up, but nothing came up.

He ran until he couldn't run any farther. Tree branches tore and clawed at him, vines tripped and thorns scratched him. All the while he heard his father following.

It was so dark now he couldn't see where he was going and couldn't see how close David was behind him. Normally Billy wasn't too afraid of the dark, but it terrified him now.

It struck him then that if he couldn't see, then neither could David. Perilously close to exhaustion, Billy crawled up beneath a thick bush and hoped that his father didn't carry a flashlight.

He heard him still coming, smashing grass beneath his feet, swatting limbs with the backs of his hands, cursing softly beneath his breath.

Billy sat perfectly still. He knew how to be quiet. He'd spent the first four years of his life knowing that silence was his friend, that being quiet protected him from the father with the mean eyes.

"Where are you, pissy boy? I'm going to find you." Closer and closer David's voice came. Billy closed his eyes, willing himself not to move, not to breathe.

"I'm going to find you, pissy boy, and when I do, Daddy has a big surprise for you." The soft laughter sent goose bumps across Billy's skin. "Come out, come out wherever you are." Again that laugh. Billy bit his tongue to keep himself from crying.

Terror. Billy didn't know the word, but he knew the feeling. He was more scared than he'd ever been in his entire life.

"Pissy boy." Soft as a whisper, the voice came from so close Billy thought he could feel his father's breath on the back of his neck.

Billy squeezed his eyes tightly closed as he peed his pants.

Juliette stood at the front window, staring out into the dark of night. Nick came up behind her.

"I'm worried. They should have been home by now." She turned to look at him and he knew she was looking for signs of worry on his face. He kept his features carefully schooled.

"I'm sure there's nothing to worry about." He was glad his own disquiet wasn't evident in his voice. "They're probably just having a good time and haven't noticed it's gotten dark. I think the park had lights on the basketball court." That was a lie, but he didn't want her to know that he was worried, too.

She turned back to the window, stress evident in her stance. He placed a hand on one of her rigid shoulders.

"I'll just grab my jacket and run down there and haul them home."

"Thanks," she murmured.

He took the stairs to his bedroom two at a time and once there grabbed both his jacket and his gun. There was no reason to think that anything was wrong, but he'd rather be safe than sorry.

He tucked his gun in his waistband, then buttoned his jacket so Juliette wouldn't see it. A moment later he stepped out the door and headed down the block to the park.

As he walked, he told himself it wouldn't be the first time Tony had lost track of time. Nick and Diane had often teased Tony about his penchant for being late to everything. Nick was certain that Billy and Tony had probably gotten involved in a game of one-on-one and didn't notice that the sun had set thirty minutes ago.

The night air chilled without the warmth of the sun. He pulled his jacket collar up around his neck and began to jog.

As the park came into view, his disquiet grew into a full-fledged case of nerves. The basketball court wasn't lit. In fact, the whole park was dark except for the faint illumination cast by the streetlights along the curb.

"Tony? Billy?" Nick's heartbeat raced as he gazed around the empty park. Where could they have gone? He would have met them on the street if they'd gone home.

"Billy? Tony?" he yelled again.

A faint cry rode the night air. Nick drew his gun, heart pounding now as a terrible dread swept through him. "Tony?"

Again, a noise, a human noise. It came from the area by the basketball court and Nick approached cautiously. As his eyes began to adjust to the darkness, he saw his brother lying on the ground.

"Tony!" He shoved his gun back into his waistband and raced to Tony's side. He saw the blood first. It painted the front of Tony's sweatshirt like a puddle of black shadows. Nick grabbed his cell phone from his pocket and dialed 911.

"What happened?" he asked his brother before a dispatcher answered his call.

"Blankenship." Tony's voice was faint. "He . . . he must have followed me from the hospital . . . stupid . . . stupid of me . . ."

"How bad is it?"

"Bad."

The dispatcher came on the line and Nick requested an ambulance. Tony reached a bloody hand out and grabbed Nick's jacket. "Give me the phone. I'll stay on the line with them. Find Billy. He ran toward the woods. You gotta find him, Nick. Blankenship ran after him."

Torn between the need to remain with his brother and find Billy, Nick hesitated. "Go . . . go," Tony exclaimed.

Nick handed him the phone. "You just hang on, Tony. They'll be here for you any minute." Nick left him there and raced toward the woods, terrified that he was too late and he'd have to tell Juliette that her son was dead.

Juliette was in the kitchen when she heard the front door open and close. "It's about time," she said as she stirred the saucepan on the stovetop filled with hot chocolate.

"I always did love to see you working in the kitchen."

She gasped and whirled around. David stood in the doorway, a paper bag in one hand and a knife in the other. His hair was dark and whatever he'd used to darken his eyebrows had begun to run down the sides of his face.

For a moment her mind couldn't wrap around his physical presence here, in this kitchen, in their safe house.

"Whe— where's Billy?"

David smiled. "You don't look happy to see me."

"What have you done with Billy, you bastard?" She wanted to know. She needed to know, but yet was afraid. She saw the blood on his knife. Whose blood?

"They're all gone now, Juliette. It's just you and me, the way it should have been forever."

No! her heart cried out and she didn't want to believe him. She couldn't believe him, for if she did she'd curl up on the floor and just die. Then he would win, just like he'd always won.

He took a step toward her. "It's time to pay the piper. You've been a very bad girl." He took another step toward her and began to whistle.

She recognized the song and a wave of icy terror raced up her spine. "Ain't Misbehavin'." He'd always whistled that tune when he'd hurt her.

In the space of a split second, a battle raged inside her. Just let him kill you, a little voice whispered inside her head. Just give up the battle, let him win. Your life is worth nothing without Billy anyway.

Another voice yelled louder in her head. If you give up, if you let him win without a fight, then everything Nick did, everything Tony did meant nothing. Nick. Her heart cried. Billy.

Her death by his hands would not be a painless one. That wasn't David's style. He would make her suffer, but that wasn't what made her want to fight. She wouldn't give up easily. He might win, but he wouldn't win easily.

As he took another step toward her, she frantically looked around for a weapon, something she could use to try to protect herself. There was nothing. No knives on the counter, no mallets or ice picks or forks, nothing that could be used as a viable weapon.

She backed up as David approached. She backed against the stove and when he stood directly in front of her, she grabbed the handle of the saucepan filled with hot chocolate and threw it at him.

The hot liquid splashed across his face and shoulders and he roared with rage. Juliette didn't stand around waiting to see what his next reaction might be. She ran toward the doorway of the kitchen, hoping to get through the living room and to the front door before he recovered.

She made it to the living room, then was tackled from behind. She crashed to the floor and screamed as loud as she could.

David laughed, the sound of exuberant madness. "That's it, scream. Scream and cry and kick and fight." His eyes blazed as he crawled on her chest. In horror she realized he was sexually excited.

She stopped screaming, not wanting to feed his sick excitement. He got up off her and grabbed her by the hair to pull her to her feet. He shoved her into a chair, then reached down and grabbed the bag he'd brought in with him from where he'd dropped it.

He moved to stand next to her and pressed the point of the knife against her throat.

"Go ahead," she said. She was weary, more weary than she'd ever been in her life.

This man had stolen everything from her: the dreams of a young woman, the child of her heart, and the man she had just begun to love. There was nothing left but the weariness, the hollow emptiness of a shell.

"Just do it, David. What are you waiting for?" A numbness had spread through her and she just wanted this finished.

"I'm waiting for the final act." The knife point pricked her skin and she heard the sound of the paper bag once dropping to the floor. "You should have never left me, Juliette, and you should have never promised me all those things you did when I was in the day care center. Don't you know that the price of broken promises is death?"

"Then kill me, David," she said dully.

What difference did it make now? Tony would never get his chance for a happily ever after with Diane. Nick would never hold her in his arms once again, and Billy would never be able to get to be a Boy Scout. "Just do it, David," she said wearily.

Nick crashed through the woods and called Billy's name, his gun held tightly in his hand. He wanted to find Billy yet was afraid what he might find.

Over and over again he cried Billy's name, but there

was no answer and the answering silence stabbed like a spear through his heart.

Juliette. Her name screamed in his head. She was at the house alone and vulnerable. But, she'd made him promise. If he could just save one of them, save Billy, she'd said and Nick knew he had to honor his word.

"Billy! Billy, where are you?" He screamed the words over and over again as he fought his way through the darkness, through the woods and prayed that it wasn't too late.

Tears stung his eyes. Not another one, he thought. Please don't take another child from me. Not Billy, with his radiant smile and sweet disposition, not Billy who hadn't had a chance yet to have a real life.

Again and again he cried Billy's name. He stopped to catch his breath and that's when he heard him. A soft whisper coming from behind a nearby tree. "Nick?"

A sob caught in Nick's voice as Billy ran to him. He opened up his arms and pulled the boy into his embrace. "It's okay," he said as he hugged him tight. "You're safe now."

Juliette. Her name exploded in Nick's head. She was in the house, alone and vulnerable.

He scooped up Billy in his arms and as quickly as he'd crashed into the woods, he crashed out.

He hit the street and ran, hoping he wasn't too late. Blankenship had been smart enough to get rid of part of Juliette's support and protection by going after Tony here in the park.

The neighborhood was so quiet. People had gone inside their homes to catch a little television time before bed, to have a last little bit of family time before calling it a night.

Meanwhile, death had entered the quaint little neighborhood and nobody had a clue that in one of the perfect little houses with its perfect little yard, a murderer had come to visit.

Desperation drove him to run faster than he'd ever run in his life. He couldn't be too late for Juliette. Maybe David was still in those woods, hunting his son. He squeezed tighter to Billy's trembling body. Maybe Blankenship hadn't gotten to the house yet. Nick prayed this was so.

When he got to the house he saw nothing amiss, at least from the exterior. He cursed as he saw both the house on the right and the one on the left were dark. He placed Billy on the ground on the side of the house and crouched down in front of him.

"Listen to me, Billy. You have to stay right here. I think your mom is in trouble and I need to help her. Stay here and don't move until me or your Mom comes for you."

Billy nodded and Nick went to the front door and grabbed the doorknob. It turned easily in his hand and he eased it open as he pulled his revolver from his waistband.

Too late. The words screamed in his head. Juliette sat in the living room chair and standing just beside her was David, a knife pressed to her throat. A trickle of blood ran down her neck where the knifepoint had penetrated her skin. Her eyes widened in surprise when she saw him, then took on the dull glaze of a woman in shock.

"Ah, finally. The man of the hour has arrived. We've

been waiting for you." David's voice was exuberant. His hair was dark and wet with what appeared to be chocolate milk. Black lines ran down from his eyebrows, giving him the look of a punk kid with a strange makeup job.

"Drop your gun, Nick."

Nick didn't immediately comply. Instead he assessed his options, wondering if he could get off one good shot before Blankenship stabbed Juliette.

"You shoot me, I'll stab her. It will be perfect. We'll once again be together only this time in death. Is that what you want?"

He was right. In Nick's gut he knew he was right. There was no way he could get off a shot without Juliette getting hurt. He simply couldn't chance it. He clicked the safety on his gun and lowered it to his side.

"Good. Now toss it on the floor toward me," David said.

Nick leaned down and slid the gun on the floor. It came to rest midway between the two men. He hoped that David would leave Juliette long enough to pick it up. The moment that knife left her neck, Nick would attack.

David seemed to read his mind. He laughed. "We'll just leave it right there for now. Sit down on the sofa, Nick. I promise you it's going to be a long night."

Nick tried to catch Juliette's attention, but she stared straight ahead, her eyes empty. She'd gone into a place inside her where she couldn't be reached.

Maybe it's for the best, Nick thought as he moved to the sofa and sat on the edge. It might be a blessing that she'd disappeared into herself.

"What do you want, David?"

"You know what I want, Nick. I want to kill this betraying bitch."

"If you kill her, then you'll never be with her again," Nick countered. Every muscle in his body was ready to pounce. If the bastard would just move that knife an inch one way or the other, Nick would spring. As long as the knife pressed so intimately into Juliette's neck, he was helpless to do anything.

Again David laughed. "Maybe I'll kill her, then eat her heart. Isn't that the way primitive tribes used to do it? If I eat her heart then her spirit will be with me forever."

"You're a sick bastard." Anger shook inside Nick, an anger and fear he'd never before experienced.

He had only one hope. He knew that a patrol car would have been summoned along with the ambulance for Tony. If Tony was able to speak by the time the officers got there, then maybe he'd be able to tell them what was going on.

The important thing was for Nick to keep David talking. He needed to make things last as long as possible to give help time to arrive.

"I'm not sick, Nick. I just knew the moment I first laid eyes on Juliette that she was mine. Isn't that right, darling?" With his other hand, David reached across her shoulder and cupped her breast.

Nick came half off the sofa and the knife pressed deeper against Juliette's skin as a new trickle of blood made its way down her throat. She didn't even flinch. Filled with rage, but recognizing the consequences of indulging the rage, Nick sank back down.

"I'm going to kill you, you bastard," he said.

"Ah, Nick, another one of your empty promises.

Just like all the ones you made to me that day at the day care. You remember? You promised me no handcuffs. You promised I could take my lovely wife with me and just go home. And I got news for you, Nick. You aren't going to talk me out of this, so don't even try."

Nick wanted to make contact with Juliette. If she'd jerk out of the chair, lean to the opposite side of the knife, the point would be displaced. But she didn't seem to be aware of anything that was going on in the room.

She looked dead with her eyes wide open. Even if he managed to somehow get the upper hand on David and save her, what would he be saving? A woman shoved over the edge into catatonia?

Nick was a cop and his job, his calling was to save lives and he knew if he didn't do something he'd lose Juliette and probably be killed himself. He also knew if he lost Juliette and lived, he'd have a hole inside him too big to bear.

"I'm going to tell you how this is all going to go down," David continued. He used a conversational tone, as if he were talking about the weather, or a movie he'd seen.

"We're going to tie you up real tight, so you can't move. Then I'm going to fuck my wife in every way possible. If you close your eyes, I'll cut her. If you try to look away, I'll cut her, but not deep enough to kill. If you're good and cooperative, then maybe I won't eat her heart. Maybe I'll give it to you and you can hold it while I kill you."

Evil. It emanated from him even though it didn't show on his features. It filled the room and Nick smelled it, felt it surrounding him. One thing was sure. There was no way he intended to let anyone tie him up. If he was bound, then it would be the end for both of them.

"What happened to you, David? Your mama didn't nurse you long enough? Maybe she made you wear her underwear? Did your daddy drink and dance naked on Saturday nights?"

"Nice try, Nicky. But you won't make me mad enough to do anything stupid."

There had been only one other time in his life when Nick had felt this kind of helplessness and that had been after the smoke had cleared in the bank that day and he'd found Miranda dead. That same helplessness hit him now.

If he didn't think of something fast he and Juliette were going to die.

"Mom?"

The voice came from the front door and in that instant several things happened. Billy stepped inside. David's attention shifted. The knife momentarily left Juliette's neck and that was all Nick needed.

As he sprang off the sofa, Juliette came alive. She fell over the side of the chair, away from David. Nick hit David in the midsection and the two men rolled to the floor.

David slashed across Nick's back and Nick felt the cold metal slice through his jacket and to the skin beneath. It might hurt later, but at the moment adrenaline kept the pain away.

As he struggled to gain control of David's knife hand, he was vaguely aware of Billy running to his mother's outstretched arms.

Physically, David was stronger than Nick expected. The two men grappled for control. They rolled across the floor, first David on top of Nick, then Nick on top of David. The knife cut Nick's arm before he managed to grab hold of David's wrist.

He banged the wrist against the floor over and over again, attempting to dislodge the weapon, but David held fast. The man's eyes glittered and he laughed, as if enjoying every moment. "I'm going to cut your throat, then I'll take her," he gasped.

"Give it up, you bastard," Nick said. "It's over." He slammed David's hand once again against the floor and the knife flew out of it.

"It's not over until I say it's over," David replied.

A gunshot resounded and both men froze. "It's over when I say it's over," Juliette said. She stood above them, the gun steady in her hand. "Get up, both of you."

Nick stood and kicked the knife well out of David's reach. "Give me the gun, Juliette."

"Get up, David." Her voice was low, her eyes the arctic blue of winter winds.

The front door burst open and Sammy stepped into the living room, but froze at the sight that greeted him. Nick held up a hand to halt him from doing anything. David rose to his feet.

"Juliette, honey, give me the gun. You don't want to do this," Nick said. Billy moved to stand next to him.

"Tell me why I don't want to do this." Cold. He'd never heard her voice so cold, so utterly void of any emotion. There was no tremor in her hand, no unsteadiness at all.

"Do it, Juliette," David said. "Come on, you know you want to. Pull the trigger."

"Shut up," Nick snapped. "Juliette, Billy is standing right here next to me, safe and sound." Nick placed a hand on the boy's shoulder and he leaned into Nick's side. "Now is the time for you and Billy to make that life we talked about. If you do this now, you won't get to fulfill those dreams."

A deep, wrenching sob escaped her.

"Just do it, Juliette," David urged.

She stood for another long minute and Nick held his breath. With another sob, she dropped the gun to her side. Sammy rushed to David and Nick grabbed Juliette.

He held her tight with one arm as the other held onto Billy. "It's over now," he murmured. "It's finally over." He held onto them long after David was led away in handcuffs.

"I hate him," Billy finally said. "He made me hide in the woods and I peed my pants."

Nick leaned down and eyed the boy soberly. "You were a very brave boy, Billy. If I'd been in your place, I would have peed my pants, too."

"Really?"

Nick pulled him into a full embrace. "Really," he replied.

It was a seemingly endless night. They went from the house to the hospital to check on Tony. Thankfully, David's knife had missed every vital organ, although the doctor told Nick that if the ambulance hadn't arrived when it had Tony would have died from loss of blood.

He was sleeping when Nick checked in on him, Diane seated at the side of his bed.

They went from the hospital to the police station to give statements. It was there they learned what had happened at the park, how David had stabbed Tony, how Billy had thrown the lucky rock which had distracted David enough for Billy to get a head start toward the woods.

Billy lamented the fact that the lucky rock was lost, but Nicky assured him it didn't matter. The rock had saved his life and had, indeed, worked its magic.

Nick also realized why David hadn't been picked up by the local authorities before he'd shown up at the house. Diane, who had never seen David before, hadn't realized the man had changed his hair color, and therefore hadn't told the police they were looking for a dark-haired man instead of a sandy-blond-haired man.

It was near dawn when they finally arrived back at the house where the three of them tumbled together into Nick's bed and slept.

Nick slept hard, without dreams, and awakened at noon to find himself alone in the bed. He got up and went down the stairs to the living room. The first thing he saw was their suitcases standing next to the front door.

He turned as Juliette and Billy came out of the kitchen. "Oh, you're awake. I was just writing you a note."

"You're leaving?" He asked the obvious.

"I've contacted a women's shelter. They've agreed to let us stay there for a few days until we can get things squared away. They're sending a cab for me."

"So soon?" The hollow ache he'd sensed was just around the corner had arrived.

"Billy, go look in your room and make sure we haven't forgotten anything," she said. As he raced up the stairs, she turned back to Nick. "I figured each moment that passed would only make it more difficult."

"It feels pretty difficult right now." He jammed his hands into his pockets. "You know I'm in love with you."

She blinked, but didn't avert her gaze from his. "I need time, Nick. Time to find out who I am without all this. I need some time with Billy, when we aren't running, aren't hiding. Can you understand that?"

He didn't want to understand. He had a feeling if he talked long enough, fast enough, he could change her mind. He could make her stay. But that wasn't what she needed. And that wasn't his kind of love.

A horn honked outside. "That's your cab," he said as Billy raced back down the stairs.

He leaned forward and kissed her on the forehead, a long, lingering kiss. At the same time he drew the scent of her into his lungs. When he drew back from her there were tears in her eyes. "Build a life, Juliette," he said softly. "Build a life of happiness."

She nodded and picked up her suitcase. Nick bent down to Billy. "You're going to be all right, my little man. You're the bravest soul I know."

Billy threw his arms around Nick's neck and squeezed tight. "I love you, Nick."

Nick closed his eyes, for a moment unable to speak as emotion filled his throat. "I love you, too," he managed to choke out.

"We have to go. The cab is waiting," Juliette said.

Nick gave Billy one last squeeze, then straightened. Nobody said good-bye, as if the word itself would be too painful if voiced aloud. Juliette picked up the large suitcase and Billy grabbed the smaller.

Nick stood at the door and watched the two of them as they walked away. He was reminded of another day when he had watched the two of them walk away, their backs rigid with pride and strength.

He stood at the front door until the cab pulled away, and then he went upstairs to pack his bags.

Epilogue

It was a perfect Christmas Eve with enough snow to transform Tanglewood Lake into a winter wonderland. Nick warmed his hands over a fire burning in a barrel and watched his brother execute a perfect figure eight on the ice. Nearby Diane clapped in appreciation of his form.

There were few skaters on the ice. Most people were home, enjoying out of town company or family time. Skating on Tanglewood Lake on Christmas Eve had been Diane's goal for a very long time. Tonight she had achieved that goal.

Nick had been pleased that the two of them had included him in the evening festivities, which included ice skating, then hot chocolate at the house where Tony and Diane now lived.

Each time he visited them there he couldn't help but think about Juliette and Billy and wonder how they were doing, if they were even still in town.

Tony motioned for Nick to join them on the ice and he left the frozen shoreline and glided out to meet them. For the next thirty minutes they skated as if they were once again kids.

The cold air burned in his lungs and his fingers became numb, but Nick loved the physical exertion and the glide of the ice beneath his skates.

Long before Diane and Tony were finished on the ice, Nick returned to the barrel to warm his face and hands. A dog barked in the distance and he turned his attention in that direction.

He froze, for a moment wondering if he was hallucinating.

"Nick!" Billy waved with one hand, the other hanging tight to a leash that connected to the collar of a black puppy.

Her hair was blond again, as was Billy's—that beautiful pale blond that shimmered like silk and swung around the collar of her navy coat as she approached.

He thought it was the cold that made it difficult for him to breathe, but he knew better. It was the sight of her, with that beautiful smile of hers so open and warm.

They stopped just in front of him. "Hi," she said.

"Hi, yourself," he replied.

"I was hoping you'd be here."

"Nick, I got a dog," Billy said.

Nick crouched down. "I see," he said as he held out a hand toward the rambunctious dog. "What's his name?"

"I wanted to name him Nick, but Mom said that might get confusing, so his name is King."

Nick frowned. "Confusing?"

Billy shrugged and held the leash out toward his mom. "I gotta go say hi to Tony and Diane."

"Be careful, the ice is slippery," Juliette said. Billy nodded and took off toward the others.

"Confusing?" Nick rose and looked at her.

"You know, if you wanted to come around." Her gaze held his, then she looked toward the ice where Diane and Tony had Billy between them and were guiding him across the ice. "It's good to see Diane."

"Yeah. She's made a lot of progress." Nick shoved his hands in his pockets. He didn't want to jump to conclusions, although what he wanted to do was reach out and take her in his arms. "She still has some bad days, but more good than bad."

"But she's out of her apartment."

Nick nodded. "She's taking things slow. She's okay if there isn't a big crowd around and she's working real hard with her therapist. What about you? How are you doing?"

"Good. Very good. I've rented a house not far from the one we all stayed in. I'm substitute teaching during the day and have started night school to finish up my degree."

"What about Billy? He doing okay?"

Her smile widened. "I have him going to therapy. I'm going, too. But he's doing terrific. He has a new best friend named Robby and he's in preschool."

"You know the trial has been set for February."

She nodded. "The district attorney called me to let me know. They're requesting the death penalty."

"How does that make you feel?"

She drew a deep breath and released it slowly. "To be honest? Indifferent. Whether he lives or dies, I know he's out of my life forever."

Nick pulled his hands out of his pockets and held them out over the heat of the barrel. "So, you're building that life you wanted."

She nodded. "I needed some distance. I needed to know, Nick. I needed to know whether what I felt for you was gratitude or love."

"And did you figure it out?"

That beautiful, sexy smile curved the corners of her lips. "I know one thing for certain now. It wasn't just gratitude. I've missed you, Nick. I've missed you desperately."

That was all he needed to hear. He wasn't sure whether he reached for her, or she reached for him, but she was in his arms and the dog was barking and they were kissing.

"You're right," he said when their kiss ended.

"About what?"

He smiled and patted the dog on the head. "Two Nicks in one household would be confusing."

And with that, their life together began.

"Welcome to hell, Blankenship." The prison guard unlocked the gate and shoved David through. He scooted down the long corridor, hampered by his leg shackles. He was flanked by two guards.

Life. That's what they'd given him. Those smug jurors with their smug faces had sentenced him to spend the rest of his life in the Leavenworth Penitentiary.

Life in jail while awaiting his trial hadn't been too bad. The guards had left him alone and he'd had a cell of his own. He'd even been given access to law books in order to help with his own defense. But of course there had been no help.

He'd been charged and convicted of one count of murder and four counts of attempted murder, along with myriad other charges.

No, jail hadn't been too bad, but this place was different. The gates clanged with a more resounding echo, the guards appeared bigger, meaner, and the whole place smelled of badness.

Still, David wasn't too worried. He was a smart man, a hell of a lot smarter than most of the losers in this joint. He figured within six months he'd be running the place from the inside.

"Here you are, hotshot. Home sweet home." He opened the door of a cell where a tall, dark-haired man sat on the top bunk. One of the two guards leaned down and unfastened David's leg shackles while the other one unfastened the handcuffs.

A hard shove in the back sent David through the doors and into the cell. The door clanked shut behind him. At the same time the big man jumped down from the upper bunk.

"Hey man," David said to the man who would be sharing his space. "How you doing?" Jesus, the man was a moose, with biceps bigger than David's thighs.

"I'm doing just fine."

David stuck out his hand. "I'm David Blankenship."

The man ignored his hand. "Yeah, I know who you are." The punch the man delivered to David's stomach dropped David to his hands and knees and brought bile into his throat. He choked and spat on the floor.

"Oops, I forgot to introduce myself, didn't I?" The big man's deep voice came from right next to David's ear. "The name is Maynard—Big John Maynard. I believe you knew my daughter."

SuEllen's father. There was a mistake. This all had to be a terrible mistake. He crawled on his hands and knees to the bars. "Guard," he yelled. "Guard!"

Maynard laughed. "Ain't nobody gonna help you now. But, don't worry. I won't kill you—at least not today. Hell, we've got the rest of your life to sort things out between us."

For the first time in David Blankenship's life, he knew terror.

Into the Fire
by Jessica Hall

A warehouse fire in New Orleans' French Quarter
kills a local politician—and ignites intrigue and
pent-up passion between former lovers...

PRAISE FO THE NOVELS OF JESSICA HALL:

"AN AMAZING THRILLER THAT IS EXOTIC, PASSIONATE,
AND EXHILARATING. DON'T MISS THIS BOOK!"
—*ROMANTIC TIMES*

"DO NOT MISS READING THIS RIVETING,
PASSIONATE NOVEL. IT'S FANTASTIC!"
—*BEST REVIEWS*

"A FAST-PACED SERPENTINE OF HIGH TENSION,
STEAMY SEX AND JUST THE RIGHT TOUCH OF ROMANCE."
—LISA JACKSON

**Available wherever books are sold or
to order call 1-800-788-6262**

"A soul-deep love story and
wild adventure."
—Catherine Coulter

Jessica Hall
The Steel Caress

Raven had no intention of ever returning to
her life as an undercover government agent.
The stunning beauty didn't doubt that years
ago she'd been betrayed by the agency she
worked for—and by her devastatingly
handsome boss, General Kalen Grady.

Now, Raven has launched a new
career—and a new life. But just when she's
certain the past is behind her, Kalen
turns up on her doorstep with one final and
crucial assignment.

0-451-20852-8

Available wherever books are sold, or
to order call: 1-800-788-6262

ANNE FRASIER

SLEEP TIGHT

"There will be no sleeping tight after reading this one...Guaranteed to keep you up all night."*

> A female FBI profiler is up against a killer who may have ties to her own tragic past.

"A riveting thriller...laced with forensic detail and psychological twists, Anne Frasier's latest intertwines the hunt for a serial killer with the personal struggles of two sisters battling their own demons and seeking their own truths. Compelling and real—a great read."
—*Andrea Kane

0-451-41077-7

Available wherever books are sold or to order call: 1-800-788-6262